WHAT HAPPENED TO FRANK?

WHAT HAPPENED TO FRANK?

A MEG SHEPPARD MYSTERY

BOOK ONE

VICKY EARLE

ISBN: 978-1-78324-218-4

www.vickyearle.com

Published by Wordzworth
www.wordzworth.com

This book is dedicated to my father,

Douglas Frederick Symes,

1917-1998,

who knew how to love, live and laugh.

1

Dreaded Anniversary

I pull on my tight, stretchy riding pants, grab a couple of carrots, and step out into the bright, crisp air. Kelly, my beloved border collie, trots in front, leading the way on the well-worn path to the barn. The dog wags her silky tail, glancing back now and then to make sure I'm following. It's as if she's beckoning to me.

My trustworthy thoroughbred, Eagle, has helped me to cope during the past months. When riding I have to devote my full, undivided attention to what I and the horse are doing, focussing my thoughts and channelling my energy.

It had soon become clear that Eagle didn't have the makings of a racehorse, with not one ounce of competitiveness in him, but he loves being ridden. And as soon as he sees the carrots, Eagle trots across the paddock to the gate, showing off his springy steps. I clip on the lead-rein and give him a carrot at the same time. He is handsome, and he knows it. A broad white flash runs down his face, contrasting with his dark bay colouring, standing out like a snowy ski-run on a brown hillside.

I lead him into the barn and soon have him clipped to the cross-ties and immerse myself in grooming.

I've known that this dreaded anniversary would be a challenge. Memories that I've struggled to control flood to the surface and threatened to overwhelm. It will take enormous effort, and all my resolve to continue functioning, to keep raw emotions in check. I am hopeful that this early ride will help me focus on more positive things, but my hand trembles as I pick up the mane comb. Eagle senses my uneasiness and dances around on the rubber matting laid between two rows of well-maintained, solidly built horse stalls. Despite his jitteriness, I pause and reflect.

When I arrived from England over twenty years ago, alone and barely an adult, I never dreamt that I would be living in a stylish, renovated farmhouse, riding my own horses and romping in the undulating fields with my loving dog. I still have to pinch myself now and then. I am fortunate; I know. But the sudden and tragic loss of my husband, Frank, exactly one year ago, has darkened my thoughts, feelings and actions every day since. And I have dreaded this day, this anniversary of raw shock, pain and loss. That's why I've planned a busy itinerary. Nevertheless, I hesitate, and wonder for a moment if it's wise to get on a spirited thoroughbred when I'm vulnerable and stressed. But I mustn't start the day in defeat, and recommit to following my schedule and comb Eagle's thick, black mane.

The sound of my phone ringing makes me drop the comb, and I curse myself for not having left it in the house. I don't know why I feel compelled to answer when I see Sharon McDonald's name.

"Hello," I say.

"Hi, Meg. Have I got you at a bad time?" Sharon's raspy voice grates on my ears as I picture the tubby, drab-looking accountant. Her looks must be deceiving though, because she is the Vice President, Finance and Administration, at Sandy's Waste Retirement, which is a euphemism for Sandy's garbage dump, a large, successful and growing business.

"I'm in the barn grooming a horse, I can only take a minute."

"How are you?" asks Sharon.

"Not too bad."

"Have you got plans for lunch?"

"I have actually. I'm meeting Tom."

"That's great. I'll take a rain check then," Sharon says. "What are you doing this afternoon?"

"I'm planning to see Speed and Rose at the racetrack. So, you needn't worry, I've got lots to do. I won't be alone." Eagle escalates his show of impatience by shaking his head and swishing his tail.

"That's good. You know what they say in our group about the first anniversary."

"I know, you don't need to remind me." Why did I answer the phone?

"I thought you did really well in our last support group session. You sounded like you've finally accepted that it was an accident."

"I have to go. My horse is getting restless. Thanks for calling. See you next Tuesday!"

"Okay, just as long as you're all right."

"Yep, I'm fine, thanks. Bye!"

I'm relieved to put the phone back in my pocket. Sharon has agitated me. My heart beats too quickly as I ditch the mane comb and settle for the dandy brush, which I lift out of my well-organized grooming box.

Sharon's comment about "accepting it was an accident" replays in my head and takes my concentration away from Eagle. My thoughts, despite all my best intentions and effort, drift back to the same day one year before. My stomach lurches and my eyes well up as I relive the unbearable memory of being told of Frank's death. Frank was the only person I ever truly trusted. Before my relationship with him, I'd believed that my best and most faithful friends were the animals in my life. But Frank became especially beloved to me.

And, despite Sharon's observation, I'm still convinced there was more to Frank's death than a simple car accident. My conviction remains as strong as it was on that awful day.

I've always been a person to act. If there's a problem, I invariably seek a solution. While tacking up the fidgeting Eagle like an automaton, my shakiness disappears and my heart settles into a more sedate rhythm. Something, some emotion or feeling, works its way through my body, like an alien force gradually taking control of me. It's as if I'm standing on the outside, observing a change in my body and mind. It takes me a couple of minutes to understand what's happened, that a wave of determination has washed over the pebbles of my mind, agitating them into action. I am going to find out exactly what happened to Frank. Perhaps Sharon has done me a favour by bringing my frustrations to the surface and stirring up my resolve.

But, at the same moment that I am empowered by my determination, I reproach myself for not taking any action during the past twelve months. I should have been doing something rather than wallowing in self-absorbed, self-pitying helplessness brought on by the overwhelming grief and shock at the loss of my husband.

As I get into the saddle, Eagle whinnies to his stable-mate, Bullet, snapping me out of my self-criticism. And, sustained by my new sense of purpose, I have one of the best rides ever. The thoroughbred catches some of my newfound spirit and trots with confidence and style, with a beautifully arched neck.

* * *

Energized, I put more effort into getting ready than I have for the past year. I curl my shiny black hair and put on a smart pant suit. I rummage in my neglected jewellery box and unearth a pendant. It has faux diamonds around the edge which catch the dancing spring sunshine, and the large shiny stone in the centre reflects the browns of my eyes. On the rare occasions when I've gone anywhere socially since Frank died, it has been obvious that my sense of style had evaporated. I've usually thrown on the nearest thing and given no thought to the overall effect.

As I inspect my appearance in the full-length mirror, I reflect on how Frank liked to play a role in selecting, or at least approving, what I proposed to wear at a function or event we were to attend together. He said he wanted me to look my best, that appearances matter in the world of politics. It's all about image. I am fortunate that it's easy for me to maintain my slim figure, partly because I ride Eagle and walk with Kelly almost daily. But I remember Frank wondering aloud if my thighs were growing larger because of all the riding. I valued his attention and wanted to fulfil my role as the wife of the Minister of the Environment, but I didn't think that bigger thighs were a sufficient reason for me to change my daily routines. So, I didn't and thankfully no more was said.

* * *

The next item on my busy agenda for the day is to talk with Chuck, the gardener. I've decided that it's a good time to plan the planting of pansies and the addition of more bulbs to the garden. I don't remember last spring. Chuck must have planned, planted and nurtured, but I couldn't see anything through the fog of grief which shrouded my eyes. I'm trying to be more positive about things this spring. I used to get a lot of pleasure out of seeing things grow and blossom, especially after the long, colourless winter. The green shoots pushing their way through the near-frozen earth, as if pulled up by invisible strings, would fill me with anticipation. And the bursts of vibrant colours that followed would amaze me. On the few occasions that Frank could take a break from his demanding schedule, we might sit together on the deck, soaking in the garden's ever-changing beauty.

Chuck usually shows up mid-morning about three days a week. I give him a lot of freedom to decide what time he needs to do things, and call upon him to use his initiative. But I know little about him. Frank hired Chuck about three years ago, saying that he badly needed a job. Although I now have more time on my hands, since I'm on leave from the humane society and have given up my volunteer work, I feel I'd somehow be betraying Frank if I dismissed Chuck. In any case, aloof as he appears, it's nice to know that someone comes to the property a few times a week, especially since I've had little interaction with people after Frank's death, except that I've recently been attending support group sessions once a week. And Chuck is willing to do some of the maintenance jobs that I find challenging.

He arrives at the kitchen door just as I plug in the kettle. I'm about to make myself what seems like the millionth cup of tea since Frank died. It's soothing to sit with a mug of something hot.

Kelly wags her tail. She knows it's Chuck before I open the door.

"Hi, Chuck. I'm just making tea. Would you like some?"

"That would be great, thanks."

Chuck looks more sombre than usual. Silence hangs over us like a grey rain-cloud as I pour steaming water into each of the mugs.

"I want to talk to you about the spring flowers," I say as I sit down opposite him. He doesn't look up.

"Yes." He sighs, almost inaudibly. "This must be a difficult day for you, I'm sorry."

"It is." I fiddle with my mug. I'm surprised that he's remembered that this is the anniversary of Frank's death. "I miss Frank."

"He was good to me," Chuck says in a soft voice. "I expect you've wondered why he left me so much money. You've never asked." He looks up at me. His face is lined beyond his forty years, and his large green eyes look tired.

"Frank was a generous and kind man, and I assumed he felt you deserved it. It wouldn't have occurred to me I should question it."

Chuck looks down again, into his mug. "I don't feel like telling you my story today, but I'd like to tell you soon. I think you should know. I owe it to you because Frank was so kind, and you've been keeping me on. After all, it was Frank who hired me and knew me, not you."

I have to admit that I'm curious why Chuck is still working here. Not that Frank left him a fortune. It was only $50,000, which doesn't go far these days. But it appeared a lot to leave a gardener when the only other beneficiaries were charities, Frank's brother and, of course, me. I definitely received the lion's share since Frank and I had agreed that I should have no financial worries if he died first.

Given my determination to find out what happened to Frank, my curiosity is roused. I'd love to hear Chuck's story right now, but I respect his desire to postpone it. I just wonder what's prompted him to want to share it after all this time.

Chuck breaks the silence at last by making a few well-thought-out suggestions for pansies, bulbs, seeds and perennials. I like all of his ideas and plans. I always do. My imagination conjures up an exciting image of the garden bursting with all the colours of the rainbow. I can hear the breeze rustling the shiny, green leaves of the plants and can smell the musty loam that's almost overpowered by the sweet-smelling scents of the many flowers. I love the pungent daffodil, the honeyed lilac and the perfumed hyacinth.

After our tea, there isn't much time for me to clear up and get to the restaurant. As I get ready, I realize I haven't told Chuck that I'm on a mission to find out exactly what happened to Frank. But perhaps it's wise not to share this with anyone other than Tom at the moment. In fact, I can't wait to tell Tom and see his reaction. I scramble into my pickup truck and drive down the long, treed driveway.

My senses are reawakened, making me more alert. It's as if my body has been rewired. I'm taking more notice of the sprouting trees and the new green grass. With the window down, I enjoy the cheerful songs of the chickadees as they flit among the branches of the road-side shrubs in the sweet spring air.

But the fresh air will only be a memory as soon as I reach the outskirts of Vannersville, an industrial city which produces most of the pollution in the province. And I'll have to pass the steel mill. I reluctantly roll up the window in anticipation of an assault by acrid smells.

As I slow down to take a sweeping bend, I decide that the big-shot owner of the steel mill, Timothy Westmount, is somewhere to start in my quest to find out what happened to Frank. I know he's highly regarded among the old boys' network of Vannersville, and Frank had liked him well enough. But they clashed over Frank's push, as the provincial Minister of the Environment, to introduce new pollution control regulations. I'm not sure if I'll be able to get a meeting with Timothy, but it's worth a try.

The truck knows this part of the road well, but my stomach knots. They still haven't put up the promised safety barrier around the bend, and I imagine I can see deep grooves in the soft shoulder. But I know they can't really be there, not after a year.

I can see the city now. At least, I can see the industrial belt. I understood and respected Frank's concerns about pollution, and his dismay at what these large industries can get away with. The pungent smog can nearly always be seen hanging over the city, with its ominous orange tinge. Although cars contribute a significant amount to the pollutants, the large industries are churning out poisons with inadequate controls, at least according to Frank. I can hear him now, telling Tom that they could do a lot to decrease the pollution levels, if they cared enough, but the incessant drive for return on investment for shareholders is the constant, over-riding priority.

Once I reach the busy city streets, I change my focus to my lunch meeting with Tom. Having parked my dirty truck next to some noticeably clean cars, and having got out of it without messing up my pant suit, I walk briskly towards my favourite Italian restaurant. I choose a seat next to the window. I need to be able to look out and see my surroundings, whatever they are, otherwise I feel trapped and disoriented like a fly in a sticky spider's web.

The smell of garlic, which pervades the whole room and hangs in the air, increases my hunger pangs. As the minutes pass, I finish my cup of tea and wonder if Tom is going to make it. But I look up from my empty cup just as a tall, slim, energetic man jay-walks across the road with large strides. Tom is soon standing in front of me. He takes off his jacket and drags the heavy metal chair out from under the small table. He rubs his hand through his fair fuzz, which is all that remains of his hair, although he's only in his late thirties.

"Hi! Sorry I'm late." His familiar face is brightened by a broad smile which reveals his even white teeth. I can't help feeling more relaxed as soon as he sits down.

"Thanks for coming, I know you're busy."

"You look great!" I detect a note of surprise in Tom's voice. Have I really been looking that dreadful?

"Thanks. I feel better."

I'm interrupted by a chatty server, who reels off a long list of specials, none of which interest me.

"I'm going to have a glass of white wine, please," I say. Tom raises his eyebrows with his soft, brown eyes mocking astonishment.

"Well, I'll join you then." Tom has a love of life which can be infectious. I can see why Frank enjoyed his company so much.

Finally, the server finishes buzzing around us for a bit, having delivered the cool, golden wine and taken our order.

"You seem to be coping well," Tom observes. "I'm so glad." I'm touched by the sincerity in his voice. Not being one to beat about the bush, I get right to the point.

"I think I'm seeing things more clearly. I know what I have to do. I have to find out what really happened to Frank." Tom picks up his wine glass, as if in slow-motion.

"I don't share your belief that it wasn't an accident, but you know that." He twirls his wine glass around, so much so that I think the wine might escape. It's clear that he doesn't appreciate my enthusiasm, and I'm a bit taken aback. But my resolve doesn't waver.

"I'm quite determined to get to the bottom of it, Tom. As I was driving round that damn bend on my way here, it seemed so obvious that Frank couldn't have misjudged it. I know the road sweeps down, and sharply around, but he knew it so well. And he hadn't been drinking. You know he didn't drink. And the road was dry." I stop while the server delivers the meals.

"Would you like parmesan cheese on that?" I almost regret liking parmesan cheese. The interruptions from the server are eating into the time available to speak to Tom.

"I actually wonder why I haven't done anything before this," I continue, once the server has left us again.

"Losing a spouse is a traumatic event. In fact, I don't think you ever get over it."

At least Tom isn't ridiculing me, even though it's taken me a year to come up with the resolve to find the truth.

"What do you plan to do?" Never one to sit still for long, Tom piles the little sugar packets into one precarious pile.

"The smell of the steel mill helped me to remember that Frank planned to introduce those strong pollution control regulations. I bet he had some fierce opposition from the powerful industries round here." I finish my wine but haven't eaten much, despite my initial hunger pangs.

We both know that Frank had been an influential and successful Minister of the Environment, and had introduced several new pieces of legislation during the Government's first term of office. And, not long before his death, the party had been successfully re-elected on a platform which included enhanced pollution control regulations. These regulations were championed by Frank and were to be introduced by him.

"Why don't you research the newspapers? Perhaps you'll get some names of the people involved in that pollution issue," Tom suggests, as he jostles with the salt and pepper shakers.

"Before I do that, I'm going to visit Timothy Westmount, just to see what happens."

"Be careful, Meg. Those guys are hard-nosed businessmen. They can be pretty ruthless. While Westmount might be a reasonable type, his COO, Susan Kingsley-Black has a reputation for being aggressive and hard-nosed, and even a bit whacky. They both have strong links with MMB Aggregates and Sandy's Waste Retirement. A guy called Brad Buckthorn, Marshall Moncton-Brown's Assistant at MMB, is a nasty piece of work." Tom warns.

"How do you know?"

"I've done some management training sessions for the front-line supervisors at both Westmount Steel and MMB, and had to deal with both Susan and Brad. They are full of their own self-importance and autocratic. In fact, that was what was causing most of the challenges for the supervisors. They're tough to deal with and don't care much about the employees, it seems, or anyone else for that matter." He sighs. "I wish you'd reconsider this."

You won't dissuade me, Tom, but I promise to be careful." I fold up my crisp linen napkin wishing Tom was a more enthusiastic supporter of my plan. "You know, they still haven't put up the safety barrier along that bend."

"That's surprising. I suppose it hasn't got on top of the priority list. There are lots of roads in very poor repair around here. What are you doing for the rest of the day?"

"I'm going to the racetrack to see Speed and Rose. The trainer has been pestering me ever since Frank died, asking me to go there more often to see the horses. Then I'll see Murray, Frank's brother, and probably stay there for supper, although I'm not looking forward to that. I've only visited Murray once since Frank's death. And then I'm going to put my thinking cap on. I want to determine how Frank's car crashed and who caused it and why. We know where and when."

"You know, I'd very much like to help you. I can schedule some time," Tom offers. "I owe it to Frank as well as to you."

"That's kind of you, but I'm going to do this myself."

"I'd be glad to help, so if you change your mind, just let me know. But at least let me know how you're getting on, okay?"

"Thanks." I appreciate Tom's offer, but I'd like to do this on my own. I value my independence. In any case, I don't have a plan and I don't know what I'd ask him to do.

"Are you going to the racetrack now, or are you going to see Westmount first?" Tom stands up, letting his napkin slide to the floor, and puts his leather jacket back on.

"Oh, I haven't got time to do both, and I promised the groom, Linda, that I'd go. Besides, I want to see the horses. I haven't been for such a long time. I've had this planned for a while, you know."

"When will you see Westmount?"

"I suppose I'll have to figure out how to get a meeting with him."

"Don't forget to call me and let me know how it goes. Good luck!"

"Thanks. Bye!"

Tom turns and leaves the restaurant. His long, athletic legs appear to dance as he dodges the vehicles on the busy street, and I can't take my eyes off him until he reaches the other side in one piece. It's hard for me to understand why Tom, Frank's best friend, doesn't share my scepticism about the accident. I assume he just wants to put the tragedy behind him. I know he wants me to.

I leave the restaurant, having lost none of my resolve. Nothing is going to shake me off my quest for the truth. But I still have this day to get through. Following my itinerary, I get back into my muddy truck, which sticks out like a sore thumb on the city street, and head in the racetrack's direction. The backstretch is somewhere where my truck will fit right in.

2

Backstretch

Frank and I would visit the track together a few times throughout the racing season, but he was the one with the stronger love and passion for the horse-racing business. He was vocal and influential on racing ethics and humaneness, as well as being actively involved with our racehorses. Never a man to accept the status quo, Frank questioned, challenged, and pushed for change. I admired and respected his commitment to help make the world a better place, especially his efforts to improve animal welfare.

The track brings back many memories. It's a place that we both enjoyed being a part of, even if our appearances weren't frequent. The painful knowledge that there won't be any more of those happy days with Frank has kept me away, except for a couple of quick visits.

I show my badge to the security guard and try to keep my mind on the present as I drive into the backstretch. It's as if I've entered another world, full of captivating and differing characters. It seems that every race, class, religion and personality is represented. I love to watch these fascinating people working with the horses as I drive along the familiar dirt tracks between the long barns. I see hot-walkers leading horses round and round inside the barns to cool them off after their daily exercise, a timed work or a race. This is an important job, since a horse not properly cooled can succumb to colic, but hot-walkers are usually the lowest paid, working wherever they can find a hot horse and a trainer willing to use them. I see a couple of the wealthy racehorse stable owners, who have their own private trainers, riders, grooms and hot-walkers, each driving a flashy, expensive car towards the barns.

Frank told me he'd once thought of expanding his stable so as to be in that league, but decided he was too busy to enjoy the benefits. He admitted he had too many irons in the fire. There was no mention of the incredible expense of maintaining a large stable. There is no guarantee of return in the horse-racing business, just the certainty that lots of money will go out.

Watching and listening to the interesting and vibrant life of the backstretch is like being in the audience at a live theatre, with its schemes, intrigues, characters, tragedies and triumphs. And sometimes I join the play. It's easier for me to be more outgoing and sociable in the backstretch because the horses are the focus of everything and everybody, and there's always something to talk about. But I've only come twice during the past year, despite Shane the trainer pestering me more than daily.

Yielding to horses and their handlers on the way, I find the right barn and recognise Shane's green and white training colours. My dirty truck looks quite at home parked by the shed-row. As I slide off the high seat, I pick up the smell of steaming manure piled high in the dumpsters mingled with the scents of clean golden straw and fresh green hay. I step over the open ditch, which carries water from endless horse baths and numerous emptied water buckets, and enter the barn. Several horses' shiny heads turn to watch me. But they soon lose interest and resume eating their hay, snatching mouthfuls from the nets that hang just outside their stall doors. The neat barn boasts a freshly raked aisle. The feed bins hang in a row along the wall opposite the stalls, and the clean, rolled bandages are stowed tidily on the shelf.

"Hi, Linda!" I raise my voice, hoping Linda's somewhere in the vicinity.

"Hi, Mrs Sheppard," a voice replies. It came from under a horse, at the back of a dimly lit stall. Linda is bandaging the legs of one of the young thoroughbreds who worked earlier.

"How are you? I haven't seen you for a long time." I step into the deep straw to pat the horse.

"Oh, I'm fine."

It's hard to have a conversation of any length with Linda. She's an excellent groom, and my guess is that she communicates more effectively with horses than with humans. And perhaps I do too. Linda's appearance hasn't improved. She looks after the horses better than she does herself. She needs a hairstyle, jeans without holes and a sweater that isn't frayed around the collar and cuffs, not to mention without the stains. But the horses' coats gleam, their manes are short and combed, and their tails are silky-clean and trimmed.

"What's Shane up to?"

"He had to go to the racing office," Linda replies.

"How are Speed and Rose?"

"Fine."

"I'll find them." I turn to walk down the barn aisle. It isn't hard to pick Speed out from among the eleven horses Shane has in training. He's tall and active, always keen to know what's happening around him. His dark bay head is hanging over the half-door to his stall as he watches all the comings and goings. He recognizes me and tosses his head with a soft whinny.

It isn't long before Linda's rotund body and florid face join us.

"How's Speed doing?" I ask.

"Fine. You know he's entered into the Seaton Stakes Race?"

"Of course! I can't think why I didn't remember that. Well, Shane must be pleased with him, then. Where's Rose?" Linda waddles towards Rose's stall, which is on the opposite side of the barn. It is a puzzle how Linda manages to stay overweight when she works hard physically every day. She starts work at 5am and rarely quits before 4pm, and I wouldn't be surprised if some of that time is unpaid. Rose looks good, as usual.

"She looks in excellent condition and she's grown since she was at home. Perhaps we'll have some luck at the races this season." I stroke the velvety nose of the chestnut thoroughbred. "When's Shane likely to show up?"

"Don't know." Linda hesitates, as if she wants to add something.

"Is something wrong?"

"I think he's in some trouble like, with the officials."

"Do you know what sort of trouble?"

"You might not want to see him." Linda has taken over the stroking of Rose, who loves attention.

"What do you mean? Has he done something to one of my horses?"

"No. But it's something to do with that drug rule Mr Sheppard brought in." Linda goes into the stall with Rose, and before I can think of a response, she adds, "He's coming back now." I wonder how Linda knows that Shane's on his way, but, sure enough, when I turn to look outside, I see the trainer appear from behind the administration building. I recognize the grubby baseball cap with the fringe of straggly looking red hair. I've always thought he looks less professional than virtually all the other trainers. His shabby, well-worn and somewhat grimy clothes would have you assume he's one of the poorer hot-walkers. His dominant nose and long, ruddy face give him an uncanny horse-like resemblance. I find him unappealing.

I call out to him. "Hi, I finally made it here!"

"That's great! Excellent!" Shane replies, as he quickens his pace to almost a run. He holds out his hand and shakes mine for what I think is an unnecessarily long time. I can smell nicotine and coffee on his hot breath, which increases my aversion to the man.

"Is everything all right with Speed and Rose?"

"They're great. As I said in my email to you a couple of days ago, I've entered Speed into the Seaton Stakes Race. It won't be a tough race for Speed, and he has a good shot at winning." Shane walks towards the stall and I follow. We have to step swiftly to one side as a hot-walker, leading one of the many beautiful thoroughbreds, almost meets us head-on round the end of the shed-row.

When I reach Speed, I stroke his neck. Shane positions himself so that he's leaning against the stall door, almost touching me. I move to the other side of Speed, who's craning his neck towards me, hoping for treats.

"Sorry boy, I forgot the carrots." Seeing his big, doleful eyes, I wish I'd remembered. Speed loves his treats. But I'll not beat myself up over it, because I know this is a difficult day. I'm allowed a few mistakes, and Speed will forgive me.

"Doesn't he look grand?" I notice that Shane's narrow light-brown eyes are on me and not on the horse.

"Yes, he does," I agree. I'm about to ask Shane about his meeting with the racing officials, but think better of it. It was decent of Linda to tell me, but Shane will guess that Linda let me know, and poor Linda has to work with Shane. I certainly don't want to cause the girl to lose her job. I can easily find out from the officials.

After a few minutes, I excuse myself from Shane and say a quick goodbye to Linda. I drive a circuitous route to the administration building and park out of the direct line of vision from Shane's barn.

Fortunately, Frank was so well-known and respected that I'm not the least bit concerned about entering the building to ask some questions. While not all the officials agreed with Frank's goals, they respected him and didn't feel threatened by his approach. He was careful to do his homework. From what I could to gather through various conversations he had at the track, Frank researched what racetracks were doing in other jurisdictions, he consulted with the key stakeholders including owners and officials, and he attempted to develop a reasonable and practical position with which it was hard to argue. However, a few trainers were threatened by what they saw as a probable decrease in wins, and consequently, in earnings. When I asked Frank about this, he told me that there is only a small minority who thought this, and that most saw his goals as good for the well-being of the racehorse. And they agreed with him that, as long as everyone complied, it would be fine.

So, Frank dismissed the vocal objections of the minority, giving them little credence. His stance didn't jeopardize his success in pursuing the specific anti-drug regulation he was working on. He actively lobbied to have StartSmart, in particular, added to the list of banned drugs. I read about his work in the Thoroughbred Bulletin. The article explained StartSmart contains an anti-inflammatory drug, as well as a stimulant and I can't remember what else. The drug can cover up injuries and give the horse an increased adrenalin-boost, but there have sometimes been serious and potentially life-threatening consequences after a race. A few horses even had a bone suddenly snap or some other tragic injury during a race, resulting in immediate euthanasia on the racetrack.

I remember being proud of Frank's work on this. The new regulation, banning StartSmart, came into effect about ten months after he died, in time for this year's racing season.

* * *

I enter the dingy corridors of the administration building, and it doesn't take long to find the racing official I hoped would be here.

"Mrs Sheppard, how nice to see you." An older man, with a kind face, greets me. I appreciate Bill Price's warm welcome. After a brief exchange during which I ask him to call me Meg, I get to the reason for my visit.

"As you know, Shane Parrington is my trainer. I understand that there are some concerns?"

"Unfortunately, yes. Of course, you'd know all about the new drug rules that came into effect, since Frank was instrumental in having them put in place, in particular the banning of StartSmart."

I nod.

"Well, right from the start, Shane Parrington has been vocal in his disapproval, and he continues to be so. He can be quite aggressive at times. I can't understand it."

"Frank must have been aware that Shane opposed the impending regulations, but he didn't mention it to me."

"I can't see how Frank would not have been aware. I have to confess that I'm shocked, and I don't think that's too strong a work, that Frank's own trainer would show such bad judgment. He stood to lose Frank's good business, not to mention tarnishing his own reputation with other good owners. Also, the research is clear. The data are staring us in the face. All the provisions in the new regulations make sense and StartSmart is dangerous. Frank did a good job of educating everyone in that regard." Bill leans back in his chair and sighs.

"It's hard for me to understand why Frank didn't fire Shane." I'm surprised to feel a twinge of annoyance at Frank. Bill shrugs his shoulders. I try to come up with a plausible explanation, and add, "I think Frank would have respected Shane's opposition, to a point, when the regulations were being proposed and debated. But he would never have presumed that Shane would defy the regulations once they were put into effect. I don't think Frank would ever believe that someone in Shane's position would not obey the law."

"I agree. That sounds plausible. Frank always gave people the benefit of the doubt. He was a reasonable and honourable man."

"Yes, he was." Bill is right, Frank had integrity. And what also meant a lot to me was Frank's genuine and active commitment to the welfare of racehorses. There's a lump in my throat and my eyes are watering up. I need to tighten my grip on my emotions. I'm pretty good at reining in my feelings. After all, I've had a lot of practice.

"I'm also absolutely certain he would have instructed Shane not to give any drugs to the horses without his okay, including approved drugs. He cared so much about our animals."

"You and Frank were so well-regarded here that I will be bold and make a suggestion to you. If I were you, I'd check what Shane Parrington is doing. I feel absolutely certain that you wouldn't want Speed to fail the drug test after the upcoming Seaton Stakes Race. Not only would it be dangerous for the horse, and I know how much you love your horses, but it would be a disgrace to your husband's memory, and I assume it would be very upsetting for you."

"Absolutely."

"Officially, I can tell you that Shane has raised the suspicion of the officials. There is an investigation going on regarding claims made by a veterinarian and a hot-walker, that Mr Parrington is using SmartStart. He hasn't had a horse test positive after a race but, to be honest, the testing is not without its teething problems. There is other evidence that appears to support the allegations. You should have received notification of the investigation in the mail." Bill leans forward over the worn metal desk and clasps his hands together. "As I mentioned, Mr Parrington's objections to the regulations have continued, despite them being finalized and introduced. And the manner in which he chooses to make those objections known has become increasingly unpleasant, including personal attacks on some officials. Rather odd behaviour, if you ask me. I'm being direct with you because I'm concerned for you and your horses." He leans back in his chair and waits for my reaction.

"I appreciate you being direct with me. I haven't received the letter yet. I've not been here nearly often enough to know what's going on, or to know what Shane is doing. He calls me frequently, but doesn't give much information. He's usually just pleading for me to meet him at the track."

Shane's behaviour is perplexing. I can only think that Shane's opposition to the drug regulations and aggressive behaviour must have started after Frank's death, despite what I said to Bill. And I'm certain that Frank would have found another trainer if he'd suspected Shane of breaking the rules, even ones which were only in the process of being introduced. I resolve to email Shane, when I get home, making it crystal clear that I do not authorize the use of any prohibited drug for Speed or Rose.

By the time I get back into my truck, the backstretch is no longer a hive of activity. The horses have been groomed, exercised, cooled, bathed and fed, and are resting in their stalls. Many wear leg bandages enveloping various preventative poultices and ointments which emit strong antiseptic odours that hang in the air. Leaving the familiar smells, sights and sounds behind, I make my way home to do the barn chores and to get ready to see Murray, Frank's brother.

Murray has no family left. Although it should have been obvious as soon as Frank died, I've only recently registered that I am now his sole living relative in Canada. While I'm changing my clothes into something more suitable for leading the horses in and feeding the animals, some mixed thoughts about Murray play around in my mind. Frank told me that Murray always compared himself to his successful older brother and came up short. This started back in primary school. Murray had difficulty with schoolwork and trouble making friends. Frank was a year ahead of him in school and was a star pupil. Murray couldn't measure up and presumably gave up trying. Frank knew that he, and not Murray, had been his parents' favourite. I could see this would be hard on Murray, but I still don't understand him. He is so different from Frank.

I have composed an image of Murray's character in my mind, sketched from my memories of the few times I've met him and the several times Frank has talked about him. The image is of someone who is self-obsessed, negative and unstable. So, it isn't without some misgivings that I get changed again, get back into my truck, leaving the comfort of my home and the loving companionship of Kelly, to go to the Lighthouse Rehabilitation Centre.

It's difficult to drive round the deadly bend yet again, too many times on this tragic anniversary. I didn't consider this when I planned the day. Perhaps it would have been best to stay at home. After all, that's where I feel most relaxed, partly because I get more comfort from the animals than I do from humans. Humans often deepen my wounds. But I've set myself a mission to find out what happened to Frank, and I'll have to meet with people to get the answers I'm searching for, so it's likely a good idea to get out and about, to not only occupy my mind but also to stretch and strengthen my shrunken social skills.

My thoughts drift back to Murray. I remember Frank mentioned that he'd had a heated argument with him. This happened a couple of years ago when Frank wrote his will. Frank had been pretty upset. He'd said that Murray had made him feel cheap and uncompassionate, despite all of his efforts to do the best for his brother. I'm not sure why Frank had raised the subject of his will with Murray. Perhaps he thought it would give Murray some sense of security, and prevent him from worrying about the (unlikely) eventuality of Frank dying before him. When I read Frank's will, I thought that the establishment of the trust fund was a good idea. Frank left Murray

$750,000. His brother would have access to the interest only. On Murray's death, the interest would then go to various charities which Frank had selected.

Murray wasn't happy with this at all. He accused Frank of not trusting him. Despite the argument, Frank didn't change his will, although in the heat of the moment I heard him tell Murray he'd consider it. Soon after this, Murray admitted himself to the Lighthouse Rehabilitation Centre, but it was an abbreviated stay. He left and started drinking again. I remember there was another argument. Because Murray left the Centre without completing the program, Frank reduced his financial support. Murray accused Frank of being callous and selfish. I remember Frank repeating some of the awful things that Murray had said. Such things as Frank having too much money and not enough love for his own flesh and blood, that he just wanted any excuse to keep all the money himself when Murray deserved his fair share – after all, hadn't the inheritance from their parents paid for much of Frank's schooling? Murray hadn't had such a great education handed to him on a plate.

Frank didn't give Murray the money he demanded. He didn't go into details, but said that he was managing Murray's portion of the inheritance (which was not large) on his brother's behalf, in accordance with the wishes of his parents. He knew that his parents had wanted Murray to get better. And, during their argument, he said he wouldn't give Murray any more of his own money, other than through the trust fund included in his will, unless Murray committed to a rehabilitation program. I recall how upset Frank was with this altercation with his brother. He was afraid matters were going from worse to worse.

But after Frank's death, Murray admitted himself to Lighthouse Rehabilitation Centre and this time, from what I can gather, he has committed to completing the program. Perhaps Frank's death has had some life-altering impact on him.

The Lighthouse Rehabilitation Centre is nothing like a lighthouse and is nowhere near water. It is situated in beautiful, well-maintained and carefully landscaped grounds a few miles out of the city. It offers protection from where you're headed, if you're an alcoholic. It is luxurious. Frank paid the full fees for Murray when he was alive, for the short period that his brother stayed there. The trust fund interest might be just enough to cover the costs now that he is dead. At first, the Centre admits the client into a private room, similar to a hospital room. The client then progresses through various stages to an apartment, and then the Centre encourages occasional trips to Vannersville and back. Murray has just graduated to an apartment.

"Meg, it's so nice to see you!" Murray stands on the steps of the apartment complex and waits for me to walk across the driveway from the parking lot. He looks a lot better and sounds glad to see me. His features bear no resemblance to Frank's, for which I am thankful. But he looks too thin. His face is gaunt, and his skin has a mottled complexion.

"I'm glad I could come!" I kiss him lightly on the cheek. "How are you doing?"

"I'm doing well, thanks. How about you?"

"Not bad, thanks."

"I thought we'd have a cup of coffee or tea first, and then we'd go to the dining room. They actually serve some pretty good food here, although I don't always bother to go. I often snack in the apartment." Murray leads the way along the muted corridor with its thick cream and gold carpet and soft lighting.

I had been concerned that I'd find conversation difficult with Murray, but he's friendly and chatty, although he wants to reminisce about Frank. He reminds me of Frank's love of the dramatic, and how he could imitate people, often mocking them, and could put on acts. Although I find it hard to hear all this, I can't help chuckling now and then. Frank was a talented and entertaining guy. And, in the telling, Murray is coming across as much more tolerable and pleasant. I've not seen him like this before.

Then Murray changes tack and brings up their childhood, of which Frank had revealed little to me. He tells me that their parents had struggled financially and had lived tough lives. They had left England in search of more opportunity and a better standard of living. But it wasn't easy for them. Frank didn't mention his parents' disappointments, and since he was clearly wealthy when I met him, I'd assumed that his parents had been well off. Apparently not. Murray says that their father worked in construction and was killed when some scaffolding collapsed. Frank and Murray were in their early twenties when this tragedy happened. Then their mother, not long afterwards, died as a result of a severe asthma attack. Murray tells me that Frank believed that the thick, soupy pollution hanging over Vannersville at the time exacerbated her condition. They couldn't afford to move. He feels these tragedies inspired Frank to become active in environmental issues, as well as to earn considerable wealth.

"And my solution to all this catastrophe was to start drinking," Murray says. I don't have the strength of character that Frank had. But I'm now committed to making a real effort to get back on track."

And I find, as the evening goes on, that I do grow more optimistic that Murray's participation in the Lighthouse program will make a real and life-changing difference for him. As I drive home, I think how pleased Frank would have been.

But in my new frame of mind, my thoughts shift, and I wonder if Murray's apparently favourable progress might have something to do with Frank not being here. How jealous and resentful was he of Frank? Did Frank's successes rub salt into the wounds of Murray's failures? Is the trust fund giving Murray more freedom and more money than begging from Frank had done? If Murray is responsible for Frank's death, if he is the murderer, then perhaps his entertaining stories featuring his brother were told to convince me he's innocent. But I didn't tell him of my plan to find out what happened to Frank, so I'm not sure if it's fair to suspect him.

* * *

I'm back home, and finally this dreaded day is over. With a tremendous sense of relief, I sink into the warm, soft mattress on my welcoming bed. But, despite my weariness, my eyes won't close as I ponder what lies ahead and what I might find out.

3

Painted Dog

My eyes refused to close for most of the night, my eyelids reluctant to even blink. But they must have relented during the early morning hours, just before the dawn chorus. The alarm rudely interrupted a dream in which I'd lined up all the suspects in Frank's murder. There were too many faces, and each was jeering at me or taunting me. But even this dream was more welcome than the flashbacks that so often invade the night, the ones that torment and rouse me, and coat me in a soggy sweat.

I wrap my thick towelling robe around me and walk downstairs to let Kelly out. What do I know about Frank's accident? Precious little. A tingle of shame shivers up my spine. But there's no point dwelling on what I haven't done, and reproaching myself. It won't get me anywhere. Anyway, before I can do anything about it, I must look after the animals.

As I put on my barn clothes, I look out of the bedroom window and notice the dark brown soil of the flower beds. Chuck has turned them over, avoiding the sprouting bulbs and the remains of perennials planted during the past two years. Soon there will be some pansies and other new flowers to add colour to the spring garden.

Although I haven't given much thought to Chuck, I depend on him, not only for the gardening but for lots of other useful tasks. And just knowing he's around helps to lift my spirits a smidgen. Perhaps I take him a bit too much for granted.

Frank told me a little about his circumstances, but not much. I know Frank went to school with Chuck, but he hadn't seen him since then, until he bumped into him at the racetrack. Frank barely recognized Chuck. I remember him saying he looked more like a hobo than he would have expected of someone with Chuck's education and background. Anyway, I'll probably have to wait until tomorrow to get the story since he's unlikely to come to work in the garden two days in a row. But it's hard to be patient.

After the barn chores, I have a quick, warm shower and decide to visit the steel mill, hoping to meet Timothy Westmount without an appointment. It will be interesting to find out more about him and his involvement with Frank.

* * *

There is dampness in the air, and the silvery clouds are undecided on how to play out the day. I'm glad of my bulky scarf, which I've wrapped twice around my neck.

As I drive round the infamous bend, having the steep drop-off in my mind's eye, I can see Westmount Steel's large, shiny buildings that dominate the industrial section of Vannersville. The buildings grow larger and shinier as my truck gets closer. The tall chimney stacks belch out something, I'm not sure what. The gigantic complex of buildings, with their angular shapes, lack of windows, and invisible people, creates a sinister and ominous atmosphere. It is easy to feel intimidated and unwelcome here. However, the visitors' parking outside the administration office is a relief from this cold and colourless environment. Cheerful and vibrant pansies, packed into several curious steel planters, line each side of the walkway. There are some small patches of green grass. The colours and softness of the plants contrast vividly with their grey and hard surroundings.

"Can I help you?" the receptionist asks as I open the door.

"I've come to see Timothy Westmount."

"You have an appointment?" The receptionist is scanning the computer screen in front of her.

"No, I was hoping he would see me. It's important," I stress.

"Your name?"

"Meg Sheppard."

"Oh, Meg. I thought I recognized you. Frank Sheppard's wife. I'll let Mr Westmount know. But he's meeting with Susan Kingsley-Black at the moment, so you might have to wait for a bit."

I didn't expect it to be this easy and don't mind waiting. I choose one of the plush chairs in the lobby. As I get sucked into its thick, soft cushions, the image of a fly being devoured by a

Venus's fly-trap flickers in my mind's eye. I am close to sitting on the floor and hope I'll be able to extricate myself without excessive exertion. Several of these over-stuffed armchairs surround a shiny rosewood coffee table dominated by a large, exotic silk flower arrangement of various shades of purple and green.

I might have met Timothy Westmount at one of the many functions I accompanied Frank on. But his grey, lined face doesn't look familiar. His handshake is firm and friendly, and his hand feels smooth and elegant. His unkempt fine white hair doesn't look like it belongs to the slim body which wears a tailored, dark-blue, three-piece suit.

He came to greet me personally, in the lobby, and leads me into his imposing office. Panels of oak, stained mid-brown, line the walls. What intrigues me are the various art-works created out of steel, hanging on the wall, each one framed by the oak moulding of a panel.

I'm so distracted by the steel sculptures that I don't immediately realize that a woman is in the room.

"Meg, I'd like to introduce you to Susan Kingsley-Black. She's my Chief Operating Officer." Susan's lithe body, taller than mine, comes towards me topped with a half-smile. It's hard to read the expression in her dark eyes since they're diminished by thick lenses set in heavy-looking black frames. But I sense some irritation and that I'm unwelcome. She sits on the edge of Timothy's desk and folds her arms.

"To what do we owe this pleasure?" Timothy asks, after some very brief general comments to which I merely nod. I'm usually glad to get straight to the point, but I falter. I'm not sure how to broach my belief that Frank was murdered, and have no prepared questions to ask. I should have thought ahead. On a whim, I decide to distort the truth and make out that I'm thinking of seeking the nomination to be a candidate for the by-election, and that I'm planning on picking up where Frank left off, including the introduction of the pollution control regulations. As I explain why I'm keen to follow in Frank's footsteps, the elegant man sitting in his high-backed leather chair twirls the expensive gold watch on his wrist. His blue eyes frost over as he clenches his jaw. Susan picks up her smart-phone and appears to send a message to someone. Her long, red thumb-nails click on the mini keyboard at a rapid rate. Her lips are not visible – she seems to have sucked them in.

"I know you have good connections and are well-respected in Vannersville. I thought you might have some ideas or suggestions which would help me," I say. "I'm quite determined to make a difference."

"I don't see a need for any more regulations. I think the concern about greenhouse gases and climate-change are simply scare-mongering. My advice would be to leave well alone. You won't get support from business people in this community or from the workers who want to keep their jobs." Timothy is now sitting on the edge of his chair and has his long thin hands clasped together, making his knuckles white.

"I understood Frank had garnered significant support for improved pollution controls as well as for other environmental issues."

"If I were you, I'd get on with your own life rather than trying to continue with your dead husband's work." Timothy is leaning back in his chair again and twirling his watch twice as fast."

"It's not good to dwell on the past." He forces a smile as he tosses his head back. "Next you'll be telling me that Frank's death wasn't an accident."

I say nothing and keep my face unmoving. He suddenly jumps out of his chair as if he's received an electric shock.

"We have another meeting. Run out of time." With that, he ushers me out. Susan doesn't even acknowledge my departure. The receptionist bids me a cheery farewell though, before I stride out to the car park.

My keys have made their way to the bottom of my purse. Just as I retrieve the jangling bunch, someone moves between me and my truck.

"Meg Sheppard?" asks a short, chunky man, with a sneer in his voice and on his face. Despite his apparent attempt to be intimidating, I think he looks comical. He is short and square. His face, including his jaw, his frame and even his penetrating eyes are angular.

"Yes," I reply.

"Timothy Westmount has asked me to warn you to stay away. He doesn't wish to speak with you again. You aren't welcome here." His eyes don't blink as he keeps eye-contact with me. I push past the melodramatic man and get into my truck. I suppose he must be the person Susan texted. But why this crazy reaction to my visit?

* * *

"It seemed so ridiculous," I tell Tom later, on the phone. "The way they reacted makes me think there must be a link between Frank's death and these people. It can't just be about regulations and the possibility of me being a candidate in the by-election. If they want me to stop, then they've failed. And the silly encounter with that man in the parking lot has just made me more suspicious and more curious."

"Sounds like Brad Buckthorn to me," Tom says. "But it doesn't make sense."

"Timothy obviously got uneasy when I raised the subject of the regulations and my plans to run for the by-election. I could tell by his body language. And when he tried to make out that it would be utterly ridiculous if I had any thought that Frank's death wasn't an accident, and I hadn't mentioned it by the way, and I didn't answer, that seemed to clinch it. He suddenly ushered me out of the door. The way he behaved makes me think there must be a lot at stake."

"How odd of him to raise it. Be careful, Meg. These guys can be ruthless. Why don't you let me help?"

"No. Thanks anyway. This is something I feel I have to do."

"What are you going to do next?"

"I'm going to act on your suggestion. I'm going to go through the papers and newspaper clippings on the accident, and search on-line, this evening. I haven't planned anything beyond that, yet."

"Well, at least let me help you go through that stuff."

"Maybe that's a good idea. Would seven o'clock work?"

"Yep, sure."

I'm surprised that I'm relieved that Tom's coming over. Despite my bravado, Brad has made me uneasy. But at least he didn't grab me.

And I feel somewhat vindicated. They don't want me asking questions, so they must know something or have been involved in Frank's death. So, I conclude that I'm right to believe it wasn't an accident and I'm right to pursue the truth. I'm glad I visited the steel mill.

With increased determination, I bring the shoeboxes down from upstairs, which have all the items I and Murray collected immediately after Frank died. I remember how Murray was helpful in going through Frank's things, although it was only for a couple of days, and then he left somewhat abruptly. Murray even brought a few newspaper clippings that he thought I might not have seen. I'm not sure why I had decided to collect the clippings of the crash, but I'm glad I did. Going through them, especially the photographs, might just trigger some questions that should be asked. They might even answer a few questions. I know I didn't go over them carefully at the time. Looking at the photos and reading all the accolades about Frank were too painful. Being a politician often brought criticism and negative press, however good, dedicated and sincere you are. However, Frank rarely had poor press. They seemed to like him. Perhaps it was because he was a social, talkative kind of guy. He always made time to answer questions. The Vannersville Times devoted the whole front page of one issue to photos, with several articles on Frank and the accident included in the body of the paper.

Kelly has been following me everywhere. I put all the shoeboxes and some of Frank's files on the dining room table. I turn the laptop on and look down at Kelly's big brown eyes.

"You want to go for a walk, don't you?" I've been out a lot during the past 48 hours, and Kelly isn't used to it. There is some daylight left, being early in a spring evening, although it's still dull. So, we venture out in the truck, and park outside the forest about two miles down the road.

I'm warm and cosy in my lined raincoat, and secure with my sturdy hiking stick in hand, which Chuck whittled for me just before

Frank died. The smell of the pine trees is strong, tangy, and fresh. There are tiny bright-green blades of grass peeping through the decay of last year's growth. Kelly runs to and fro, obviously enjoying everything.

* * *

I remember when Kelly arrived at the humane society. She was a neglect case, and her owner was charged with cruelty to animals under the Criminal Code of Canada. Kelly was a matted mess of filth, with fleas and lice attacking her outside, and worms attacking her inside. With lots of tender, loving care and excellent veterinary services, she put on weight, gained strength and blossomed. I grew deeply attached to her and I could tell that she trusted me. Frank and I had just moved to the farm, so I assumed we'd adopt her. But Frank resisted. He wanted a puppy, and he wanted a German Short-Haired Pointer, complete with registration papers. I just couldn't understand him. I was flabbergasted when he said that he didn't want other people's rejects. To me, his position on Kelly was dissonant with his voiced concern for the welfare of animals, his pursuit of enhanced drug rules for the horseracing industry, and his apparent love of racehorses. My adoption of Kelly was the first of only a very few occasions when I defied him.

I shake my head as if to rid myself of the unwanted memory. I watch Kelly trotting ahead on the trail, and think how lucky I am to have her warm, limitless, unconditional love. She is my treasured companion.

We've been out on the trail for about twenty minutes, and it's time to head back to the truck. Just as I'm about to turn round, I hear something thundering up behind. A huge German Shepherd tears past me and lunges at Kelly with a fury that turns my stomach. My heart pounds as I rush towards the hairy, growling, rolling mess. The noise is terrifying. As soon as I get the opportunity, I hit the dog as hard as I can manage with my stick across the side of its body. Its enormous, bared, white teeth turn towards me, and he leaps with a blood-curdling growl. I have the stick out in front of me, holding it near to each end and thrust it towards the dog as he charges, which prevents him from reaching my face. But he's ready to spring again. Just as he prepares to leap for the second time, I swipe the stick across the dog's head as hard as I can manage. This time he falls limp to the ground, but I sense we have little time to escape.

It's too far to get back to the truck safely. But I know there's an old telephone booth at the corner of the intersection, next to an abandoned gas station, about five walking minutes from this part of the forest. I hope the booth has a door and will provide us with a safe haven – if we can reach it in time. Kelly is obviously shaken and presses against my legs, looking for protection. I'm relieved to see her on her feet, and thankful that she doesn't appear to be injured.

"Come on, Kelly, we have to run!" She's as eager as I am to get out of here. We run. I'm pretty fit, but I lose my footing a couple of times on the wet, decaying leaves which cover slippery mud. The forest has transformed into a fearful and forbidding place. My heart thumps and my face is flushed and sweaty. It's as if we've strayed into the filming of a horror movie, and I desperately want the director to call "cut".

I can't make up my mind whether it's good or bad that the escape route is straight. Likely it doesn't matter. The dog will pick up our scents on whatever path we take. I glance back. The German Shepherd is shaking itself.

I can see the telephone booth at the corner of the intersection. Kelly glues herself to my side, and is able to keep up, despite having been attacked. I'm tiring and breathless. I turn and see the German Shepherd gaining ground with long, easy strides. Somehow, we find some extra energy and at last we squeeze into the booth. I yank the folding door closed, bracing my foot against it, just as the German Shepherd emerges from the forest.

It bounds over the road to the booth and circles us. Now and then it pauses to scratch at the walls of the booth, its claws making piercing screeches, and its paws smearing muddy streaks over the colourful graffiti. The walls rattle and shake. Kelly whimpers.

"Tom, I need your help." I'm relieved that I have my phone.

"What's going on?" Tom sounds alarmed.

"A large, vicious German Shepherd attacked us in the forest for no apparent reason. Kelly and I are okay, but we're trapped in a telephone booth, which this damn dog is circling. He doesn't look like he's going to let up in the near future, that's for sure. Could you get us out of here somehow?"

"Where are you?" asks Tom. I'm relieved that he's calm, despite the concern in his voice. He can be highly strung at times. Thank goodness for a friend like Tom.

I can't easily bend over in the booth. There isn't room. I want to check Kelly. I notice some blood smeared on the inside of one of the walls, and there is a little on the floor. Kelly is crouched down, tight against my feet, and whimpers each time the dog thumps the side of the booth. It's too difficult to examine her, and wouldn't serve any useful purpose at this stage in any case. There's nothing I can do until we get out of here and home to safety.

As I move my feet, I kick something. I see two cans of spray paint on the floor. I scrunch myself into a contorted fold so that I can reach them. I test them, and find that they each have some paint inside. I pull the folding door slightly towards me, creating a small gap. The dog takes the bait and leaps towards the door, and my reactions are quick enough to spray paint in its face. Undeterred, it leaps again and I spray with both cans at the same time, keeping the door ajar just enough with my foot. I've now turned him into a blue and yellow freak. He backs off. I'm sure there's some of the paint in his eyes and perhaps up his nose and certainly in his mouth.

Tom arrives in record time. It seems like seconds. He parks the car about ten feet from the folding door. Roused by Tom's arrival, the German Shepherd turns, voicing his disapproval with slobber-laden aggressive barks. Tom rolls the window down, and my mouth drops open as I see him point a handgun at the dog and fire. The noise of the shot sends a shockwave through me and Kelly. I now wonder if I did the right thing to call him. I know that he often over-reacts, and perhaps the dog would have eventually left us. I need to have more confidence in my ability to deal with situations like these. I like to think that I'm resourceful and strong.

"Hope you're okay," Tom says, as I open the door to the booth. "A dog like that should be put down."

"Why do people have aggressive dogs? It's been a bit like something out of a horror movie for Kelly. Look at her shaking. Her eyes are as wide as saucers."

Kelly won't move, and cowers in the booth. For the first time that I can remember, the dog won't obey. She won't come to me. Tom squeezes into the booth and picks Kelly up. He seems to have no trouble carrying the sixty-pound dog.

"You'll get blood on your nice raincoat. She's bleeding." Why did I say that? I can't stop my eyes welling up with tears for Kelly. I can smother most of my feelings and emotions most of the time, but not when my beloved Kelly's hurt.

"That's the least of our worries. I can sponge the blood off when we get to your house." Tom says.

"Thanks for coming so quickly. And it must have been horrible shooting that dog." I'm relieved to get into Tom's smart red sports car.

The German Shepherd lies in a pool of blood, quite still, with paint, drool and dirt all over its head. I'm surprised that I'm not upset by its death. I'm relieved. I love animals, but that was a dangerous beast and innocent Kelly has been hurt. I can't fathom how an animal could be so vicious for no apparent reason. Tom picks up the dead dog and heaves it into the trunk.

"I assume there's somewhere on your farm I can bury it?" asks Tom. "He hasn't got a collar, and I don't think for a second that he's microchipped, so we should deal with his body."

"Animal Control Services would probably do something. But I agree we shouldn't leave him. We can bury him at the farm. Let's get out of here." I can't bear to move my eyes away from Kelly, although I have to twist around to watch her.

"And don't worry about blood on the back seat. It's leather. It'll wipe off." Tom drives us away from the gruesome scene with a surge of acceleration which thrusts Kelly into the back of the seat. My aching for her grows. "Good thinking to use the spray cans. It might have ended differently if you hadn't. By the way, I won't report this to anyone, just because I think it might be linked to your meeting at the steel mill."

"You really think so?" I haven't given it a thought and certainly haven't made a connection. If there is one, then it's my fault that Kelly got hurt.

"I don't mean to be dramatic, but how many times do unattended vicious dogs attack for no reason in a forest? Somebody's obviously very concerned about what you said about planning to follow in Frank's footsteps. There must be a lot at stake with the pollution control regulations issue. I know it sounds crazy, and I'm having trouble getting my head around it, but I reckon someone is trying to shake you off something."

"Perhaps you're right. But there's got to be more to it than that. It must also have something to do with Frank's death and that his crash was no accident."

"As you know, I don't agree with you about Frank's accident, but it does seem odd that you and Kelly were attacked on the very day you go to visit Westmount, and after Brad threatened you. I think you should be careful. This could be dangerous. As I said, there could be a lot at stake here."

I've twisted myself sideways in the car so that I can now reach Kelly and stroke her. She's whimpering. I'm shaking, but it's mostly to do with the shock of realizing that Tom is capable of doing something like shoot a dog.

"I didn't realize you have a gun," I say.

"I'm sure you know my Dad was a cop."

"No, I didn't. At least, I don't remember."

"He didn't like guns, but he was a realist. He knew he had to be able to handle one well. At one time, I thought I'd like to follow the same career as my dad. Part of this interest resulted in me joining a shooting club. Just indoor target practice. After my dad got shot, rather than put down my gun, I decided I should know how to use one and should keep my gun registration up-to-date." Tom pauses and looks at me. "But this is the first time I've shot a living being. It's a bit different from hitting a target."

"It's awful." I can't help wishing he'd keep his eyes on the road. "But it was the right thing to do. I'm glad you did. I hope it hasn't upset you too much."

"I'll get over it." We finally arrive at the farm and Tom parks his car round the back of the house, near the kitchen door. "I'll carry Kelly in," he says.

4

Likely Suspects

The warmth and familiarity of the house wraps around me like an old security blanket as I step through the back door. Tom puts Kelly down gently on one of the kitchen floor mats. It's such a relief to get her home.

"Are you going to call the vet?" he asks.

"I'm going to check her over myself first. Kelly hates going to the vet. It's traumatic for her. I think it might remind her of the humane society and she might think she's going to be left there. And we country folk learn to do a lot of basic first aid ourselves. I'm hoping it's nothing more than puncture wounds."

I gently ferret through her furry coat, looking for blood and wounds while her wide eyes search my face, as if seeking answers and reassurance. I talk to her in as calm and soothing voice as I can muster, hoping her trust in me will help her settle. "Probably the shock of the whole thing is going to be more of the issue. It certainly was frightening." Kelly lies quietly as I continue my search. At least she isn't bleeding profusely. "I've found three puncture wounds from the beast's teeth on the back of her neck. But I see there's also a scrape on her leg, which is where most of the blood came from, I think. It's quite nasty and still bleeding a bit, as you can see, but not deep. I can't understand how she got that, but it's nothing serious. The puncture wounds will have to be flushed out with hydrogen peroxide and the scrape kept clean, but I think these wounds will heal quickly. I've got antibiotics on hand and I'll give her a course of them, just to make sure." Of course, she's up-to-date on all her shots, including her rabies vaccine.

* * *

"Still sounds gruesome. Poor Kelly." Tom is pacing around the kitchen, fiddling with things by the sound of it. His agitation is hard to ignore. I'm relieved when he asks, "Is there an old jacket and some boots I can borrow, so I can bury that dog while you're attending to Kelly? And then I'll sponge the blood off our raincoats and the back seat of my car."

"That would be great." The atmosphere will be calmer and quieter with Tom busy elsewhere for a bit. But I'm grateful to him, especially for disposing of the vicious dog. "There are extra clothes and boots in that cupboard by the kitchen door, and there is a shovel in the garage and if you can't find it, there should be another one in the feed room in the barn. And for sponging off the seats, there are some clean cloths under the kitchen sink. Cold water should work."

"By the way, I think I might as well stay, now that I'm here. I was going to come over later this evening, in any case. Just thinking you both might like some company."

"We'll take you up on your offer, thanks." I notice that Kelly's breathing has slowed down to a near-normal rate, and she accepts the cleaning of her wounds with no fuss. At last, I'm finished and I settle in a chair and the dog curls up, covering my feet with welcome and comforting warmth. I can't help feeling that I should have been able to protect her from the attack. After all, that's what family is all about, or should be. This thought reminds me of my so-called family, which wasn't a family in the loving, protecting meaning of the word. It was a hurting family. But I delayed leaving because I couldn't abandon the dog, Bertie, who I knew wouldn't be safe without me. He and I were family, the kind that counts, that watches your back, that picks you up when you're down. I told Bertie my secrets, my deepest feelings, my plans for escape. But I couldn't find a plan which included him. Where could I go? No youth shelters or hostels accepted dogs. And I didn't have enough courage or resourcefulness to live on the streets. That life sounded untamed, uncovered, and unkind.

One morning I found Bertie dead in his bed, and, despite everything, I believe he died peacefully in his sleep. The pain precipitated my departure the next day. It was impossible to endure without Bertie's unfailing, unconditional love.

I do hope Kelly forgives me for not watching her back.

* * *

I must have fallen asleep for a few minutes. I'm woken by Tom setting up the laptop, which announces its start-up by singing loud tones like doorbell chimes. I rouse myself and rummage through various papers.

"Nothing is in any order. I'm not even sure why Murray and I collected all this. Perhaps in some weird way it helped me to cope. There were loose papers on Frank's desk and I didn't know what to do with them, so I put them in those larger boxes. I don't even know where all these boxes came from."

The real doorbell chimes echo through the house. It takes me a second to realize what the noise is, since I rarely have visitors who ring the bell. Anyone who knows me comes and finds me, or I'm expecting them and greet them as soon as they get out of their car. Kelly pricks up her ears but makes no attempt to move. Tom offers to go, but I say it's fine and I'll go to the door, although I'm sorry that Kelly has to move so that I can use my feet.

I'm more than surprised to find Susan Kingsley-Black on the doorstep. She smiles with tight lips as if it's a struggle for her. Her dark, well-tailored pant suit and her upright posture give her the appearance of self-assurance. I ask if she'd like to come in, but she declines.

"I'm here, far too belatedly, to give my condolences to you on your loss of Frank."

"Thank you." How strange she looks, standing on my doorstep in her Chief Operating Officer garb.

"I've lost someone close to me in the past. I have some idea what you've been going through."

"Is this why you came here?"

"Yes. You coming to the office today reminded me I hadn't conveyed my sympathy to you. It was very tragic that he died so unexpectedly in that awful accident."

I don't reply. I maintain eye-contact. Her dark eyes flicker behind the thick lenses. I just want her to leave.

"As Timothy said, it was an accident, you know." She continues. "Thinking anything else will just stop the healing process."

"Let me worry about that. Thanks for coming." I'm in no mood to deal with her. I try to close the door, but she keeps it open with a foot in a shiny leather pump and a hand with long, bright red nails which look something like talons to me.

"If I was you, I'd let sleeping dogs lie." The woman's forced smile, such as it is, reveals a line of incongruous yellow teeth. I try again to shut the door. "And you'll do yourself no good trying to get Frank's pollution control regs back on the table. It'd be best for you if you got on with your life." People keep telling me this.

She lets go of the door, and I close it with a bang and relock it.

When I relate the episode to Tom, he isn't amused. He thinks Susan tried to threaten and intimidate me, and that she was letting me know that they, whoever "they" are, know where I live. Perhaps he's right, but it isn't going to work. I convince him we should get back to what we planned to do. So, Kelly curls up on my feet again, and we get down to business.

"How about you go through the papers, and I search the web," Tom suggests.

The very first newspaper cutting brings back vivid and painful memories, some of which I realize I'd managed to bury. The picture of Frank's smashed-up car attached to a winch, which was about to drag it up the long steep rugged slope to the road, reminds me of how horrific the crash had been. The car plunged into large rocks and it was speculated that it had been going at such a rate that it had tipped on its crushed nose and crashed back down. It was amazing that the car had made it all the way down at such a speed, especially since it had to miss several large trees on the slope. The article mentions the search for Frank's body, which they believed had been flung from the car into the frothing, churning river. It was running high and fast, as it does every spring. It narrows and deepens along the bottom of the slope, past large, dark-grey smoothed boulders which came to rest many hundreds of years before.

I remember the deep shock I felt as my world was blown apart that day. Frank was the only person I had allowed to get close to me, physically or emotionally, since I left England. The memories are like thorns pricking my skin and piercing my heart. I'm shivering and have a lump in my throat.

"Are you sure you want to do this, Meg?" asks Tom.

"I must." Tom's words and presence help to snap me out of my grave reflections. I gather myself together, reining in the intense emotions which have resurfaced, although I can't stop my voice from trembling. "I'd love a cup of tea though." Tom goes off to the kitchen to make some.

I stare at the picture, and mull over the words in the article. It's sadly ironic that Frank had been driving his beloved 1963 Cadillac. Although it was large and sturdy, it had no seatbelts or airbags.

Some words leap out from the article underneath, including "well respected", "one of the few honest, hard-working politicians", "solid member of the Vannersville community" and "well regarded by the horse-racing industry". Despite my resolve, I have tears in my eyes and put my hand over my mouth. What a tragic loss of such a good person, and he was my husband. I'll need a lot of strength to go through these cuttings and papers. I need a break already.

While the tea is brewing, Kelly and I visit the barn. I find some solace and comfort as I listen to the horses calmly munching their hay. I hear the occasional snort as they clear their nostrils, which reminds me of the fascinating fact that they can only breathe through their noses and not at all through their mouths. It doesn't take long for me to feel soothed and nearly as calm as they are. And it's a relief to see Kelly wagging her tail again when I say it's time to go back to the house.

"Here we go. I probably should have found cups, shouldn't I?"

"Mugs are fine. Thanks, Tom," I reply.

"What a god awful day you've had," Tom says, as he sits down in front of the laptop.

Something catches my attention at the end of the newspaper article I've been reading, as I'm about to put it aside.

"It says here, that another car was at the scene. It says 'A second man was also seriously hurt. Vannersville Police Services has not yet released his identification. Although the man was conscious, and able to give a brief report to police, he was immediately transferred to hospital, where he is reported to be in serious condition. It is believed, according to police reports, that this man, as yet unidentified, had been driving behind Minister Sheppard. The man apparently told police that Minister Sheppard abruptly plunged down the slope. As a result, he was startled and lost control, and crossed the road to the opposite side from the Minister and crashed into a large tree.' I bet he could give us some useful information, assuming he pulled through."

"It seems though, that he's an eyewitness, who supports the accident theory," Tom notes.

"Well, if that's so, explain Buckthorn and the beast from hell!" I don't mean to be melodramatic, but the events of today have left me more convinced that Frank's death was no accident. I reach down and pat Kelly's silky head. "And what about the very strange visit from Susan?"

"There might not be a connection between Frank's accident and what happened. It likely has more to do with their fear that you might be working towards having the pollution control regulations introduced, or picking up some other work of Frank's. You said Susan mentioned the regulations just now."

"She also mentioned the so-called accident." I really don't want to argue with Tom about this. I don't see the point. "Perhaps the other man who got hurt saw something. But I suppose he would have told the police."

"I'm sure he would have," Tom says.

I pick up a letter from Frank's papers, which has a letterhead I'm not familiar with.

"I've found a letter from a lawyer, but it isn't from our lawyer, it's someone called William Porter."

"What does it say?"

"Something about his clients having concerns about the stands Frank had taken on environmental issues. Something about the proposed new pollution control regulations and how they would do serious damage to the economy, businesses, and jobs, and therefore people, aka voters, and that Frank should meet with him to hear another, more realistic side to the argument, as presented by his clients. I'd say it sounds somewhat threatening, which is odd. I thought everyone respected Frank."

"I'd say that lawyer should have a visit. But I'd recommend a day off." He smiles and stretches back in his chair, with his arms over his head.

"Well, tomorrow is the Seaton Stakes Race. The trainer says that Speed has a good chance. So, I was planning to go. I wondered if you'd like to come."

"That's a great idea. I'd like to."

"There's a table reserved at the restaurant. The racetrack does that for owners with horses entered in to that race."

"I'll look forward to it."

"We'd better keep going with this. I'd like to get as much of this reviewed this evening as we can manage."

Tom returns his focus to the laptop. "I've found some articles on the internet. A couple about the election campaign, and one about the pollution control regulations Frank drafted," Tom says. "And one short newspaper article quotes Timothy Westmount as saying, 'Of course, we share the Minister's concern regarding the environment, but the controls he is proposing will shut us down. That would be a loss of 1,200 jobs for Vannersville'. It goes on to give Frank's response, saying that the regulations would have a lengthy phase-in period, and that the technology is readily available to comply with these laws."

"There are some similar articles here that must have been in the papers on Frank's desk. Some of them are photocopied. It must have had something to do with his campaigning," I say. "There's a short one here that mentions Sandy's Waste Retirement. That's where Sharon works."

"Well, you have a good contact then."

"Perhaps. Not sure I trust her though."

"There's a press release I've found on Frank's campaign website. It mentions a public forum planned for about nine weeks before the accident. It says that he will present his ideas for enhanced pollution controls to the public, and give them an opportunity for feedback."

"I've got a clipping here on that. It says there were some disruptive, noisy hecklers, and that the police had to be called."

"Oh, I remember Frank talking about that,"Tom says. "I remember him being quite concerned. He hadn't come up against such strong and vocal opposition before."

"But the article is pretty positive. It says that his ideas were well received."

"That points to the possibility of the hecklers being hired by someone, with the plan to disrupt the meeting, which Frank suspected, by the way."

"I suppose that makes sense," I say. "Here's something about the new drug rules Frank was advocating for at the racetrack. It quotes some animal welfare group as being totally behind the new rules, but says a few trainers were opposed to them. It doesn't mention which ones. That's interesting. I found out yesterday that Shane is being investigated by the racing officials. They've received allegations that he's using SmartStart, which is a drug that is now banned and that Frank was instrumental in having added to the regulations. Apparently, Shane continues to attack supporters of the new drug rules personally, and vocally. The steward I was talking to said he had been 'quite aggressive'. I think those were the words he used."

"Well, he's a definite for your list."

"I can't figure out why Shane would be so opposed, and why Frank continued to use him as a trainer, given his opposition."

"Perhaps Frank didn't know at the time."

"That's possible, I suppose. I've finished going through most of these papers. Do you have anything else?"

"There's a letter from Marshall Moncton-Brown. He's considered an autocratic businessman and very right wing. But this letter seems decent. He's inviting Frank to tour his gravel pits and concrete plant."

"I'll add him to the list, just in case. I'm looking at Frank's will and I see two names I should check out. One is Charles Alexander Murphy. That's Chuck, the gardener. He received $50,000. Then, the other name is Murray Sheppard. It might surprise you I'm adding Murray to the list, but he's had terrible problems."

"Frank confided in me some of his frustrations with Murray. He handed out money to him regularly. I gather he's an alcoholic."

"We didn't have a lot to do with him. But, as you say, Frank did give him money, and the will is quite generous. At least, I think so. He didn't get a lump sum, but, as you know, there's a trust fund set up for him, of $750,000, with the interest to be paid to him quarterly. I'm sure you remember that, when Murray dies, the money is to go to several charities that Frank specified."

"Yes, I remember."

"And Murray and Frank had arguments. The two I'm aware of were both about money. Frank just wasn't willing to continue handing over money to Murray. There were conditions. Frank didn't want to support Murray's self-destruction, is what it boiled down to, but Murray didn't see it like that. Now Murray has the interest from the trust fund and can spend it any way he wants to".

"Did Murray know what was in the will?"

"Yes, that's what they had one of the arguments about. Murray thought he should get a lump sum, rather than Frank setting up a trust fund."

"What's the next step?"

"Well, I've got several names of people I want to talk to. I want to meet the man who was in the other car, and also hurt, apparently as a result of Frank's accident, but we don't know his name yet. And William Porter, the lawyer. As far as suspects, I've listed the ones that objected to Frank's stand on pollution which includes Timothy Westmount, Marshall Moncton-Brown of MMB Aggregates, and Sandy Bingham, owner of Sandy's Waste Retirement where Sharon works. I'm going to put Brad Buckthorn's name down as well because I'm not sure if he's following direct orders or not. And I'm going to add Shane because of his opposition to Frank's initiative on the horse-racing drug rules. And I suppose I should add Chuck because he's benefitted from Frank's will, although it's hard to think that way. This is getting to be a long list." I sigh and Kelly gets up and puts her head on my lap, as if she understands. I put my hand on her head and ask her if she's feeling better.

"It's probably best to have too many on the list at first, then we, I mean you, can scratch them off when you've ruled them out."

"And I need to add George, Frank's Assistant, to the people I should meet. I haven't seen him since the memorial service. I'm sure he'll have some thoughts on who might want Frank out of the picture and why."

The possible motives that have risen to the surface so far don't appear compelling enough for murder. If I could uncover the real motive, I'm sure I'd be much closer to identifying who was responsible for Frank's untimely death.

Tom offers to help again. I'm hesitant. I want to do this on my own, and I certainly don't want anyone else staying in the house. I've grown used to having my privacy, solitude and freedom. I like it that way. But I come up with a compromise, since I don't want to push Tom away in case I need his help again, and I don't want to hurt his feelings.

"Since you're coming to the track tomorrow, you can help me keep Shane at bay. I feel uneasy about him." Shane makes me uncomfortable. Perhaps it has something to do with the fact that he texts or emails me at least once daily, usually to ask when I'll be going to the track.

"Okay. By the way, I realize that I've met Chuck at Westmount Steel – he was a manager there and I'm pretty sure he has an MBA. Now he's a gardener of all things!"

"And what's wrong with that?" I raise one eyebrow and give Tom a sideways glance.

"Okay, you have a point."

"It's just that with an MBA and $50,000 you'd think he'd find more lucrative employment."

I start to tidy up the papers. "I think I know how I can find out who the man in the other car was, the one that also crashed. I was a volunteer at the hospital and got to know Dr. Milton reasonably well. I imagine he'd know about the man. I'm sure I'll be able to find out something."

"I doubt that man will be helpful. He was reportedly seriously injured. The fact that he was in a terrible accident himself makes it unlikely he saw anything. And even if he did see something, he has probably forgotten it, because of the shock and trauma he must have experienced. In any case, as you said, he would have reported what he saw to the police."

"Yes, I suppose so." I now want my space back to myself, and to enjoy some relaxation with loyal and loving Kelly. We are both tired. It has been a challenging day. "I think that's enough for this evening. I can clear up this mess. Thanks for helping. You've been great."

"I'm glad I was some help. I'm looking forward to the race," Tom says. "Will you be okay here alone?"

"I have a fancy security system I can activate from inside. Kelly will be with me. I'll be fine, thanks."

5

Broken Glass

Echoes of the snarls and growls we'd heard the day before haunt my sleep and wake me with a start a couple of times, but Kelly's rhythmic snoring reassures me and I manage to doze off again. As dawn breaks, I emerge from the warm cocoon of comforter and blanket and brace myself against the cool air of the bedroom. Kelly paddles her front paws as if marching on the spot and wags her tail. It's time to go to the barn. Well, at least the dog seems to be in fine shape and ready to tackle another day.

As I glance out of the window, grey clouds with dark undertones scurry across the sky. The sun hides close to the horizon and looks as if it will stay concealed for the day. I feel as unsettled as the weather. I can't decide whether I want it to rain because Speed likes the sloppy track, or if I want it to be fine so that we'll have a pleasant, dry afternoon at the races.

It would be smart to arm the alarm system before I go down

to the barn. I usually do, if I remember. Not even Kelly can hear someone coming up the driveway when we're busy working in the stalls. Frank had a siren installed which sounds like an enormous, sick fog-horn, hoping it would scare off intruders. It isn't connected to a service or to the police, but it gives me some peace of mind.

I'm at ease in the barn. The horses have been more effective therapists than any people I've dealt with. People have said some stupid things! These large and powerful animals comfort me with their honesty, trust and loyalty.

Frank's death stunned me, and the subsequent grief shattered me. I hadn't realized how much he meant to me until he was gone. I wonder if he loved me. Our marriage had been one of convenience. His first wife died of cancer. It was quick. A shock. I know it cut through him like a knife and left him staggering to regain control. But he was a tough, driven man, and for the sake of his political career he believed he needed a wife, and that's where I came in, about two years later.

We'd met at a meeting of a provincial violence prevention coalition. Yes, he was keen to do something about violence, as well as increase protection for the environment and improve the welfare of racehorses. He had a lot of passions. He was the provincial government's representative on the coalition, and I was there to make a presentation on behalf of humane societies on the link between animal cruelty and human violence. It's obvious when you think about it, which is what Frank said to me at the end of the meeting. We started chatting, and things grew from there. But it took a long time for me to let him touch me. He seemed to understand and knew what to say and how to say it. He gained my trust, which no-one else had been able to, ever.

He once said to me that I helped to fill an aching void left by his dead wife. But I wonder by how much. His love for her had been deep and honest and had utterly consumed him. I knew that. So, what had I meant to him? I will never know.

I turn my focus back on to the needs of the horses. I've almost finished the morning chores and toss a couple of flakes of hay into the corners of each of Eagle's and Bullet's clean stalls in preparation for when I'll bring them in for the night. I shut the stall doors just as the wail of the alarm's siren drowns out the soothing sounds of the barn. I peer through a barn window and see a black pickup truck disappear down the driveway, spewing gravel as it goes.

I jog down to the house, with Kelly close at my side, barking, and shut off the security system which is operated from a panel adjacent to the kitchen door. The piercing noise stops but leaves my ears ringing.

The invader has smashed the tall thin window that runs parallel to the front door so he could reach through and round to unlock the door. The shattered glass litters the entrance and jagged pieces stick out from the frame, suspended and surprised. I usher Kelly into the relative safety of the kitchen and check to see if there is any other damage, any other signs of invasion. As I clear up the sharp, shiny pieces, I decide that there's no point in contacting the police. I'm sure that nothing is missing. I have no positive identification and there will be no fingerprints. In any case, I don't want the police involved.

* * *

Usually a warm bath, laced with aromas that promise to calm and soothe, helps me to relax. But it isn't working. My jaw is clenched and the rest of my body feels taut and stiff. The invasion of my home was offensive and personal. But if the intruder has the notion that he can scare me off, he'll have to think again. It makes me more resolved than ever. I stomp down the stairs and fill the kettle.

Kelly whines. Chuck's at the back door.

I haven't done anything to cover the jagged opening into the front hall. Without my asking, and with no fuss, Chuck finds some thick plywood, and measures, cuts and screws it in place before the tea gets cold. He listens to the whole story and agrees that there isn't much point in calling the police. I offer him a mug of tea and, after being reassured that Kelly and I are okay, he starts to talk.

He went to school with Frank, which I already know. They kept in contact from time to time, just touching base. Most of the MBA graduates were active networkers, including Frank, but Chuck chose to stay on the periphery. His career got off to a good start, and it wasn't long before he secured the position of Vice-President Procurement at the Steel Mill, reporting directly to Timothy Westmount.

"It was through one of my colleagues there that I met a woman and we eventually got engaged to be married. I'm cutting a long story short, of course. Just one week before the wedding, I got a text from my fiancée, breaking off the engagement and cancelling the wedding. She didn't respond to any of my attempts to reach or see her. This was nearly four years ago. I felt as if I'd been flattened by an avalanche. I was frozen and disoriented, with no future and with a past that had suddenly become irrelevant. I couldn't dig myself out. I couldn't function at work or at home. I lost my job."

"Probably what you really lost was your self-esteem and your sense of worth."

"Perhaps. I thought I must be a bad person because this happened to me." Chuck gazes into his tea, which is now definitely cold. "People tried to help me, but usually their attempts made me feel worse, or at least didn't make me feel better. I wallowed in self-pity and I don't think I even wanted to be pulled out of the pit of cold despair I found myself in."

"I can understand that."

"But eventually I wanted to do something. Something that would help me move on. I remembered Frank saying how much he enjoyed the racetrack, how it was a different world and that the backstretch was like family, a community. I didn't want anything too challenging, and I thought that working with horses might do me good. So, I got a job as a hot-walker which led to cleaning out stalls and then grooming. I enjoyed it. People didn't ask questions, didn't judge. They and the animals just accepted me as I was. Then I bumped into Frank in the backstretch. He was good enough not to probe, which was a tremendous relief. The next time I saw him, he joked he was looking for a gardener. I'm sure he thought I needed the money. I wasn't doing much about my appearance at the time, so I probably looked pretty down-and-out. As it happens, and as you know, I love gardening, and I thought I'd do both jobs for a while and see how things went. So, I said I'd be happy to be his gardener. Well, he said, you'll be working for my wife. So here I am." We let the silence hang in the kitchen, for a minute, with the buzzing of the fridge and the ticking of the wall-clock in the background.

He lifts his green eyes for a second, and I feel a sense of kinship, a bond of understanding.

"I suppose Frank left me money in his will because he thought I needed it. I didn't confide in him and, as far as I know, he nothing about my financial affairs. I have wondered though, what made him think I would outlive him? I was only a few years younger."

"I suppose he was covering for possibilities."

Chuck unwinds his long, fine fingers from round the mug he's been clutching and unfolds his lean body. His eyes look tired, and his face drawn.

The noise of crunching gravel distracts us. Kelly wags her tail as she waits by the back door. Of course, she knows who it is before we do.

Out of the side kitchen window, I see Tom get out of his sleek red sports car. Chuck grabs his work gloves and brushes past Tom as they each mumble greetings.

Tom takes his jacket off and puts it on the back of one of the several padded chairs. He's often told me he loves the kitchen. The understated décor, with its subdued colours and rounded edges, and glimpses of countryside out of every window, is soft on the senses. Although modern, it is relaxed and invites its visitors to linger. Tom and Frank often chatted over endless cups of coffee with their elbows leaning on the great oak table. Frank would make Tom roar with laughter with his clever imitations of people, usually business and political leaders in the community. Although Frank was about ten years his senior, I remember thinking on one particular late summer evening that they both looked fit and healthy, tanned and vibrant. They both showed even white teeth with their infectious smiles. Although I wasn't part of their camaraderie, the warmth of their joyous friendship couldn't help but seep under my skin. And it made me feel good that Frank felt and looked so good.

When I tell Tom about the intruder who'd apparently been frightened off by the alarm, his eyes narrow.

"This is getting serious. He, or they, know where you are."

"Well, they've known for a while, because they followed me into the forest with that dog, and Susan Kingsley-Black has the address for sure."

"Yes, I suppose you're right." I notice a deep frown on his forehead and a twitch under his left eye. He's agitated and I think my involving him might be a mistake. I know he can get stressed by some things. But on the other hand, Frank had said that he could be great under pressure. Well, it's too late now. He's here and part of this, whether I like it or not.

"I checked no-one followed me, and I didn't see any vehicles parked anywhere near," Tom says. "I parked out of view from the road. I thought it might be best if they didn't know I was assisting you. You never know when the element of surprise might come in useful."

It sounds as if Tom has transformed into some kind of agitated action-figure. I think this is over-dramatic. After all, we've just agreed that they know where I live. The scales are tipped in their favour. They know who I am, but I'm not sure who they are yet, or what they don't want me to find out.

But nothing is going to prevent me from going to the Stakes Race. I have my heart set on it. So, I think it's best to go along with Tom's dramatics.

"I don't suppose there's another way off the property, is there?" he asks.

"Actually, there is." I stand up and walk to the kitchen window that looks towards the barn. "Do you see that lane past the barn? It goes through the forest, and enters a side road, which then joins the road into Vannersville. It could be pretty swampy in the low part of the forest, though. I'll have to take the truck. It's got four-wheel drive."

"How do we get the truck to the barn without being seen, in case they're watching?"

"I take it down there for lots of reasons, including unloading feed. I don't think that'll draw attention."

"I should hide my car."

I'm convinced that they already know that Tom is working with me, but I don't argue and suggest he put it in the drive-shed. I point to the old grey wooden building, which had belonged to the original 200-acre farm of which the Sheppards' property had once been part. Frank had considered demolishing it at first, because it's quite close to the house, and is in view of most of the back windows. But it provided a haven for his immaculate old Cadillac, which was too large for the garage. And it's still used to shelter all sorts of miscellaneous items which don't have another home. And now it will be a hiding place for a shiny red sports car, under an old winter pool cover just in case flashes of red could be seen through the many gaps in the wooden siding.

Tom scans the area as we walk back to the house. As we enter the kitchen, I burst out laughing. I can't help but see the funny side of skulking about on my own property, hiding fancy cars in dingy sheds and planning escape routes. It's all a bit too much. Tom's face doesn't flinch.

"Well, let's go to the track," I say.

Tom's determined not to be seen leaving the property. He crouches behind the front seats, in the small space which qualifies the truck as having an extended cab, as I drive down to the barn. I'm wearing my coveralls, and Kelly is beside me on the other front seat. We go round to the back of the barn, and then make our way to the track which leads towards the maple forest. Frank spent what I assumed to be a lot of money on maintaining the forest, clearing out old wood, planting new when needed, felling trees that had fallen on other trees, amongst a myriad of other caretaking activities. I often saw the man he hired, with his powerful but docile horses, who pulled the huge logs out. It beat using destructive machines. Frank tried to "walk the talk" in his own life, and I respected him a lot for that, as well as many other things.

I stop the truck.

"Unless they're following, which they aren't, we can't be seen here." I writhe and struggle out of my coveralls.

"Has Kelly been to the racetrack before?" asks Tom, as he exchanges seats with the dog.

"No, but I didn't want to leave her in the house, just in case. I don't think they'll try breaking in again, but if they do, I'd rather Kelly wasn't there. Also, I wouldn't be going down to the barn without her, would I?" I straighten out my pantsuit. "Okay, are we all ready?"

The swampy part of the forest is wetter than I'd expected. We make it through by keeping up momentum, and eventually reach the side-road which leads to the main road. I know the truck is now covered in mud, not just dirty. Clods of mud thump against the wheel arches.

As we drive into the grounds of the racetrack, the rain starts.

"Did anyone follow, do you think?" asks Tom. I'd noticed that he was craning his neck to see out of the side-mirror for most of the trip. I'm pretty sure he'd have seen someone if anyone had been there.

"No, there's been hardly a sign of anyone, and no-one's behind us now. We're early, so let's go to the backstretch and see Speed."

"I haven't seen him for over a year, when he was at your farm last spring," Tom says.

"There's Shane. He's certainly dressed up today. I hardly recognized him. He must expect to be in the winner's circle."

"Looks like a shifty character to me."

I introduce Tom to Shane. The trainer grunts and shakes Tom's hand with one sharp down-stroke, as if whacking a bug with a fly swatter. And, with a few long strides, he retreats to his office without a word.

"Not very friendly, is he?"

"Perhaps he sensed you didn't take to him." I find it somewhat amusing that the two men appear to have taken an immediate dislike for each other. "However, I think the main reason could be the trouble that Frank's drug rules have got him into. Linda might know something." I soon find Linda, who walks with us to the end of the barn, where Speed is leaning out of his stall to watch all the action.

"What's the matter with Shane?"

"I think he thought he was going to the restaurant with you," Linda whispers to me. Tom wanders along the shed row, looking at the horses.

"With me and Tom? I was only offered a table for two. And he hasn't come to the restaurant in the past."

"I think he thought you'd be alone, Mrs Sheppard." Linda draws in a big breath and sighs.

"Well, we didn't talk about it, and he's never come to the restaurant before." I turn my attention back to the horse. "Speed looks great. Thanks for taking such good care of him." There's something soothing about stroking Speed's soft, sensitive nose. Linda smiles and gets back to her work.

"Perhaps Shane shouldn't have seen us together," Tom says, when he reappears in front of Speed's stall. "He might be involved with Brad and his friends. They share a common concern after all. They all hate the various regulations Frank was introducing. And if they believe you're picking up where Frank left off, you never know, perhaps Shane's training horses for them and he's part of their circle."

"They could know one another, perhaps. But I honestly think we can forget about Shane. He'd assumed that he was going to the restaurant with me, and I think he's disappointed that you showed up. I don't think he'd behave that way if he was involved."

"Sorry if I've caused a problem for you with Shane," Tom says.

I chuckle. "No, no. You've prevented one. Come on, let's enjoy the day. I'm sure no-one will bother us here."

We make our way to the grandstand. The rain comes down as a light spring shower and doesn't dampen my spirits. It feels great to make it to the track, at last, to see Speed run.

We have a clear view of the track from our table in the restaurant. It brings back memories of sitting across the table from Frank as he perused the racing program, studying horses' times for works and their racing histories. We rarely visited the restaurant, but when we did, I felt it was Frank's world, rather than mine. Every other person seemed to know him. He saw people there from all of his various walks of life, whereas I don't remember seeing a single soul from my small life-circle.

Despite everything, I feel relaxed. And it gives me a boost to convey some of my knowledge and understanding of horse-racing and betting to Tom. We place a few bets and win a bit of money. But Tom is like one of the grey clouds in the unsettled sky outside and refuses to brighten up. He gets up about a dozen times to select something from the enormous buffet table, and a dozen more times to place bets, go to the washroom and I'm not sure what else. And he keeps glancing around the restaurant as if someone could be planning to attack us right there.

He isn't any more at ease by the time the Seaton Stakes Race comes up. It is the ninth of ten races. The track is pretty sloppy by now, and the wind has picked up. My heart is pounding as Speed comes out onto the track for the post parade. His official racing name is Scarfin. I don't understand what made Frank choose that, but I can't help feeling proud when the track announcer calls out his name. He looks elegant but powerful, feisty but controlled. While the horses are parading in front of the grandstand, I contemplate Speed's racing name again, as well as Rose's, which is Alusio. I feel like smacking my forehead as it dawns on me.

"I've just realized why Frank chose Scarfin and Alusio for racing names."

"Oh?" Tom is absorbed in the post parade announcements, and for just a couple of minutes, isn't glancing over his shoulder.

"They're anagrams of Francis and Louisa."

"That's nice."

Frank must have named them after our marriage. A tinge of sadness dampens my spirits. And I'm surprised by an unwelcome pang of envy for his obvious deep love of Louisa. I quash these disturbing feelings. I won't allow anything to distract me from Speed's race.

The weather has deteriorated, but the wind-driven rain isn't bothering the horse. Despite the drenching conditions, we stand outside near the edge of the track, close to the finishing line.

"I wonder where Shane is? He's phoned so many times, pestering me to come to the track, and when I do come, he's nowhere to be seen. He always used to watch the race with me and Frank, when we were here and had a horse running."

"He looks an odd character to me," is all Tom says as he pulls his raincoat collar up over his ears and reverts to glancing over his shoulder again.

"Just about anyone who has anything to do with the horse racing business is odd. And yes, that includes me. I have to be crazy to spend money on racehorses. I hardly came to the track at all last season." I know why I keep the horses. There are several reasons, including the fact that the racehorses were Frank's and I can't bring myself to sell them. But I also don't want to cut myself off from the inner-world of the racetrack. I've isolated myself enough as it is. I need to get out more. I make a promise to myself to visit more often.

The horses finish their warm-up and gather behind the starting-gate. Speed, or Scarfin, doesn't need much encouragement from the gate staff and loads calmly. It's a relief to see them all in the gate, poised for the race. And then they explode out onto the track as if they've been shot out of cannons. I stood by the gate once and was startled by the incredible noise as it crashed open and the thundering hooves took off at a gallop. The ground vibrated under my feet and I could almost sense the oxygen being sucked out of the air as the horses took off. I felt humbled. The experience gave me greater respect for the power, determination and competitiveness of the racehorse.

Speed is now in the middle of the pack along the backstretch. Mud-laden spray is spewed up by the hooves in front of him, and he'll be caked in mud by the time he reaches the finish line. The jockey finds a gap and he and Speed seize the opportunity to gain some ground. At the final turn he still has four horses ahead of him, but he has a clear path and stretches out his stride a bit.

Tom jumps up and down and yells "Come on, Speed! You can do it!" I've never seen him so excited. I wave my arms in the air like a maniac, and I'm not sure what I'm shouting. In the final stretch he does his best, but is beaten by a nose by the favourite. But I'm pleased. He has earned some money and ran a good race. In fact, he's earned his keep, and a bit for Rose as well. And he is "Stakes Placed" again, which is always good.

And Tom has finally forgotten to check if someone is watching or following or both. But I'm sure it won't last.

6

Home Invasions

I set up the pull-out sofa bed in the family room and retrieve bedclothes and sheets from one of the spare beds and the linen closet. I'm relieved that Tom insists on being downstairs and didn't accept my offer of a bed upstairs. But I curse myself for not having the courage to tell him I'd rather be on my own. I'm sure he thinks he should support and perhaps even protect me. I like to think I don't need either.

Even though Tom was Frank's closest friend, it feels like another invasion of my house and an intrusion into my personal domain. Murray stayed for a couple of days after Frank's death, and I was relieved when he left. Other than that visit, I've been on my own for the past year.

But as I get Tom a glass of water, I reflect that perhaps I haven't been as tough as all that since Frank's death. I gave up my job, stopped my volunteer work and even quit riding for a while. I have lost touch with friends, few as they are, and have been close to living like a recluse. And I reluctantly admit that joining the support group has helped me, despite its frustrations.

I return to the family room.

"I'll be able to hear someone coming more easily if I'm downstairs. And I'll have the element of surprise on my side," Tom says as he slips his gun under his pillow. The presence of his weapon is even more disturbing than his staying in my house. I don't like guns at all, especially in my home.

Hoping that I'm concealing my true feelings, I hand him a glass of water with a smile on my face. "Is there anything else you need?"

"I can't think of anything. This is great. I'm just going to read for a bit." Tom pulls a book out of the wall-to-wall bookcase, which is one of several in the house, and tightly packed with Frank's favourite reads. The crowded bookcase reminds me of how I marvelled at Frank's ability to cram so much into each and every day. He invariably had several missions on the go at the same time and, what's more, he made a difference, not always in a big way, but a difference all the same. Which is more than most of us can claim.

What had he thought of me? I knew he thought I was beautiful. But he didn't share his innermost thoughts with me. It felt a bit like I was watching the movie of his life from behind the camera. I wasn't often included in the action. But I don't know what a good marriage is supposed to be like. So, what should I have expected? All I know is that the family I grew up in had been diabolically bad. And, to be fair, Frank had said it was a marriage of convenience for both of us. But my grief suggests that I may have fallen in love with my husband.

I leave Tom to read, and search for something to do to stop my head from spinning with thoughts of the past. I decide to play some opera arias Frank used to listen to when he was working at home. I've gradually grown to appreciate their musical beauty, and their familiarity makes me feel warm and relaxed. They have become my music now. And even Kelly looks content, curled up on Frank's side of the bed. Yes, Frank and I slept in the same bed. Not at first, but from time-to-time in the latter part of our short marriage.

I'm woken abruptly by Kelly's furious barking as she bounces over me to reach the top of the stairs at break-neck speed. I can't hear anything above her racket, but grab my robe and follow her.

"Whoever it was, has gone!" yells Tom. I check the clock in the hall. It's 2 am.

"What happened?"

"Someone threw a brick through the front window." Tom holds Kelly back since shattered glass is scattered over almost half of the family room floor. The sofa bed is at the other end of the room. I'm relieved that Tom isn't hurt.

"Did you see anything?"

"It could have been the same black pickup truck you saw before, but it happened so quickly, and the lighting is so poor, I can't be certain." Tom's face is pale and drawn.

"They seem bound and determined to get to me." There is an edge of anger in my voice. "They're wasting their time. It actually makes me more intrigued."

"The stupid thing is I forgot to pick up my gun as I rushed to see who it was." I'm relieved to hear that. So far, no-one has got seriously hurt. There's one vicious dog dead. I want to keep it that way.

Tom starts to clear up the glass, and I help once I've convinced Kelly that she must lie down and stay in the hall. Finally, the last fragment of glass is sucked up the vacuum cleaner and the larger pieces safely placed in a cardboard box. Tom's been working like the Energizer Bunny. I have to admit I'm glad of the help.

I remember Chuck used some tough sheets of plastic to cover a frame for a small greenhouse early last spring, but we'd agreed not to do that this year. The plastic is in the drive shed and Tom finds it and tapes it over the jagged hole before I finish putting the glass in the large garbage pail in the garage.

"I need a cup of tea. Would you like some?" I ask. I'm wide awake and not sure if I'll be able to get back to sleep, even though the tea will be camomile. "I'm sure they won't try anything else tonight."

"Yes, thanks." Tom follows me and Kelly out to the kitchen and sits down at the table. He has sweat on his brow, and his right leg bounces up and down. His agitation could be contagious if I let it be. I wrap myself in an impervious cloak of numbness as if to protect myself from infection. He looks up at me with a deep frown.

"What are you going to do tomorrow?"

"I'm going to visit William Porter, the lawyer. Then I've arranged to meet Sharon for lunch, because of her connection with Sandy's Waste Retirement and because she keeps asking me."

"Someone could have got hurt tonight. You should consider quitting."

"I don't think we need to be that concerned."

"Well, I'm not happy about this. Two attacks here in one day. It's unnerving. Who knows what they'll try next? None of it makes any sense to me."

"They're just using scare tactics."

"What's it all about though? I wish I could come with you to see that lawyer but I've got to go to the office in the morning. Could you call me as soon as you leave Porter's office?" His frown looks as if it's pulling his eyes closer together, and their dark circles contrast with the paleness of his high cheekbones. His thinning fair hair stands up on end as if he's seen a ghost, and he's behaving as if he has. A ripple of laughter wells up inside me. I quash it and give him a mug of steaming tea. He peers into it with his hands gripped tightly round the hot mug. I need to escape from his agitation because I'll either be infected or laugh out loud and the latter is more likely.

"I'm taking my tea back to bed. See you in the morning."

* * *

I slept well despite the earlier rude awakening and am relieved that I forgot to set the alarm. As I get dressed, squeaky doors and heavy footsteps tell me that Tom's on his way out of the house. I glance into the family room on my way to the kitchen and stop in my tracks. Kelly comes close to bumping into me. Tom must have had a restless night. There are several of Frank's treasured books scattered around the sofa bed. Various papers, clothes, blankets and throws surround a mug and a glass, which are plonked in the middle of the floor. Frank had been such a tidy and organized person that this chaotic mess seems like an assault on our home. But I decide there's no point in tidying up until Tom leaves. And that won't happen soon, because I don't have what it takes to ask him to go.

The weather is about as unsettled as I feel. Haphazard patches of sunshine light the emergent grass, showers are on the horizon, and nippy breezes dance all over.

Chuck shows up with trays of pansies to plant in the tubs and in the beds. He knows I love their bright cheery colours and the fact that they can handle the late frosts. They look sad, beaten and dark when frost hits, but the warm spring sun works like magic, and their faces soon smile up at you again. He puts the trays down by the kitchen door and comes in.

"I thought I'd put the pansies in today. The ground's quite wet and there could be some sunshine."

I encourage him to sit and talk. I want to reduce my list of suspects and my intuition tells me he shouldn't be one of them. I hope I'm right. So, I take a bit of a gamble and give him an update on what I've done and what I hope to do, including my list. But I don't have to get to the point. He beats me to it.

"So, that's your list of suspects. You didn't include my name, but I think I'm on the list. And I understand. I'm not offended. It would seem odd that Frank left me money in his will. He didn't know my financial situation and he must have assumed I was broke. I'll just say that I have significant funds. So, I don't have a motive."

"You're right. You are on the list."

"And, by the way, just so you know, I love gardening. I live alone in a condominium townhouse. I treasure the opportunity to design, plan and plant your gardens, and enjoy the results. But it's not all I do. A couple of years ago I took a writing course, and got inspired. I'm now a freelance copywriter. I find it stimulating, challenging and rewarding. I'm actually doing quite well, and earning six figures, which has pleasantly surprised me."

"Well, I think you've convinced me to take you off the list." I chuckle and feel a great sense of relief. "I appreciate you being so open. It really helps to narrow things down. And it's also nice to get to know you a bit better."

"And another thing. I gave the money to the Vannersville Children's Centre. I've always enjoyed children. I thought it would be worthwhile to support children with special needs, especially those who need technology to communicate."

"I think that's wonderful."

"There was an article in the Vannersville Times. You should be able to check it out. I didn't want it to be public, but they convinced me it would encourage others to give, so I reluctantly agreed. I'm sure it'll be on their website."

"You've convinced me. Really."

"I'd be grateful for a chance to help in any way I can, by the way. I agree with you it was no accident. So please keep me in mind, if there's anything at all I can do."

"I will. Thanks. Now, tell me what you're planning for those pansies."

My mind wanders as Chuck outlines what his planting plans are. His mention of his enjoyment of children has triggered a twinge of sadness. Frank didn't want children because he thought the world was too violent, corrupt, and polluted, although that didn't stop him from believing he could improve things. And the marriage, Frank reminded me, was a marriage of convenience, and he was career-minded, almost to obsession. He liked to put on a public face of being a family-man, but he didn't live up to the true, intentional meaning of the term. And, to add to this, I've always been terrified that I would be an abominable parent. The only role-models I've had were damaging and loveless. Would I be different? I would cherish the chance to raise happy and healthy children, but I suppose there's no point thinking about it. I'll never have the opportunity to find out what kind of mother I'd be.

Chuck has wrapped up his suggestions, and I readily agree, although I haven't been paying full attention. I have to cut the conversation short because I have the barn chores still to do before getting ready to see the lawyer, William Porter.

* * *

Before I get back into the house, I glance at Eagle and Bullet. The horses are on the fresh pasture, ripping at the grass at a great rate, consuming mouthful after mouthful. It amazes me that such large animals can flourish and grow on grass. I always give them grain in the morning and evening, and hay for the night, but likely they don't need the grain at all when they have such luscious pasture. That's what their bodies are designed to digest and use. You can see it in the shine and beautiful dapples of their coats. I can't help but hesitate and lean on the fence to watch them for a couple of minutes. A contented sigh emerges and I know a smile has grown inside me.

* * *

A couple of hours later, I emerge from the house carrying Frank's slim black leather briefcase, dusted off and containing the letter that William Porter had sent. I step into the muddy truck and drive into Vannersville. On the way into town, I reflect on how anxious I used to be when I met a man alone, and especially one I knew. (I suppose this isn't surprising, since the man who violated me, and damaged me, was a member of my family). My anxiety could escalate to full-blown panic if the man was between me and the door. Frank helped me to conquer my fear, or rather, terror. I am thankful for that.

Perhaps Mr Porter is hungry for clients because when I phoned no questions were asked, and I have an appointment at 11 am.

The outside of the office appears hungry for attention. The building is four storeys high and has a half-empty look. There's garbage in the planters, in stark contrast to the spring flowers which decorate the Westmount Steel's entrance. It's in a part of town where light and life have faded, where gradual decline is evidenced by increasing grime and decreasing occupancy.

I'm not even asked to wait in the dimly lit waiting room, but immediately directed to the lawyer's office by his nondescript assistant.

"Glad to meet you. Please have a seat," William Porter bellows. The large solid rosewood desk is dwarfed by the size of the office. Dark oak panelling, deep blue carpet and hefty leather chairs might have conveyed stable prosperity at one time, but they don't now. Perhaps it's the dirty windows that betray him, or is it the worn patches in the carpet, or could it be the soiled arms of the chairs? It's likely all of the above. The lawyer notices my eyes scanning the room.

"Don't be fooled by these surroundings, Mrs Sheppard. We're moving shortly to improved accommodation. I can assure you we have superior services to offer you. I'm sure you won't be disappointed. How can I help you?" He moves his large head towards me. His intense black eyes look directly into mine. He appears to be so eager that I'm almost sorry I don't have a case for him. But, on the other hand, I'm glad he's keen to get down to business without a whole bunch of unnecessary preliminaries.

"I expect you recall Frank Sheppard, Minister of the Environment, who died one year ago?"

"Yes, of course I remember Mr Sheppard." I don't pick up the slightest flinch. He leans back in his familiar chair which groans with the movement of his bulky body.

"Well, I don't think you've realized that he was my husband."

"Oh, oh, I'm sorry." He leans across the desk again and the chair squeals at the sudden change in position. He doesn't blink as he stares at me for a couple of seconds. "It was a terrible accident. I remember reading about it in the papers."

"Well, that's just the point. I'm convinced that it was not an accident. I'm trying to find out what really happened." I go straight to the issue and it doesn't appear to faze him.

"I'm not a private investigator. I'm a lawyer." He stressed the last word. "I could perhaps provide some guidance, though. What help do you want?"

"I'd like you to provide some information to me regarding this letter you wrote on behalf of some clients." I hand the letter to him. It's difficult to stretch far enough to span the polished wooden desk, despite the lawyer's hand extending towards me more than halfway.

"I'd have to charge a modest fee, you understand."

"That's expected."

"Especially since I would be divulging information about clients, even if they aren't my clients anymore."

"Quite understandable."

"Fine. In that case, I'll tell you what I know. It isn't much." He places the letter to one side, but I reach out my hand with a smile. He returns the letter to me.

"Thanks. You were going to give me information regarding the circumstances surrounding the letter."

"As I was saying, it isn't much, but it could be important. You'll notice that the letter doesn't mention who my clients were."

"It says something about representing the interests of many of the key businessmen in Vannersville."

"Well, since we've agreed to a fee of, say, $500, I'm willing to tell you who they were." In a lower voice he adds, as he scans the room this time, "And I have my reasons." I think this is a bit silly, but I want to hear what he has to say.

"That would be helpful."

"They were Marshall Moncton-Brown, the owner of MMB Aggregates, as you probably know. He's known to be a tough businessman. My contact there was Brad Buckthorn, his assistant. Then there's Timothy Westmount, he's the steel mill giant, as everyone refers to him. He's an older man. Not sure why he doesn't retire. My contact at Westmount Steel was Susan Kingsley-Black. She's a stunner. She's the Chief Operating Officer. And then there was Sandy Bingham, owner of Sandy's Waste Retirement, a comical name for a garbage disposal company, and his side-kick is the one with the raspy voice. Oh yes, Sharon McDonald's her name. That's the lot."

"So, the representatives of the three organizations approached you to write a letter to Frank?"

"They wanted a strong, warning letter. They were, as you can tell from the letter, vehemently opposed to any proposed pollution control regulations."

"Is that all they did, that you're aware of, just get you to write a letter?"

"That's all they asked me to do."

"What about speculation? What did you think they were up to?"

"I don't like to speculate. I'm aware that the group met often. I mean, the threesome, probably with two or three of their sidekicks," answers the lawyer.

"I'd like to know what you thought might be going on. I'm sure there's more to this than a letter. Your conjectures could be helpful." I gamble on him being unscrupulous enough to reveal more.

"Okay. I think I said the fee would be $1,000." The lawyer sighs, and leans back in his chair again. It groans again. I nod. After a brief pause, he continues. "I know they were meeting regularly. I'm guessing that they were conspiring together to stop the Minister from introducing the pollution control regulations, somehow."

"Do you think they could have been planning to kill Frank?"

"Oh, no. Oh hell, that would be going far too far, even for that group. It would be ill-advised for them to risk everything for the sake of stopping pollution control measures, which we all know are going to come sooner or later. However, these guys all have egos as big as Mount Everest, and they want control. It might have more to do with power, and ego than with pollution."

"Then don't you think they could have wanted Frank out of the way?"

"Perhaps. And they would be capable of arranging such a thing. But it's more likely they would try intimidation, combined with attacks on his political persona. But he must have been pretty clean, because I don't remember seeing any dirt dragged up in the papers about him. Anyway," he says, as he lurches towards me across the desk, risking total destruction of his chair, "that's all I can tell you."

I bend down to pick up the briefcase.

"Oh, there's another thing that might have been on the agenda for the meetings. I think everyone knows that they're working on pit rehabilitation. It's a multimillion-dollar business if you can accept fill from large construction companies doing extensive excavation work. I believe your husband had concerns about the lack of controls on the quality and quantity of the fill coming in. But you probably knew about that already."

I didn't know. What did I know about Frank and what he was up to? Not much. And I didn't go with him when he went on his numerous trips. I just felt sorry that he wasn't around. I moped but didn't do anything about it. Well, I couldn't go to England, that's for sure. It would have stirred up hateful memories beyond my endurance. And he knew that, so he never asked.

As I leave the tired office and the sad building, I doubt the visit has been worth the bill. It cheers me up to see Kelly's face poking out of the truck's window as I walk back to the parking lot. I can see that she's quivering with excitement, her wet nose dabbing at the air. She gives me a quick, warm lick as I get in to sit beside her. I'm about to start the engine to drive to the ravine near the restaurant where I'm to meet Sharon, when I remember to phone Tom. He tells me he's very relieved to hear my voice. I don't know what he thinks could happen to me in a run-down lawyer's office.

"You think he knows more about that group, then?" asks Tom.

"I do. But he wasn't telling me much. They're a powerful bunch, and I suppose his livelihood as a lawyer could be in jeopardy if he got on the wrong side of them."

"He's probably just a puppet of that group."

"Well, I suppose he could be. I certainly didn't learn anything significant."

As I turn the key in the ignition, I notice a black pickup truck out of the corner of my eye. It's about three parking spots behind and there's a short man in it. I can make a good guess who it probably is.

7

Wilted Lunch

I back out of the parking space. It needs all my concentration. Vannersville has brought the parking space lines closer together yet again, cramping my truck's style. The running lights on the black pickup come on. There's no subtlety in its intent to tail, and as I leave the lot, the truck is only about two car-lengths behind. I can almost make out who's behind the wheel, but not quite. I catch myself thinking that the large chrome grill makes the truck look menacing and remind myself that they're playing at scare tactics and nothing more. In fact, they aren't being very smart about it, because they haven't explicitly told me what it's all about. I smile at Kelly.

"We'll be fine, Kelly. But I'm not going to risk you being attacked again in the woods, so we've either got to lose this guy, or go somewhere in the open for our walk."

I take a couple of detours on the way to the ravine to see if I can shake off the unwanted follower. At the first set of traffic lights, as a precaution, I lock all the doors and close the windows. I plan a route that will stick to well-used streets. But we have a black shadow wherever I weave and meander. And even though I exceed the speed limit and have a smaller vehicle, he follows my circuitous route as if I have him on a string. He dares to get within a foot of my tailgate and I can't see the chrome grill any more. I wonder what he would do if I stopped. I wish I knew what I was dealing with: how great the threat is from these people.

We arrive at the ravine, but I don't want to risk it. We would be too vulnerable in this wooded area with its steep slopes and narrow paths. Even though Kelly knows we've arrived at the ravine and wags her tail in anticipation of a walk, I go with my plan B, following the signs to the racetrack. It takes about five minutes to get to the security checkpoint for the backstretch. I tell Kelly to lie down behind the seat, as she's done a few times before. I have my racehorse owner's licence ready for inspection, and gamble on the shadow not having the authorization to enter. I'm right. The black truck hangs back, abruptly makes a screeching U-turn, churning up dust and grit, and tears back in the direction we've just come from. Not a discrete exit.

I pull off the road and roll down the front windows. Kelly and I watch a couple of horses gallop past on the training track. Seeing the streamlined athletes covering the ground with easy strides, and hearing their rhythmic puffing, helps to restore my inner calm. I could gaze at the horses for hours, whatever they're doing – being fed, led, groomed, bathed, trotted, galloped. Their beauty, grace and athleticism captivate me and their generous spirits hearten me.

The backstretch, in its segregation from the outside world, offers a safe haven. But I have a lunch date, and after about ten minutes I reluctantly pull away, and leave at the opposite end to where we entered. This is a less-used entrance, and I assume that the black shadow doesn't know it exists. There's a pleasant green space close by, which will be fine for a short walk for Kelly. Although not as much fun as the ravine, Kelly enjoys the change of scene and the myriad of fascinating scents. I wish she could relay to me what stories the smells tell her.

As we get back into the truck, it occurs to me that they, whoever they were, more than likely know I've a lunch date with Sharon. So, the black shadow, in all probability, will be back on my tail despite the shake-off. I'm irritated with the silly games they're playing and frustrated with myself. I'd like to make better progress so that I can get my life back, such as it was.

The immediate priority is to make sure that Kelly will be safe, so I decide I must park the truck in a meter parking space within sight of the restaurant. It takes three circuits of the block before I get a spot. I put the windows down a little for Kelly and enter the restaurant, determined to act as if nothing unusual has happened. Sharon is already here.

"Hi, Meg." Sharon suggested the place. I haven't been to this restaurant for well over two years. I hoped that it would have had a major face-lift. But I'm disappointed. The same hard wooden chairs, and the same worn, dingy decor greet me. I can't understand anyone liking it, especially a Vice President of a large organization like Sandy's Waste Retirement. But as I walk towards Sharon, I notice that she's almost camouflaged. Her drab outfit blends into the dreary surroundings. She fits in.

"Hi, Sharon. How are you?"

"Fine, but, more to the point, how are you?" Sharon sweeps her mousey hair off her forehead, as if to get a clearer view of me.

"Oh, I'm doing better, thanks."

"I'm glad we finally got together. But you mentioned earlier that something was bothering you."

"Well, something is bothering me."

"Oh, what?"

"Actually, it crystallized in my mind when you talked to me the other day on the phone. You know, the anniversary of Frank's death." I still have a hard time saying "death". I startle a bit as the server slams two glasses of iced water in front of us. She requests our orders. Having dispensed with the server temporarily, I continue.

"As I was saying, my conversation with you helped me to realize what I have to do. I have to find out exactly what happened to Frank."

It's now Sharon who thumps her glass down onto the table. "Oh, Meg. I was feeling so pleased for you, that you'd finally accepted Frank's death, and, of course, what is more important, you'd at last given up the crazy idea that it wasn't an accident." Sharon emphasizes the last three words in a derisive whisper and leans over the table towards me. I lean back. She's too close to me for comfort.

"It isn't a crazy idea, Sharon." I use the most confident and calm voice I can muster.

"Oh, Meg, to think of all the hours you've spent in the support group. You know that you've made so much progress. To think you're throwing all that away, just 'cause of a phone call. I can't even remember what I said, but I've always encouraged you to accept the truth, that it was an accident. We all know it was an accident. You do, really. This is probably just another stage of the grieving process." She has crumpled her forehead of her chubby face into a dramatic frown as she peers at me with unblinking grey eyes. Despite her intensity, I believe it's all an act and have an urge to leave. But I stay perched on the uncomfortable seat.

"It's not," I reply. The server plonks down a plate of limp looking salad in front of me and a burger and salad in front of Sharon.

"Well, we'll see what the rest of the group says on Tuesday. They're bound to be so sad for you. You'll feel differently then, I'm sure," Sharon says, just before she takes a huge bite of her burger.

"I'm not going." I refrain from saying that I don't appreciate being told how I feel, especially by Sharon, who hardly knows me.

"What do you mean you're not going?" Her raised, raspy voice grates on my ears. "You know how helpful it's been."

I've had enough of this conversation. I have to change tack.

"How are you coping with your loss, I mean, the death of your sister? You haven't said much about it, even in the group sessions, and I wonder, since you seem to be doing so well, if there are things which have helped you to cope, which might help me." It's my turn to look at her with unblinking eyes, and Sharon turns her face down to look at her plate.

"It wasn't such a shock for me, since she died after a long battle with cancer."

"Then why did you join the support group? You joined shortly after I did, I think." I try not to sound confrontational, just curious.

"I was told it would be a good idea." She takes another large bite of her burger. It turns my stomach to watch her devour the greasy meal with such relish. I wilt along with my salad.

"By whom?"

"Never mind." She wipes her mouth, which has a good layer of mustard and ketchup on it, and chucks the napkin onto the table. "I didn't come here to talk about me. I'm concerned about you, Meg. You really must accept that Frank's death was an accident. Only then will you be able to start healing." She clenches her puffy hands together as she bangs them on the table. Her cheeks are flushed. I'm not sure if the redness is the result of the effort needed to digest the burger, or due to her obvious frustration with me. I've had enough of Sharon.

"I have to go. I think the meter is about to run out. I couldn't get a good parking spot. Sorry I can't stay longer. I hope the group session goes well, and say hello to everyone for me," I say as I pick up my purse and put more than enough cash on the table to cover my sad meal. I leave my salad to shrivel some more on the plate, with Sharon sitting across from it with a mouthful.

I'm just about to head for the door when I realize I need to go to the washroom. Not surprising, since all I had for lunch was a glass of iced water. I push on the sticky, battle-worn brown door marked "gals" and sense someone is close behind. I turn, and am flabbergasted to feel Sharon's hot, foul breath puffing into my face.

"What?" I ask in a squeaky voice, taken by surprise.

"You must drop this whole thing about Frank." She steps between me and the cubicles.

"I'm going to the washroom." I try to pass her, vaguely noticing a whiff of stale urine and mouldy walls. She seizes my arm, but I wrench myself away. "Leave me alone, it's none of your business."

"It is my business. You're poking your nose into my business." She grabs my other arm.

"Let go or I'll have you charged with assault." I sense my anxiety rising. The primary flash point for the re-emergence of my terror is constraint. The irony is that my fear makes it hard for me to garner enough strength to shake myself free of her grip.

"Yeah, right. Who's going to believe the word of a hysterical widow against that of a senior executive?" She grasps a chunk of my long hair and yanks, and doesn't let go.

"You're not behaving like a senior executive. For the last time, let go."

"Or else, what?"

Time to pull things into perspective. This unfit, overweight woman is no match. I can handle this. What right has she to threaten me? How dare she tell me what I should be thinking and believing about Frank's death. My anxiety morphs into anger, and the ensuing rage mobilizes me into action.

"Or else, this." I punch her on the nose, enough to make it bleed a little. It's her turn to startle.

I'm determined to let her know that I'm no push-over. I won't allow her physical assault to intimidate me. I will fight my demons, fight the baggage I carry from the past. And I will find out what happened to Frank.

I'm able to free myself from her greasy grasp and lock myself in a cubicle. When I come out, she is nowhere to be seen. Now I'm absolutely sure that I'm onto something. What it is, is still mostly a mystery. But definitely onto something.

I don't see any sign of the black shadow tailing us on the way home. I turn into the driveway and, at the last second, avoid running over a mouse as it scurries across our path. My heart pounds. A haunting flashback from my earlier life flies into my consciousness. I didn't know that mice don't live very long, when it happened. I found my pet mouse dead in her cage. It was a shock and filled me with fear and dread. It must have been my fault. Ominous feelings overcame me as I buried my lifeless pet. I must have done something wrong or not done something that he wanted, and he'd killed her to punish me. After all, he'd threatened to end her little life if ever I showed any resistance to what he demanded. My whole body shudders. I desperately need to believe that it wasn't my fault.

As I park the truck, I know I must also park these negative, destructive thoughts. I wish I had an eraser to eradicate the many poisonous memories that lurk in the dark depths of my brain. Instead, I decide to wander over to the horses and talk to them. Just being with them will help to restore my spirits and to get things back into perspective.

Eagle and Bullet come ambling up to the fence, smelling of fresh grass with sweet, musty overtones. Their warm breath and soft muzzles greet me. Their kind eyes comfort me. After several minutes, they wander back to the spot of the field which they believe to be the tastiest, and I watch them graze. I am so lucky to have such loving animals around me.

I hug a mug of tea and feel no inclination to think about what to cook for supper, let alone do anything about it. I don't feel like eating a thing.

A spring thunderstorm has erupted and the water cascades down the windows. Flashes of startling light dance in the fields. The horses have gone into the shelter. I find some strange solace in watching the drama and listening to the claps of thunder as the black clouds fight in a rumbling rage above me. But I don't like the fact that Kelly is frightened. She cowers at my feet and presses against my legs. I wish she could find reassurance in the comfort and warmth of the cosy kitchen during the storm.

The supper question is answered when Tom comes crashing into the kitchen, bringing the contents of half a cloud in with him and four bags of groceries, which he drops onto the floor.

"Hi! I got soaked just getting from the car." He takes his dripping jacket off, shakes the worst of the water off onto one of the mats, and puts it on the back of a chair. "As you can see, I got the ingredients for some kind of supper. I thought you could do with a good meal."

"I was wondering what to do about supper. Thanks."

"Well, I want to be useful and I'd like to contribute." He picks up the bags and starts lining up what seems like mounds of vegetables on the counter, along with pasta and sauces and other things I can't make out from where I'm sitting. It looks enough to feed twenty hungry people.

Tom's hands work at rapid speed as he washes, peels, and chops. His exuberance has the opposite effect on me. I feel like a rag doll that has been out in that rain. Limp and unenthusiastic, and wanting to be alone, I sigh and finish my tea. I watch with my eyes barely focussed and realize he's been chattering away and I haven't listened to a word. He turns to look at me.

"I'm glad I can be here to keep you company and help fend off the bad guys." He smiles and turns back to the counter to start tossing, stirring and boiling. Thank goodness he didn't ask me something related to what he's been talking about.

"I know you don't like to ask, but I'm fine with staying here again tonight."

"Thanks," I mumble. I wish I could think of a way to convince Tom that I'd be okay alone. I'm still not happy with the prospect of Tom becoming a fixture in my home. But what can I do?

He sets a plate of salad down in front of me. It has a mixture of spring greens with berries, topped with thin, crispy noodles. It looks good and I may be able to eat it. It's a vast improvement on the sad salad I was served for lunch.

I find some energy to tell Tom about my conversation with Sharon as he compiles the pasta primavera. But I don't tell him about the altercation in the washroom and the bloody nose I gave her.

"This Sharon sounds like a pushy woman to me," he says.

"Yes, she is very pushy, and she wants me to believe that it would be crazy to think that what happened to Frank was anything but an accident. But, other than that, I didn't learn anything."

Tom delivers the pasta. The steam, laden with the aromas of pungent garlic, sweet tomato and subtle artichoke, wafts under my nose. The medley of colourful vegetables looks cheery. I might be able to eat this too. Perhaps it isn't so bad having Tom around, at least for one more night.

"What about the sister you mentioned?" he asks.

"That's a good question. I'd like to find out if Sharon had a sister. I have my doubts."

"I can help with that. I've a got a couple of contacts who'll be able to find out."

"I'm sure Sharon knows what's going on. And the lawyer told me that Sandy's Waste Retirement was one of his clients behind the letter Frank got. And no-one followed me to or from the restaurant."

"That could just be coincidence. After all, that pickup hasn't been following you everywhere, has it?"

"No, I don't believe so."

"I found out that Sandy's Waste Retirement has some hefty contracts with Vannersville and most of the surrounding municipalities for garbage pickup and disposal, and a couple of new ones in the works with Boughton."

"I wonder if that's significant. The only thing I vaguely remember Frank mentioning was a concern about illegal dumping. With all the unused sand and gravel pits in our area I think he believed it was an issue."

"Yes, I remember him mentioning something about that, I think. I wish I'd paid more attention, but what I remember best about our get-togethers was his hysterically awesome imitations of well-known people. I hurt, I laughed so much!"

* * *

Chuck arrives this morning just as Kelly and I are leaving the barn. He's surrounded by a sparkling vibrancy created by the sun playing on the droplets of moisture which bejewel the fresh spring growth. His red hat, and blue-and-red patchwork jacket, make me think he should carry an easel and paints rather than a trowel and gardening gloves.

Relief wrapped around me like a warm embrace as Tom left this morning. But I'm glad to see Chuck. Perhaps it's because he's not intrusive. I feel his presence, but don't feel a pressure, a stress.

"I think I should tell you something," he says as he pats Kelly.

"Oh?"

"I saw a pickup slow down at the end of the driveway yesterday when you were out. It hesitated and eventually moved on."

"Oh, yes. The big black one, right?"

"No, this one was white and looked beaten up. Rust round the wheel arches."

"I don't know that one. Probably someone admiring all the pansies you've planted."

"Perhaps." Chuck sounds doubtful. "I'll keep my eyes open just in case it has something to do with your investigation."

8

Out of Gas

It seems like an eternity since I last entered the concrete and glass hospital, which looks as if it has erupted from a sea of tarmac. As the automatic doors open and I enter the cold, cavernous atrium, the tangy smell of disinfectant hits my nose. It doesn't seem right to be here without Kelly at my side, in her therapy dog mode, and I promise myself that I'll get back to our volunteer work as soon as I know what happened to Frank.

I find the nurses' station on the fourth floor where the chronically ill patients live and die. It's better than some long-term units in that the staff make some attempt to improve the quality of life with music, pictures and colours. Our first visit amazed the staff. A couple of patients who'd not uttered a word since being admitted spoke to Kelly. She has some sort of magical charm which brings many of the patients out of their shells. Most want to pat her silky head and mumble endearing sounds to her. I'm irrelevant. The dog opens up their hearts and sometimes their minds. I feel ashamed that I've not brought her for over a year.

I walk up to the nurses' station, and am about to ask a nurse something, when a voice reaches me from behind a chart rack.

"Meg, how nice to see you! Is Kelly with you?" Dr Milton peers over the top of the barricade that surrounds the nurses' desks.

"Dr Milton! How are you?"

"Oh, do call me Munro. I'm fine. How are you doing?" The tall man's face appears as if it's all nose and eyes. His dark-rimmed glasses enlarge his eyes to such an extent that they seem comical. "I hope you can bring Kelly in soon. I think she gives joy to many of the patients."

"Yes, I'll do that. Is there somewhere where we can talk briefly? I won't keep you, but I have something I want to ask you."

"We can go into the case conference room." Munro beckons me to go behind the nurses' station, into a room which is set up for meetings of about a dozen people. If Munro wasn't with me, it would feel like a cold and unfriendly place. Not the place to talk about the care of people. There are no pictures on the plain, grey walls. The table is dark and bare, and the chairs austere and uncomfortable. The décor of the room needs to be transformed so that the ambience fits with the mission statement of the hospital, which I know has words such as "warmth and caring" and "human touch".

"Well, what can I do for you, Meg?" Munro asks as he leans back in the chair, and crosses his long legs. His deep voice, upright posture and calm authoritativeness convey confidence and competence. His short-sleeved striped shirt hints at his professional success. I can tell that the material is of the highest quality without needing to feel it, or knowing the price-tag.

"To come straight to the point, I don't believe that Frank's death was an accident." I watch his face for a reaction.

"Meg, I wish you would just get on with your life. If I was your doctor, I'd advise you to put this behind you. It's been over a year now, hasn't it?" I nod. "Well, it's time for you to put your life back together. I'm sure that's what Frank would want. For you." The doctor pats my hand as it rests on the table. I resent this patronizing act, and a deep frown scrunches up my forehead. I've heard this message so many times recently. For a split second I imagine a conspiracy, with everyone in collusion, to convince me that Frank's death wasn't an accident, when he was in fact murdered, and all of Vannersville is covering up the truth. Is Munro involved too?

I dismiss the paranoid-like thoughts and focus on what I need to know.

"It's going to help me more if I can put to rest the questions I have surrounding Frank's death. I'm never going to be able to get on with my life if these questions are continually haunting me." I've been more assertive in my tone than I'd intended, but he's pushed a couple of my buttons. I take my hands off the table.

"Are you saying that you think the Police didn't do a thorough job?" Despite his earlier diatribe, I sense he doesn't mean to challenge me. He's asking a genuine question. His tone has changed, and he sounds curious and thoughtful.

"I'd be happy to give you all my reasons and tell you what I've been up to, later. I'll just say that some things just don't add up and I'm determined to find out what really happened. And I must be on to something because I'm often being tailed, and they have attempted to intimidate me. Don't know what's behind all this, yet. Right now, I need your help."

"You're acting as your own private investigator." The doctor sits up straight. "I'd be glad to help. It sounds as if you think you're on to something. Fire away!"

"From the newspaper cuttings I've been going through, I found out that someone else was injured at the same time. In fact, it stated that he was seriously hurt and, as a result of Frank plummeting down the slope, he lost control of his car. He left the road, crashing into a very large tree. I need to find out who that person was. He might have seen something. The police might have missed something. I very much want to speak with him."

"I remember that man. He was indeed seriously hurt." The doctor holds his chin for a moment, and I can see his furrowed forehead over the large glasses. "I think I can share this information with you. It's no secret. The worst injury was that his spine was fractured by the impact. The damage to the spinal cord was high up. Without going into all the medical jargon, the accident left him paralysed. He is a quadriplegic."

"How awful. That's terrible. Do you know his name, and where he is now?"

"I can't remember, but I can find out his name. It might be difficult to find out where he is because he was transferred to a rehabilitation hospital, and has no doubt left there by now. Hang on a minute." He straightens out his long body, strides purposively out of the room, and shuts the door. It doesn't seem long before he returns, holding a small piece of paper.

"His name is Gerald Warren. He was transferred to Shelton Hospital, at his request. I expect he wanted to be closer to family and friends. I hope that's helpful."

"Yes thanks, that's very helpful." I rise to leave. "I'll let you know how it goes."

"I wish you the best of luck. I hope you come back here to help us out again soon." Munro extends his hand to me and gives me a firm handshake.

I'm welcomed too enthusiastically by Kelly, and wipe the wet patches off my face with a tissue. I don't much like being licked, even by my beloved Kelly. She must know we're parked at the hospital, and she probably wonders why she didn't go in with me.

"I have to smuggle you into the track again." I want to see Rose. Shane has called at least twice to tell me she's sore, although neither he nor the vet can figure out what's wrong. He seems to want me to see the horse myself. He called again, just as I was about to leave for the hospital, and wants me to visit today if possible. While I appreciate regular communication from the trainer, I'm tired of what seems like a bombardment of texts, emails and phone messages, most of which are unimportant, often just pleas for me to visit the backstretch.

"I'd like you to come. I want you to see Rose, and we need to discuss options for her," he said. Although I promised myself that I'd visit the horses more often at the track, my priority at the moment is my investigation into Frank's death. However, Shane stirred up some guilt, especially since Rose might be sore, so I relented. I told him I'd drop in on the way back from the hospital.

"Kelly, go behind, lie down and stay," I say, as we approach the security check-point. Kelly is obedient, as usual, and lies as still as a stone lion on the floor of the truck, in the extended part of the cab. I park as close as I can to the barn in which my two horses are stabled, but I still have several yards to walk in my unsuitable shoes. I forgot to bring a pair to change into. I dodge the mud and other hazards as best I can and finally reach the barn entrance. Shane emerges from his portable office and strides over to me.

"Hi, I'm glad you're here," the trainer says, as he takes off his grubby baseball cap and sweeps his rough hand through his dishevelled red hair. He seems to look right through me with his dark eyes.

"Hi. Perhaps I should see Rose, then."

"Yes, yes. She's in the end stall." Shane turns and struts ahead. I have to walk at a brisk pace to keep up with him. He opens the half door, catches hold of Rose's halter, and uses a tie which is attached to the stall wall, to secure her. He motions to me to go round with him to the side of the horse the furthest away from the stall door. Bending over in the semi-darkness, he runs his hand down the horse's foreleg.

"I can feel some warmth in the tendon. See what you think," Shane says, as he pulls himself up and steps away from the horse. I obediently bend down and rub my hand slowly down the leg. I can't feel anything unusual. There's no warmth, puffiness or apparent tenderness. I know Shane is standing too close to me, almost touching. A crawling sensation creeps over my skin as if little spiders are building webs from one extremity to another.

"Where's Linda?" I ask as I look for a space to pass the man and leave the stall. I feel pinned in and claustrophobic.

"Oh, it's her afternoon off." Without warning, he grabs my hand and firmly guides it down the horse's leg. I can feel his warm breath on my neck. My stomach lurches and my palms are wet with sweat. I can barely breathe. I pull my hand away abruptly and dive under the tie, almost touching Rose's nose, and make my escape, trembling.

"I don't feel anything unusual," I say as I catch my breath and regain my composure outside the stall. Shane releases the horse from the tie and closes the door.

"Well, she's definitely favouring the left fore." He acts as if nothing has happened. "I'd like you to come into the office. We should discuss this, and I've got some information I need to give you." Giving me little chance to reply, he marches off towards his office. With reluctance and ill-at-ease, I enter the trainer's well-used and tattered domain. There's a couch, the original colour of which cannot be determined. Faded, moth-eaten pictures of winners, including him with the horse's owners in the winner's circle, hang on all four walls. Haphazardly arranged hooks display pieces of bridles, saddle pads, bits and some other items which I can't identify. Despite the small open window, the office smells strongly of horses, but the odours of leather and human sweat also hang with heaviness in the stuffy, musty air.

"Drink?" asks Shane. He picks up a bottle of rye from off his desk and reaches into the small, battered fridge for a can of cola and another of ginger ale. I'm careful to avoid the sofa, and sit on an upright chair which has rusty legs and a padded seat with a ripped plastic cover. It's prickly and sticky. Shane pulls two white, disposable plastic tumblers out of a bag, and pours a generous measure of rye in one.

"No, I won't have a drink, thanks," I say, just as Shane's about to pour rye in the second tumbler. He pauses and then pours the rye, anyway.

"I really don't want any," I say, getting up. I walk over to his battered desk.

"You may not want any, but you need some." Shane smiles. His dry, weathered skin looks as if it will crack. "If you don't tell me what you want in it, I'll just have to guess, won't I?"

After a slight pause I say "I'll have some ginger ale." My intuition is shouting at me to leave, but I don't listen. I walk back to the chair. I suppose, at this particular moment, my curiosity is stronger than the repulsion I hold towards the man.

"Frank and I used to enjoy the odd drink," he says.

"Frank didn't drink." Why did Shane lie? "What do you want to discuss about Rose?" A sudden pang of loneliness comes over me. I miss Frank. He would have dealt with this whole thing with Shane brilliantly. Shane always treated him with respect, at least to his face, and wouldn't have dreamt of being so pushy and inappropriate towards him.

"I want to show you the vet bills first," Shane says, as he downs a large gulp of his drink. "Here, hold this." He gives me his drink, picks up some papers off the desk and drags the sister to my chair over, to be close to its sibling. He takes his drink from me, and, after taking a gulp, he puts it on the floor beside him.

"Come on, drink up. It'll do you the power of good." He leans over me and peers into my tumbler. I shift away. The smell of alcohol hangs about him like a threatening cloud.

"Let's see these papers, then. I have to go soon," I mumble. Shane pulls his chair closer. Too close. I shift mine away. He downs another large gulp of his drink, puts the papers on his lap, and stares at me for a couple of seconds.

"I can't understand why Frank would leave you on all those trips he took to England."

"That's none of your concern. It was my choice. I had no desire to return to that country." I'm taken aback. I don't know why I responded. It's none of his goddam business. My gut's now screaming at me to leave, but still I hesitate. And he doesn't reply, presumably because he doesn't like what I said. The suffocating silence that hangs between us is broken by some familiar, though muffled, sounds coming through the small trailer window. These sounds knock some urgently needed sense into me.

"What's that? I think I can hear barking. It's got to be Kelly," I say.

"You brought your dog? That's nuts. But she'll be fine. Have your drink." Shane picks up my tumbler, which I've just put down on his desk.

"No, I'm concerned. She rarely barks at anything when she's in the truck. I'll call you." I shut the office door behind me as I catch a glimpse of a sour-looking, red-faced Shane standing by his rusty, tattered chair.

I'm relieved to feel the cool, fresh spring air on my face. I jog over to the truck as best as I can in my unsuitable, unstable heels. I'm worried about Kelly but also grateful to her.

I can't find signs of anything wrong or unusual. Kelly stops barking as I reach the truck. I note the direction she was looking in, but can't see anything. I ruffle the silky fur on top of Kelly's head and find solace in her warm, dark eyes.

"We need to get out of here, Kelly." I start the engine and lock the doors with a sinking feeling in my stomach. I've loved going to the backstretch, and hoped to visit more often, but now it has become a place of discomfort. I'm discombobulated, not just because Shane behaved like such a jerk, and lied about Frank drinking with him, but because Kelly saw something, and I trust her instincts.

Just as I'm about to leave the city, I notice that the fuel gauge is showing about one eighth full. I'm annoyed that I can't remember when I last filled up. But it can't have been long ago. I stop at a one-man gas station, just on the outskirts of Vannersville, and then continue on my way home. For some reason, I want Tom to be there when I get back. I'm not sure why, and I'm surprised at myself, but perhaps I just need someone around at the moment because of the day I've had.

I glance down at the dials to check my speed. There's a patch of road, through a small community outside Vannersville, which often catches people out. It has a low speed-limit, but the road is new and straight, and the few houses along its edge are well set back. But the fuel gauge catches my eye. It's only a quarter full. I know for sure I've just had it filled up, and remember I checked that the gauge read full. Otherwise, I'd suspect the gas station for pulling a fast one. I can only assume there's something wrong with the gauge.

Then I notice that something's gaining ground at a rapid rate behind me. It looks like a black vehicle. Yes, it's a pickup truck. The fuel gauge reads an eighth full. I check the doors are locked. I've left the small community, otherwise I'd pull into someone's driveway.

I leap to a conclusion and pick up my phone. It's illegal to use a mobile while driving, but I need help.

"Hello Meg," Tom answers.

"Hi. Someone must have tampered with my fuel tank. I'm just crossing the third sideroad, and I'm being followed by, guess what, a black pickup."

"Okay, I'm on my way."

The black pickup is close on my tail now. I have a clear view of the puffed-out rear wheel arches, and the huge chrome grill looms over my tail-gate. The deep roaring of its engine drowns out my vehicle's road noise and the dark tinted windows give the truck a menacing look. I feel vulnerable. My pickup seems small and powerless in comparison. I'm not surprised when the engine begins to chug and steer the truck onto the soft shoulder. Kelly senses something's wrong and growls, which flusters me.

The black pickup doesn't stop, but speeds past. Perhaps there's nothing to this, after all. I switch the subject of my anxiety from the pickup to my call to Tom. I jumped to the wrong conclusion and called him for no reason. But then I notice a cloud of dust and a shiny chrome grill speeding towards me on the shoulder. Surely, he won't just crash head-on into my truck? I can't decide what to do, whether to jump from the truck and hope Kelly will follow, or whether it's safer to stay in the cab. Kelly's furious barking solves the dilemma. She wants out. We both jump down to the ground at the same time. I'm not sure what to do, but she knows. She runs out in front of my truck and barks at the black monster as it closes in at an alarming speed. I want to grab her and drag her into the ditch, but I don't. I join her in front of the truck and wave my arms in the air above my head. He wouldn't dare mow us both down, would he? I can't say I'm not trembling with fear as the intimidating, roaring truck looms closer. But Kelly's confidence and defiance give me the courage to stay put.

At the last possible minute, the truck swerves into the road and spins round, leaving Kelly and me with dust on our faces and grit in our mouths. I'm still shaking and my legs feel unreliable underneath me. Kelly turns her attention to behind us. She's heard the low rumble of a car approaching at top speed. It's a sleek red sports car.

"Are you okay?" Tom yells as he slows down alongside us.

"We're fine."

"Where did he go?" Tom's face is red, his jaw is clenched and his usually soft eyes are staring and glassy. I point ahead, although

I don't think it's a good idea to pursue. But he tears off, wheels squealing, engine roaring and car snaking. A couple of minutes later, Kelly and I are still standing on the road when we hear a loud bang. I shudder. I have a horrible thought that Tom might have shot the guy. I deeply regret having called him. Kelly and I handled it. Well, mostly Kelly, the super-dog.

* * *

We arrive back at the farm in the sports car, and I sigh audibly with relief when Tom says he just shot at one of the black pickup truck's tires as a warning. A gun in the hands of an angry person can do a lot of permanent damage, so it could have been a lot worse. A lot worse.

"I'm glad that I showed him he doesn't have the monopoly on scare tactics. And I saw who was in the pickup, by the way, and he saw me," Tom says.

"Who was it?" I'm sure I know.

"That guy Brad Buckthorn, who I said is a nasty piece of work. This whole thing has just got a lot crazier."

"You could say that. Brad must have somehow got past security in the backstretch so he could sabotage my truck. Kelly tried to tell me." I sometimes think she's more intelligent than I am. And it's almost as if Kelly lost her temper and decided to call Brad's bluff by barking at his truck as he careered towards us. She must have a sixth sense, knowing that Brad wouldn't mow us down. But she can't be that intuitive, can she? "Tampering with my vehicle and threatening to ram into me and Kelly does take it up a notch or two."

"What do you want to do?"

"I still don't want to go to the Police. And I don't want to give up, even though they're obviously increasing their efforts to scare me off."

"I have a suggestion," Tom says. "Let's stick together. We'll be safer."

"Okay." I hope he didn't hear reluctance in my voice. I let an involuntary sigh escape as I pour another cup of orange pekoe tea. Despite the caffeine, my eyelids are heavy. Kelly is flat out on the floor. Her paws are moving, and I assume she's dreaming that she's chasing the bad guys. What an astounding dog and companion!

"You look tired," Tom says.

"I think I must be."

"Not surprising. We're in a hellish mess. We don't have any proof of what they're doing and we don't really know why they're doing it, what's behind it all." He looks at me and changes his tune. I probably look rather fed up. He doesn't realize it's his presence which is at least partially to blame. And to complicate things, I feel badly that I don't relish his company as much as I think I should. "However, if we work together, and combine our brilliant minds, I think we'll outsmart the bastards!" He bangs his hand on the table, jolting my tea and giving me an instant headache. I suggest we move into the family room despite the mess it's in thanks to Tom's muddle. I need to stretch out in a recliner, which makes me feel better. And Tom calms down a bit.

"By the way, according to my research, Sharon didn't and doesn't have a sister," Tom says.

"As I thought, she's caught up in all this. She must have joined that support group because I did. I always thought she seemed awfully together for having had a sister just die of cancer. She's more than patronizing towards me about Frank's death. She's been quite forceful in her attempts to convince me I should accept that it was an accident, and that Frank would want me to carry on with my life." The image of Sharon's bloodied nose comes to mind, with no regrets. But I still don't share the story of my altercation with Sharon. "I'm fed up with people attempting to deter me, by threatening me or obstructing me." My head starts to throb again. I push back in the recliner and stare at the ceiling. "Is there anyone we can trust?"

"No,"Tom answers simply.

"I hope you're not right."I ease myself back to an almost upright position and grab my mug of tea. "I should tell you about the conversation I had with Chuck early this morning. It was quite interesting."

"What did he say?"

"I don't think he should be on the list of suspects. He was pretty open about why he thinks Frank left him money, and he says he gave it to Vannersville Children's Centre."

"Well, I'll check it out. As we agreed, we can't trust anyone."Tom says. "What do we do next?"

"I don't feel like driving to see the poor quadriplegic. In any case, I need to confirm where he is now. So, in the meantime I'll continue to meet with some of the other people on the list."

"I remember that Marshall Moncton-Brown was one of them. He'd sent a letter inviting Frank to tour the MMB gravel pits and concrete plant."

"That might be helpful. What about the office, by the way?" I hope that Tom might have business to attend to at the office, for at least some of the time.

"I've wound up the two important projects I had. My staff is well able to cope with the rest. Nothing's going to suffer."

"That's good then," I say. "Tomorrow it's the gravel pits."

9

Sand and Gravel

I find out a few interesting facts about MMB Aggregates as I browse some websites, while Tom watches a noisy hockey game. I wasn't raised with ice hockey and still don't understand it, but I usually pretend I do. This time I make no effort to watch, I'm much more interested in MMB.

I wonder why I didn't know that MMB has gained permission from the City of Vannersville to accept 40,000 truckloads of clean fill from a large construction company to rehabilitate one of their pits. It works out to 160 truckloads a day. I can't find an exact figure, but it has to be millions. And, as a bonus, the rehabilitation makes them look ecologically responsible since they say they intend to cooperate with the conservation authority in the construction of trails throughout the large acreage.

But I find some naysayers. They want controls on the quality of the fill, road improvements, diversion of trucks from certain roads and limits on the quantity of fill, amongst other things. I'm sure that Frank would have had concerns primarily about the current lack of controls on the quality of the fill. He would have wanted to avert the potential risk of contamination to people, wildlife, trees and plants. Since there is so much money at stake, any work Frank had been doing at the provincial government level that had the potential to threaten MMB's plans could have created some pretty powerful, and perhaps ruthless, enemies.

I stumble upon a couple of articles that were in the local newspaper which I've missed. It causes me to wonder if I've ever read any of the newspapers that have been flung out of fleeting cars onto the end of the driveway, and often into the ditch. I always retrieve them and I thought I read them. But I couldn't have. I found out that Sandy's Waste Retirement has recently entered into a contract with Westmount Steel to process scrap metal, as part of their diversification plan. This plan includes the addition of recycling as well as compost pickup and processing. There are some negative reports on this, including accusations of illegal dumping by SWR, because recycling and composting costs have escalated, with profits plummeting. There are allegations they are dumping in exhausted MMB pits which are off the beaten-track. I can't find any photos or other evidence to support the claims. I imagine myself soaring in the sky, looking down on the pits and catching SWR at it.

Tom leaps out of his chair and yells "Yes!" Apparently, the right team has just scored a long-awaited goal. Kelly barks and scampers to the front door. She's obviously just as confused as I am about the excitement. But I write a mental note to myself that I should make the effort to get some hockey education.

My truck was up on a lift the last time I saw it, and is not coming down until late in the day, so Tom's put his red car into into action. I didn't realize that it's a convertible. Its hard top deceived me. Tom looks like he's ready for some speed. He has a bright blue baseball cap on backwards, a red golf shirt which fits snuggly around his slender torso, and wrap-around sunglasses. He looks aerodynamic, just like his car.

But his driving doesn't live up to the look. He's erratic. Sometimes my foot is pushing on my imaginary brake and sometimes on my imaginary accelerator, and sometimes my body is leaning in a futile attempt to steer the car where I think it ought to go. But I don't scream or even gasp – out loud. I try to take my mind off it and guide my thoughts back to what we're doing.

"Do you think we're being followed?" I ask. I'm pretty sure we will be.

"No, we're not, as far as I can tell."

"They'll find us, of course." I pull my windswept hair off my face and look in the side mirror. I can't see anything in my limited view of the road.

"Bright red does rather stand out," Tom says. "But I can't imagine that they'd have someone watching us all the time."

"Depends on who's involved, and what's at stake." I turn to look out at the scenery passing by in fits and starts. I want Tom to concentrate on the road and not look at me, which he's inclined to do when he speaks. The leaves have sprouted on most of the trees. The soft shoulders are wet, which reminds me that there was a short, but heavy thunderstorm in the night. It made me restless because Kelly was quaking on the bed.

For some reason, Shane's face kept popping up whenever I tried to get back to sleep, and it made me feel uneasy. I was irritable by the time the morning finally arrived, and this grew to annoyance when Shane called me before I'd drunk my morning cup of tea. Just at that moment it felt like he was a frequent pest whom I needed to get rid of. He had nothing new to say. He repeated, yet again, that he wanted me to come to the track to see Rose and to talk with him about her. He even reminded me I'd left my drink.

"They'll be one ready for you when you come," he said. I try to push his face out of my mind for the umpteenth time and flit through several other topics, which somehow leads me to remembering the dire state of the food supplies at home.

"We'll have to pass a supermarket, won't we? I must pick a few things up, otherwise we'll starve to death," I say, as we reach the outskirts of Vannersville.

"Okay, I'll drop you off, and Kelly and I will drive around dodging unwanted company. How long do you think you'll be?"

"I'm getting the bare minimum. So, give me about twenty minutes max." I don't like the idea of leaving Kelly at the mercy of Tom's driving, but we need food. It isn't long before Tom drops me off and disappears. I hate shopping of any kind, but grocery shopping has to be the worst. If there was a delivery service available to the farm, I would have ordered on-line. But there isn't. So, I push the squeaky, rickety cart up and down monotonous aisles, not sure what to get. Nothing looks appealing and I force myself to focus on simple basics, but I still mysteriously end up with four heavy shopping bags which I lug out of the store. Tom's already waiting. He pops the trunk and I dump everything in it, and Tom puts his foot down too hard for my liking. I'm barely seated in the car when we take off.

"Guess what I saw," Tom says.

"The black pickup."

"No prize for the right answer. We'll have to drive past it. It's parked on the street in front of the supermarket. I haven't seen Brad. I just want to get out of here without being followed." We reach the entrance to the supermarket parking lot.

"That's Sharon with Brad!" I say. "Now we know for sure that Sharon is involved. To think I trusted her. Well, I did at first. I suppose I haven't really trusted her since her phone call when I was in the barn." Tom turns the car into a side street with a sudden jerk. For most of the time he drives with one hand on the gear lever and the other draped on top of the steering wheel, but to make this turn he gripped and yanked. I'm pushed against the side door and it wouldn't have surprised me if an airbag exploded against my ribs. Kelly loses her balance and makes a wise decision to lie on the floor in the back rather than try to keep two feet on the seat. Tom continues to take a convoluted route to MMB.

"I wonder what Brad sees in Sharon. Talk about a dull accountant!" Tom says, as he changes gear with a crunch, a grind and a jolt.

"And I wonder what Sharon sees in Brad. This business has probably thrown them together. There might be no relationship beyond that. Take us, for example." I wish I hadn't said that, and that Tom would say something. But he doesn't. He keeps his eyes on the road for a change, as he continues his complicated path towards MMB.

"It's a good job I didn't buy anything frozen. I rather thought we might not be able to pick up groceries on the way back," I mumble.

"They were rather blatant about being seen together."

"Perhaps they think I won't be out and about much, because they put my truck out of order. Brad probably thinks he scared me half to death as well. They might be enjoying a false sense of security."

"Who knows? But, assuming they really do want to find out if you're picking up where Frank left off, and also want to stop you, they should be keeping track of you at all times."

I'm profoundly relieved to see MMB Aggregates' freshly painted red and white signs appear ahead. There's a flurry of large, heavy trucks coming and going. As we approach, I can hear the low roar of vehicles intermingled with the incessant beeping of reversing trucks, and the crushing noise of gravel being processed. Dust is abundant. Apparently, the heavy thunder shower the night before wasn't enough to quash it. The protective trees and shrubs that are required by the City look like they're choking on the dust, and trying to shrink from the noise. As I scan the monochromatic, moonscape-like surrounds which spread as far as the eye can see, I have a hard time believing that the owner could have any concern for the environment, since he's created such a hostile and unfriendly landscape.

"I suppose I'm a hypocrite when I say I find this destruction of our environment abhorrent when I also want to drive on good roads and safe bridges," I say.

"He is making rather a mess of this, isn't he? Shame there aren't more people like Frank around, to keep an eye on these guys." Tom parks in front of the unassuming concrete office building. It's a relief to come to a halt.

Mr Moncton-Brown will be arriving back any minute, according to the gum-chewing, blue and red-haired, obese receptionist whose long square finger nails make loud clicking noises on the keyboard. She's more interested in her computer screen than she is in looking at us.

"I suppose they can't get anyone else to work in this environment," Tom says, as we sit down on rather uncomfortable plastic chairs in the lobby. The noise of the trucks is barely audible from inside but sounds resonate in the hard, concrete décor, which is designed to cope with volumes of dirty foot-traffic. Two workers come in, and clomp purposively down the corridor, cigarettes in hand, their untied boots shedding dust and grit. Apparently, this noise has interrupted the receptionist. She comes to life.

"Do you want coffee? There's some in the lunchroom."

"Not for me, thanks," I reply. Tom just shakes his head slightly and smiles.

"Is this Mr Moncton-Brown's main office?" I ask, taking advantage of her attention.

"Oh, no! His proper office, like, is in Vannersville. They say it's nice."

After several more minutes elapse, I get restless.

"Excuse me," I say as I get up and approach the desk, walking across the gritty floor. "You did say that Mr Moncton-Brown is due back soon?"

"Yes." The woman pauses, and then adds, "I could call him on his cell I s'pose." She reaches for a dirty, old-fashioned phone. "It's Milly." Pause. "Yeah, I know you're on your way. Two people here want to speak with you. They're like, waiting." She turns to me. I've sat down again. "What's your name?"

"Meg Sheppard, and a friend, Tom Penning," I reply.

"Meg Sheppard, and a friend. Didn't catch his name," the woman says into the phone. Tom speaks up and states his name, but it's ignored.

"Are you still there?" the receptionist looks at the receiver and puts it back onto her ear. Covering the mouthpiece, she turns to us, "sometimes the signal dies, as he's coming out the valley." Turning her attention back to the phone, "Oh, you are. Okay." Placing the receiver back, she flops back in her chair. The ordeal appears to have exhausted her.

"Is he coming?" I ask.

"Yeah," she answers.

And it isn't long before a large silver Audi SUV pulls up to the front door, almost blocking the entrance to the building. A heavy-set, sharply dressed, grey-haired man squeezes past the steering wheel and marches through the doorway. He walks straight up to me and shakes my hand long and hard.

"What a pleasure, Meg," he says, and still smiling, he offers his hand to Tom, and I introduce him.

"Come into my office. This one is just a site office. You're lucky I happened to be coming out here." He beckons us into a large comfortable-looking office, which has a view of the only patch of green for miles, I notice.

"What brings you here?" he asks as he sits behind his desk. I wonder if there is any message in his putting the desk between him and us. There are a couple of armchairs and a sofa, positioned around a coffee table by the window with the view, that appear more inviting and comfortable for a chat.

"Well, I was going through my husband's things," I start to explain.

"I was sorry to hear about your husband's most unfortunate accident." He interrupts and his smile fades.

"Thank you. As I was saying, I was going through my husband's things, and I came upon a pleasant letter you'd sent him, inviting him to tour MMB Aggregates, including the concrete plant."

"Ah, yes. I recall writing that letter."

"Tom and I were driving nearby, and I remembered the letter. I thought you might be kind enough to arrange a tour for us."

"Is there anything that you're particularly interested in?" The sunlight catches his face, highlighting the network of surface veins as well as the puffiness and wrinkles under his dark eyes. He looks tired and grim.

"I run a consulting business and am thinking of expanding into the environmental field," Tom says. I notice how relaxed and pleasant he looks and am confident that he sounds genuine. But as I glance back to Marshall, I notice his mouth has set into a hard, straight line as if he's afraid he might let something escape if he relaxes the tension. That convinces me he knows everything there is to know, including the attempts to stop me from finding out what happened to Frank. But I still play along with Tom's angle.

"Yes, I'm thinking of joining Tom's company. As you know, Frank was interested in environmental issues and some of this interest rubbed off on me. It's an exciting and growing field. I've followed a fair bit of what's been going on, especially locally," I add.

"Environmental issues, eh?" Marshall strokes his square chin. "Are you planning to continue Frank's work?"

"I've been thinking about it, but I now think I'm more suited to consulting work. Working on environmental issues could be rewarding, and could also be a way to make a contribution to the community."

"So why do you think touring MMB would be helpful?" Marshall asks.

"Since you invited Frank, we assume you have some progressive environmental projects, or perhaps policy ideas, you were planning to share with him," Tom suggests.

Marshall pushes his palms down on his desk and stands up. His large-boned, tall figure looms over his desk. He leans forward to speak to us. We're still seated. It's obvious to me he sees through our charade, such as it is, and is not willing to play along with us.

"Well, it's not convenient." His voice is now loud and gruff. "I've a meeting with my assistant, Brad Buckthorn. You might know him, Tom. I believe you did some training, of a rather elementary sort, for our front-line supervisors." His eyes have become more like slits of darkness, and his voice has become deeper, but Tom doesn't miss a beat.

"Oh, yes, I do. And you'll know that the training was well-received. The supervisors and managers have requested a couple of follow-up sessions."

I might as well play my cards.

"I think I've met him too, although I don't think we've been formally introduced." I look straight into Marshall's narrowed dark eyes. "As well as pursuing my interest in environmental issues, I've been trying to find out what really happened to Frank. I don't believe his death was an accident. In the pursuit of the truth, I've talked to a few people, including Timothy at Westmount Steel, where I almost bumped into Brad, literally."

Marshall sits down and a faint look of bewilderment washes across his face. Perhaps my straightforward approach has taken this burly man off-guard a little. He hasn't intimidated us and he's trying to figure us out.

"I find it odd that the people I've contacted so far don't want to talk about any issues which may relate to Frank's death." I pause, hoping he'll say something.

"I expect everyone believes that there's nothing to be said. It was an accident for God's sake." His face reddens. I can sense that I've pushed a button.

"What about this tour? Is there no-one who could show us around?" Tom asks.

"I'm not interested in consultants, or env.., rather, I'm too busy for this. Brad will be here at any minute. You might not want to bump into him again, Meg?" He almost leaps to the door, and we're dismissed.

"That was interesting," I say, as Tom urges me to get into the car.

"We shouldn't hang around if that Brad guy is showing up. They might be using him as a heavy and, as things escalate, Brad's orders might progress from harassment to, well, I don't like to think." Tom puts his baseball cap on, spins the car around and sticks his chin out. He even puts both hands on the steering wheel, except when he abruptly changes gear, which is associated with the engine screaming and the tires spinning as he releases the clutch. We flee the scene in a cloud of dust.

"He probably isn't even expecting Brad," I say, as I turn to check if Kelly is okay. She's crouched on the floor behind the seats. I wish she had a seatbelt. I'm glad of mine.

"I don't think we need to keep up this break-neck speed, Tom." He eases off the gas and sits back in the seat. It's a relief to be going at a more reasonable rate, but I still would much prefer to be doing the driving myself. As I do my best to get my breathing back to normal, I try to figure out what makes him drive in spurts. And now and then he comes close to crossing the line and then makes an abrupt correction. Perhaps he isn't looking far enough ahead. I'm not sure. It'll have to remain a mystery.

"We started the meeting well, but we didn't get much out of it," Tom says as he turns to look at me with one hand draped on top of the steering wheel.

"I think we did, Tom. If Marshall had been smart, he would have arranged a tour and played along. The fact that he didn't, and he mentioned Brad, means that he knows exactly what's going on. Marshall might even be a key player. He is Brad's boss, after all. But I agree we didn't get specific information and we're likely in deeper trouble as a result of the meeting. And it's not just the pollution control regulations, I'm even more convinced that there's something about Frank's death that's mixed up in all this."

"I just can't believe that. My bet is on the pollution control regulations and their fear that you're going to pick up where Frank left off."

"Well, it's obviously something big in their world. I hope we find out soon." I don't want to argue with Tom, but Marshall's reaction to my probing into Frank's death was vehement enough for me to assume that he had a role in Frank's death or he knows who killed him.

"Yeah. One of these guys is going to make a mistake. Something will crack soon, I'm sure. And then it'll all become clear," Tom says.

"I just hope no-one gets hurt in the process," I say, as I reach behind the seats and pat Kelly. "Are we being followed?"

"Nope. I don't think anyone's followed us at all today." He checks the rear and side view mirrors again. "What do we do next?"

"Well, these groceries must get put away. Perhaps we should go over what we've got so far and draw up a plan of action."

"Sounds like a good idea," Tom says as we pull into the driveway.

As I unlock the door, I can hear the landline phone ringing. I reach it just before the answering service kicks in. It's Munro from the hospital.

"I have some more information for you, on the guy who got hurt at the same time as Frank's accident."

"Oh, good."

"As I told you, his name was Gerald Warren."

"Was? He hasn't died, has he?"

"No, no. But he's changed his name to John Nelson. He was transferred out of Shelton Hospital, to a private place, called Berry Nursing Home, on the outskirts of Thornton. I think it's about 120 miles east of here."

"That's rather odd, but excellent information, thanks." I write down Gerald's new name and new location.

"I have to tell you it wasn't easy to get," Munro says. "There's a cloud of secrecy over the whole thing, otherwise I would have been able to get back to you sooner."

"Interesting."

"Well, if I didn't think there was anything fishy about this business before, I sure do now!" Munro laughs, but then adds, "Not that I didn't believe you when you suggested that Frank's death was not an accident."

"I think John could be key to finding out what really happened."

"I would think so, but be careful."

* * *

"So, what do you want to do?" asks Tom once the groceries are finally safely away. We're slurping hot mushroom soup, which Tom prepared from scratch in what seemed like minutes.

"Well, I'd prefer to have my truck back for the journey to Thornton. And I don't think I should expect you to come all that way with me."

"You may not expect it, but I'm in this thing now." It sounds as if he's bound and determined to come. I was afraid he'd say that. I don't know much about friendship, but I know enough to believe that Tom is doing his best to be a good friend to me. I feel his friendship to me is out of loyalty to his good pal Frank, but even so, I must respect it.

"You're a great friend, Tom." I smile. "I checked with the garage, and, believe it or not, they still haven't got the right part. I'm going to think they're involved as well, if they don't get their act together soon! But they said it would be ready tomorrow evening for sure. We've got one person left on the list to visit. Well, perhaps two, including the poor guy in the nursing home. Sandy Bingham, Owner of Sandy's Waste Retirement. As you know, Sharon is his VP, Finance and Administration. And I should definitely meet with George, Frank's Assistant. So, I suppose that's three."

"Okay. Do you want to see this Sandy Bingham guy tomorrow, and perhaps George as well? You might not need to drive all that way to see that Warren or Nelson guy, you never know. Perhaps you'll find out what you need to know from Sandy and George." Tom suggests.

"I don't think so, somehow. I very much want to talk to John Nelson. But I want to make some progress tomorrow. I sure hope I do because I don't feel like I've got much further ahead so far."

Tom has produced a delicious-looking fresh salad, with crunchy fresh red pepper strips and juicy cucumber chunks on top. It's a treat, I have to admit, to have a meal prepared for me. I put the soup bowls in the dishwasher. That was Frank's job. I prepared the meals for the times when he was home. Was he home very much? When I look back, he was usually doing important political or charitable work. I stayed at home, unless it was a gala or a special social occasion, when he seemed pleased and proud to have me at his side.

Was I just a trophy wife? I shut out the question and close the dishwasher.

10

Squeezed

I have woken to a bright and breezy spring day, but as soon as I get out of bed the darker memories of Frank, which have recently bubbled up to the surface, flow into my mind and disturb my thoughts. As each bubble bursts, it's as if it's revealing some hidden truth about my relationship with Frank. Each small revelation makes me feel vulnerable, and perhaps even foolish. I wonder if Frank had cared about me at all, let alone loved me. Since his death, my memories of him must have been selective, until now. I try to quash my brain's urge to search for deeper, darker memories. But despite my efforts, an unwelcome flashback flickers and flutters, then lingers.

Frank had called and said he wouldn't be home one evening when the rain outside the kitchen windows had made me think I was behind Niagara Falls. The drainpipes spurted frothy water out onto the sodden grass, where black pools grew rapidly as ripples fanned out further and further. Kelly sat with her body pressed against me as I stood with the phone in my hand. Yes, yes, I understood it was an important meeting and that it had gone on longer than expected and yes, yes I realized it was easier for him to go straight on to the board meeting, and no, no, I wouldn't wait up. This would be the sixth evening in a row when he wouldn't be home. As I hung up, the rain stopped. The unexpected burst of evening sunshine caught the drips from the trees and turned the pools into sparkling puddles. Kelly laid down and sighed. I sat down and sighed.

I open the bedroom window wider and draw in a long breath of fresh, crisp spring air. It's true, just about every evening Frank went out to some event or meeting or, if he did come home, he worked at his desk or had Tom over for a chat. It was rare that he and I would spend time together unless he thought he needed his wife at his side. No. I shake my head. It can't be true.

I know it won't do me any good to bring these memories back. I must redouble my efforts to drown them out, and the only way I'll keep them below the surface is to keep myself busy. I get dressed and walk at a good pace down to the barn. Kelly helps to lift my mood as she wags her tail and jumps up at my side. I believe she knows how I'm feeling most of the time, and does her best to cheer me up when I need it. And she's having some success.

The phone rings in the house just as I step into the barn. It only rings twice, so I assume Tom has picked it up.

Eagle whinnies in expectation of food, and there's commotion in the stalls. The barn cats weave round my legs, mewing. It's easy to get caught up in the animals' excitement at the dawn of a new day. I feed the horses their carrots and grain, and listen to their steady munching for a few minutes. I catch a whiff of sweetness from the feed on the rare occasion when one of them raises their head.

Then I feed the cats and give them fresh water. I bring a few hay bales in from the hay barn, ready to put in the horses' stalls for the evening. I lug some heavy bags of wood-shavings in from the storage room. I love the pungent smell of pine when I open the bags and spread them in the clean stalls. But the horses haven't quite finished their breakfast, so I top-up the trough in the paddock with fresh water and check that there's still enough pasture for them. I will have to move them to a larger field soon. The paddock grass shoots up in the spring, but it gets eaten quickly. Without enough grass or hay, the horses can get sick from ulcers. Horses' stomachs produce acid all the time since their digestive systems are designed for grazing for most of their waking hours.

The horses' heads are hanging over their stall doors by the time I walk back into the barn. Bullet is pawing at his rubber mat in his impatience to get outside. His stall is in an even worse mess than usual. I lead them each into the paddock and get organized for the mucking out. Bullet has somehow dug part of his heavy, tough rubber mat up. It has a mound of dirt under it that will take some shovelling and raking to straighten out. He can be a neurotic horse sometimes. He has mixed his left-over hay up with his manure, and the stall looks like someone has used a giant spoon to stir up all the contents thoroughly. I don't mind. I get some strange satisfaction in cleaning out the stalls, putting in crisp new wood-shavings and piling fresh hay in the corners. It smells so good and looks so inviting that I'm often tempted to take a nap in one of the stalls after I've finished. But perhaps not in Bullet's stall this morning, despite all the work I've put into it. It was in such a mess that the image and smell of the stirred-up manure and urine-soaked bedding won't fade for a while. Eagle's stall would be a better bet. But I should get back to the house, otherwise Tom will come out looking for me. So, with some reluctance, I amble out of the barn and double-check on Eagle and Bullet as I pass the paddock.

Tom's head appears in one of the kitchen windows and I catch myself smiling. He's making tea, no doubt. I'm no longer sure how I feel about him being in my house. Am I adjusting to having him around? I clean most of the bits and pieces from the barn off my boots on the elaborate boot-scrubber Frank bought me one Christmas, and open the kitchen door. I think the gift carried a message from Frank that it was now okay with him if I did the barn chores (rather than hiring staff). I get a small boost from recalling this fragment – it's a relatively pleasant memory involving Frank, for a change.

"Nice pot of tea, ready to be poured," Tom announces, as I take off my boots and put them on the boot-tray, and drop my work gloves on the floor.

"Great! Who was that on the phone?"

"Perhaps I shouldn't have answered it."

"No, that's fine. I just heard it ringing, that's all." I sit down to drink the steaming tea.

"It was that trainer of yours from the track. He seemed rather put out that I answered. He was gruff, to put it mildly."

"What did he want?"

"I honestly couldn't tell you. He said he'd call back."

"I haven't time to deal with him today. He'd have said if it was urgent. We have a lot to do. We said we'd visit Sandy's Waste Retirement. We should meet Sandy Bingham. And we'll have to take your bright red wheels again." I do my best to sound enthusiastic.

"One thing going for it, it can move. I bet it could out-maneuver Brad's pickup truck." Tom sounds like a proud, first-car owner, quite a bit younger than his years.

"Well, that might come in handy. Let's hope not, though." And I mean it.

It's good to get going on the quest again. Despite the uncomfortable flash-backs about Frank, I've lost none of my enthusiasm or determination to find out what happened to him.

Kelly has thrown caution to the wind and is curled up on the small backseat of Tom's car. I wonder how long Tom's driving will enable the dog to hold that position. I do my best to turn my focus to simply being a passenger.

I can hear the birds as we drive along with the roof down, especially the chirrupy chickadees. The colours are brighter than yesterday, as if an artist has worked all night to enhance the vibrancy of every tree, plant and blade of grass. The fresh growth, with its luminous shades of green, lifts my spirits. The vivid contrast to the whites, greys and blacks of my memories of the winter is dramatic and incredible. It's as if the world around me has been reborn and is eager to make the best of this fresh start. Can I make a fresh start? I try to recall how I'd felt at this time the year before. I can't remember that spring at all.

A whiff of acrid stench from the large landfill site jolts me out of my thoughts. Recycling has not put an end to dumping. We cross the poisoned River Vanner. At least I'd heard Frank say it's poisoned, polluted with run-off from the landfill which had been established fifty years previously, before any meaningful regulations. The putrid leeching has gone unchecked for decades, but there are plans in place to shut the site down in five years' time. The City is in a panic to find somewhere else to take the tons of garbage which are collected every day. To be fair, Westmount Steel, further upstream, is also believed to be a factor in the pollution of the river. I remember hearing allegations cited on a radio program that the steel mill still dumps toxic waste into the water.

As we pass the landfill, we see bulldozers buzzing around on the tops of mounds of dirt mixed with garbage, like enormous flies. The gulls circle overhead, waiting for the opportunity to settle by some tasty scraps. Doesn't everyone use the compost system? If they did, surely there shouldn't be anything tempting to the gulls? I wonder if I'm thinking more like Frank every day, as I become better informed of his environmental concerns and actually contemplate their implications.

The office building is in a curious place, just west of the landfill. Since SWR has such a variety of businesses in several different locations, and also appears to be doing well financially, I had expected the owner, Sandy Bingham, to have his office in Vannersville. But when he bought SWR it simply consisted of this one landfill site, so perhaps he's not inclined to move from the business' original location.

"Sharon hasn't mentioned much about Sandy," I say as we enter some battered double gates, which are covered in dust and lodged in clumps of emerging weeds at the side of the entrance. "But she mentioned that he's Susan Kingsley-Black's Uncle and also, through tragic circumstances apparently, also Susan's adoptive father." The driveway to the modest office building travels through a tunnel formed of maple trees that shed dappled light onto the gravel road.

"All I know is that he's a very independent person, very business-oriented but believed to be lacking in integrity. He's not one for obeying rules either. Likes to do things his way."

"How do you know all this?" I ask as he yanks the steering wheel with his right hand all the way around to his knee and pulls into a parking spot, coming to a stop with a lurch. Kelly falls off the seat, scrambles to get up in the small space behind our seats, and wisely lies down there.

"Being in the management consulting business means you meet tons of people and find out a lot. I don't gossip, but I keep my ear to the ground. It's helped me to connect with a few new clients. Boy, this isn't very pleasant. It's a bit of a shock after that shady road in."

We've emerged into a grey parking area of about a couple of acres, which is surfaced with packed limestone and has quite a slope to it. Several large, rusty and dirty SWR trucks lined up along the perimeter and a few have their engines running, spewing black fumes and emitting disquieting rumbles. About thirty cars and a couple of motorbikes are parked haphazardly elsewhere. Tom stops next to the large Cadillac SUV which has the licence plate "SWR 1". It's in front of the building, which isn't really a building, but three office trailers linked together and located at the top of the slope.

"It isn't what I expected, I have to say." I get out of Tom's car, which I notice has a layer of dust on it and doesn't look so shiny any more. He probably regrets not having the roof up since the tops of the leather seats and the dashboard already have a faded look as a result of the fall-out from the drive in.

"Not only does it all look temporary, and rather the worst for wear, but I can't imagine it's easy to navigate this slope in the winter. How odd to set it up like this," I add as I look around me. We climb the wooden steps to the entrance.

At the top of the steps, if I look in the opposite direction from the adjacent landfill site, ignore the parking lot, focus on the trees beyond, hold my nose and plug my ears, it isn't such a bad spot.

We assumed Sandy was in, because we assumed the Cadillac was his, but the sleek, perfumed and nail-polished receptionist informs us he isn't.

"But I'm sure that Sharon McDonald, his Vice President, will see you. I'll let her know that you're here." It's as if SWR is expecting us, although we hadn't called ahead.

We sit in the small reception area, breathing in the receptionist's scent. I pick up the Vannersville Times and read the headline 'Susan Kingsley-Black Nominated To Run In The By-election'. The man who'd won the by-election caused by Frank's death died of a heart attack not long after his campaign. But I admit I haven't given any thought to who might be running in his place. I point out the headline to Tom. He tosses the paper down as Sharon emerges. She leads us into a sumptuous office, in grey and dusky pink, with deep grey leather office chairs, and a large glass table, around which we're invited to sit. The décor, although dated, is a vast contrast to the drab and colourless one I left her in at the restaurant.

"I've been expecting you, Meg." I detect an edge to Sharon's raspy voice as she stares at me with her cool, grey eyes. I don't suppose she's forgotten her bloody nose, and I haven't forgotten her uncalled-for assault on me. I can see the tension in her white knuckles as she clasps her chubby hands and rests them on the glass table in front of her plump body, which is closely wrapped in various browns.

Tom offers her his hand and introduces himself.

"I know who you are." It strikes me as comical that she's seemingly trying to sound menacing. She leans across the table towards me and peers at me more intently. "Frank's death was an accident. You really need help, Meg." Her voice is as cold as her eyes. "And you've been harassing this company and two others, I've been told, and for no purpose. None of us is responsible for your husband's death. It was an accident. You just won't accept the truth. It's pathetic."

"Yes, it really is *pathetic.*" Tom and I both let out small, involuntary gasps as Susan enters the office and slams the door behind her, as if to stress her point. "As I told you before, let sleeping dogs lie." She stands close to us with her arms folded. Her small dark eyes almost disappear behind the thick, reflective lenses of her glasses, as she looks down upon us with a smirk on her red lips.

"I have to correct you." I look at Sharon. "I'm not the one doing the harassing. Brad is the one trying to intimidate me. He's not letting sleeping dogs lie, as you put it." I turn to look at Susan, who's still standing.

"Don't be ridiculous. That's crazy," Susan says. It's as if she's spitting out each word. "It's you who's been pestering us, trying to destroy healthy businesses important to this community, for no good reason. You even went to the lawyer, who's a joke, that's for sure. You're delusional. You need to get help."

"My dog has been attacked, my house broken into, my truck tampered with, and Brad's pickup has followed us numerous times." I turn to Tom, who nods.

"I'm not listening to this." Sharon says. "You have an incredible imagination. You should leave. But I hope you get some help, Meg. You obviously need it."

As we reluctantly stand up, Sharon waves us out of the office as if shooing a couple of dogs out, her face and neck reddening. Susan steps towards us and says, "And don't come back here or show your face at the mill or the gravel pits, and don't poke your nose in this anymore. You're not welcome, if you haven't got that through your thick skulls by now." Sharon is behind Susan. Her hands shake as she maneuvers towards the office door to shut it.

We stand by Tom's car.

"Well, it's almost like they're panicking," I say. "We must be missing something. They were both tense and agitated. It's odd. Makes me even more determined to keep going."

"I agree, it was real weird."

As I pat Kelly and tell her she was good for staying patiently in the car (she is an amazing dog) I hear several SWR trucks start up, and notice out of the corner of my eye that all of them are belching diesel fumes upwards, creating ink-blots on the blue sky. One chugs its way to the driveway.

"We should go," I say. "Stay on the floor, Kelly. Down. That's it." We buckle up and Tom spins the car round in reverse with limestone chips flying, but I can't hear anything over the rumble of the trucks' engines and the clanking of their rusty metal garbage compactors. Tom decides it's best to wait for them to all move out, but the driver closest to us waves us on.

We find the first truck stationary in the middle of the driveway, blocking our way out.

"Why's he stopped here?" Tom asks.

"Haven't a clue."

"Shit, the truck behind is awfully close. Makes me feel like a chipmunk about to get flattened."

"That's awful."

"I don't like this. He's almost touching my bumper, and I've got nowhere to go."

"What? I can't hear you." Tom has to repeat what he just said, at a yell, so that I can hear it. And then we move. The truck which is behind us, with a roar from its engine, pushes Tom's car. As I reach for Kelly's collar, I can see the flaky, black paint on its rusting bumper, almost close enough to touch, as it noses the little red car, scrunching the trunk which is partly under the truck. Kelly's shaking so I drag her to the front of the car, where she squeezes in by my feet. She has faith in my protection, but I don't. I'm trembling myself.

"Should we get out?" Tom yells, just as the truck pushes again. Tom has put the car in neutral so we move more easily, but then we stop as the hood touches the underneath of the back bumper of the truck ahead. Then, nothing happens.

"I'm going to talk to one of these drivers," I say. "You hold on to Kelly."

"I should go."

"No, you stay at the wheel and hold Kelly. They might be more inclined to back off if I talk to them."

"What will you say?"

I don't answer and open the car door. I decide to walk to the truck in front, but just as I'm about to emerge from behind the daunting, overpowering truck, it rocks as it changes gears and lunges ahead with a roar, and the truck behind reverses, ironically sounding its safety beeper and flashing its lights. It's as if some mysterious master has called them off. I hop back into the car and stroke Kelly as I catch my breath.

As soon as the way ahead is clear, Tom puts his foot to the floor, spinning the wheels on the gravel, and snakes down the rest of the driveway, which is almost more frightening than being pushed by the truck. It's a relief that the car is still road-worthy. He keeps the engine screaming as we head for home, the only saving grace being that his driving is less erratic when he's in full flight. It's nevertheless an unnerving and unpleasant trip as I'm thrown against the door several times, despite the seatbelt. I clutch the door handle and hold on to Kelly all the way, and am glad of the headrest.

"Your car will need a lot of work. I'm so sorry, Tom." The front is not too bad, but the trunk looks as if a giant has picked the car up and dropped it on its end. All the rear lights are smashed. "You should report it to the police."

"I thought about it, but it could make matters worse. The most important thing is that we didn't get hurt." He pats Kelly, who has her tail between her legs. She must be really wondering about the stupidity of humans right now. And Tom looks pale and his eyes have a glassy look. "But I wish I knew what the hell's going on," Tom adds.

"It could have been a lot worse, you know. The truck behind could have been one that picks up dumpsters and empties them. We could all be in a landfill site by now." I smile, but Tom grimaces. It was a weak attempt to make light of the situation, and I regret saying it. "Let's go inside and try to relax for a few minutes," I suggest.

"I could do with a drink." Tom sinks into a chair in the family room, as if he's a puppet and someone has cut the strings.

"I have to admit, so could I." I flop down into a chair just across the room, trying to ignore Tom's created chaos around me. "Kelly, go pour a couple of drinks. Poor dog, she's as exhausted as we are." Kelly curls up, pressing against my legs, quivering. "I wonder if she'll be as keen to come with us for a drive next time?" I hate to see her upset and want sanity restored into all of our lives.

"How about I pour the drinks? What would you like?" Tom heaves himself out of the chair, stiff from the tense drive, letting his hat fall to the floor to add to the array of clothes, books, papers and glasses.

"What about some brandy? Frank told me that his mother swore by it for medicinal purposes." I smile.

"Sounds just the thing."

"We must be on to something, but we don't know what," I say, as I stroke Kelly's silky head.

"Yep, it's frustrating, and I've no clue."

"The way they behaved makes me think there is a connection between Frank's death and the environmental issues and their businesses."

"I don't think so. To me, getting rid of Frank would be futile. They must know that pollution control regulations will eventually come into place in any case."

"Perhaps it has something to do with timing. What if MMB couldn't proceed with its contract with that construction company to dump those 40,000, I think it was, truckloads of so-called clean fill into one of its pits once the regulations Frank was working on were introduced? And you mentioned SWR was working on some new garbage pickup and disposal contracts with Boughton. What if SWR wanted the life of the landfill site extended, or at least not shortened with new regulations, if that's what's in the works? Also, many believe that Westmount Steel is contaminating the river. What if they were buying time so that they could delay the installation of water treatment facilities? This could be what it's all about. Perhaps it's all about delaying things."

"It still doesn't make sense to me. I just can't believe that any of the people we have on the list is capable of murder."

"It's astounding what people will do for money. And there are millions at stake here, and some ruthless businessmen, and women, affected."

Despite our discussion, I enjoy the warming and calming effect of the brandy trickling down my throat. But as I hold the glass in my hand, turning it round and watching the liquid swirl, an unwanted memory seems to rise up out of the disturbed brandy.

I sat by myself at the head table, at my wedding, as Frank talked with everyone else in the room. There were about one hundred guests, only three of whom invited by me. Frank wanted a "low-key" wedding, since it was his second. I have no family here, and no-one I would have invited anyway, so I asked Munro (Dr Milton), a colleague from the humane society, and Kelly's vet, each with their partners. So, I left the head table and sat next to my guests. It felt like it was Frank's event, not mine at all. But I suppose that's what our marriage was. It centred on Frank and revolved around Frank, and I'd accepted all that because I'd never been the centre of anything and didn't think I deserved to be, and still don't.

Kelly nudges me as if to shake me out of my thoughts. Tom has been talking and I haven't been listening.

"Sorry, Tom, I wasn't listening."

"I was saying that I want to keep on, even if my hot red car has to go into the shop for a bit."

"That's good of you, but I feel really awful about your car. I'll pay any costs not covered by insurance, of course."

"No, no. That's not an issue, but thanks. I chose to get involved in this. I'm doing it for Frank as well as for you." He puts his legs up on the coffee table and I curl my legs up under me in the large chair. Kelly is stretched out and looking more relaxed, much to my relief.

11

George

"I wonder what they're going to do about finding a new landfill site once this one is closed. That might have something to do with it as well." I say as I finish the last drop of my brandy, and Tom opens his eyes. He might have dozed for a couple of minutes.

"One of the problems," Tom says, as he lets his head fall back onto the chair again, "is that no-one wants a dump-site in their backyard, and no-one likes these incinerators. I think the new ones are very efficient, and are probably quite safe, but the general public doesn't agree."

"I was thinking. It wouldn't be easy for SWR to dump illegally because they'd need to do it in large quantities to make any decent money, and that would be hard to carry off. But I suppose they could illegally dump some of the recycling and compost and perhaps the garbage from the smaller contracts, so as to extend the life of the current landfill site for the City garbage. After all, the City has grown so much. I have thought it might be worth getting air-borne somehow to check things out. They could bury tons of garbage in those empty gravel pits north of Vannersville. You'd only know from the air, and not even then, if they're smart. They'd have to dump at night. Oh, I expect that's ridiculous. It's just the brandy talking."

"No, I don't think it's ridiculous. It could be Sandy's Waste Retirement driving this. Sharon asks Brad to help. It might not involve the steel mill, though. But, on the other hand they might all be involved, you never know. I really want to get to the bottom of this. I'm going to call my doctor," Tom says as he gets up from his chair with renewed energy.

"Why are you calling your doctor? Are you all right?"

"Fine, considering." He chuckles. "My doctor flies for a hobby, and it's Wednesday. She always takes the afternoon off. So, we may be able to arrange a flight over the gravel pits. She owes me one, so we'll see." I'm impressed with Tom's attitude and his leap to action, especially since his precious red car is smashed.

But my stomach churns at the thought of going up in a little plane.

"I get sick up in planes though," I say.

"I'll ask her to recommend something for motion sickness, and we'll pick it up on the way. She's handy like that!"

I can see why Frank thought of Tom as a good and loyal friend. But it's difficult for me to develop trust, and therefore difficult for me to build friendships. It's as if there are barriers encircling me which prohibit me from getting close to anyone. But it's a good feeling to know that the barriers have lowered between me and Tom.

Kelly and I are captured in the welcome warmth radiating from the beams of spring sunshine. They brighten the room and lift my mood. I am so glad that I didn't sell the property and move, as so many urged me to do. Not only would I have lost my husband, but

I would have lost my lifestyle, my beautiful home, and the many therapeutic benefits of living in the country. And I'm enjoying and appreciating my home even more, now that the rawness of my grief is easing.

"It's all arranged," Tom says. "We have to be there at three thirty. Where are you going?" I have pushed myself up out of the chair.

"Remember, I was to meet with Frank's assistant today, while you went to the office. And you were going to try to dig up something about Chuck."

"Oh, that's right. I'm going to arrange a tow and a rental first. I shouldn't drive the car in the state it's in, especially with no lights. Should be able to get them to bring a rental in less than an hour, then I'll drop you off. Will that work? What are you going to do about lunch?"

"That would be nice. Thanks a lot. I was going to get a taxi. I won't bother with lunch. I'll grab a snack in the cafeteria in the government buildings, if I need to."

"What about Kelly?"

"I'd rather not leave her here."

"I can look after her until I pick you up to go to the airport. My staff will love her." He even thinks of Kelly. I'm grateful.

* * *

A little later, I look up at the large stone parliament buildings. They are familiar, yet they seem strange at the same time. I've lived through a lot of my own history since last trudging up the steps worn from millions of shoes over the ages. As I walk along the corridor leading to the Members' chambers, I wonder at what the darkened oak walls have witnessed, and wish they could talk. The cool, mottled marble floors look like they could last forever and convey a sense of timelessness. The subdued lighting is more pleasant than the glaring brilliance in most other buildings. The atmosphere is stiller, warmer and more inviting than that in the much newer concrete and glass office buildings housing the civil servants.

Frank's assistant is competent, so he's not been relegated to the office block after Frank's death, but has found a new responsibility in the familiar old parliamentary buildings. Others come and go, but George is always there. I assume I'll find him in. Frank sometimes asked me to fetch a document or to deliver one in the evening, rather than use the courier service, which he distrusted for important matters. George would always greet me and make time to ask about the humane society or the horses.

"Meg, how nice to see you. What a pleasant surprise. Do come in. Would you like a cup of tea?" George greets me with genuine warmth, making me feel welcome and at ease.

"That would be wonderful. I've had quite the day so far." I settle into a comfortable easy chair, of which there are two separated by a solid, ornate coffee table. "I hope this isn't a bad time for you, George." He looks just the same as I remember, with his thin, finely featured face and sparkling eyes. He's a smart and classy dresser with his dark tailored suit and polished black shoes.

"Goodness, no. It's so nice to see you. It can get lonely here sometimes, when the House isn't sitting. And I still miss Mr Sheppard. He was so wonderful to work for. I could really feel proud of what we were doing. Anyway, tea will be here soon. How are things going with you?" George sits down, with the coffee table between us, and his desk piled with papers behind us.

"Well, I've been having some excitement."

"Oh, I hope you can share it with me. I could do with some excitement." George moves forward on the chair, and perches on the edge with his hands clasped in front of him.

"You can have some of it. I think there's enough to go around!" We both chuckle. "Actually, I was hoping you'd help me out," I add.

"Wonderful!" George slaps his thighs. "Oh, here's the tea." It arrives in a silver tea service which George's mother left him. He told me previously that it didn't suit his modern apartment, but looks quite at home in the old and dignified parliament buildings. The bone-china cups and saucers gleam on the silver tray. The tea is bound to taste delicious.

"Do tell me all about it!" George says as he pours the steaming brown liquid into a small amount of milk he's already put in each of the teacups.

"I'll get right to the point. I've had suspicions that Frank's death was no accident. Well, now I'm absolutely convinced that it wasn't."

"Wow!" George says, replacing his cup back onto the saucer without a sound. "I can't imagine Frank having enemies. Well, actually, that isn't true. I know lots of the big businesses saw Frank's initiatives as costing them money. Some of them were blatant that money was all they cared about. What makes you so convinced that it wasn't an accident?"

I summarize the key events, and it's clear that George is captivated. He hardly moves a muscle until I finish, and the tea in our cups has surely gone cold.

"I can see what you mean. Wow! It sounds dangerous, Meg. You be careful."

"Tom is helping me out. I think you've met Tom Penning?" George nods. "I know I can count on your help, too. We're still not certain who's behind this. We know Brad is doing the dirty work, but we're not sure on whose behalf. You knew everything that went on in Frank's office. Have you got some ideas?"

"Yes, I think so. Frank's proposed new pollution control regulations were upsetting some powerful, and dare I say arrogant, businessmen. You've mentioned them. Sandy Bingham, Marshall Moncton-Brown and Timothy Westmount. But I think a larger concern was Frank's investigation into the pit rehabilitation issue and his belief that there should be controls on the quality of fill. That seemed to set off all sorts of alarms. There were big contracts in the offing with the huge subway project. Millions of dollars to be made by hauling out the dirt and dumping it into exhausted gravel pits. But, as you know, part of the subway is planned to go through old industrial land which is suspected of having high levels of contamination."

"Yes, I think I've heard about that."

"And another project Frank was working on was the issue of illegal dumping. When word got out that he was looking into this and doing some international research – it is an issue in most countries – sparks flew. He had several people here, including Susan Kingsley-Black, who you mentioned, who's Timothy Westmount's Chief Operating Officer. They wanted dumping regulations relaxed rather than strengthened. I thought that was interesting and, well, short-sighted. And Frank didn't seem to be able to make them see reason. Makes you wonder what these people are up to in the pursuit of the almighty buck."

"Yes, it does. Did Frank seem concerned about any of these meetings? Do you think any of the people involved seriously threatened him?"

"All I know is that Frank didn't appear ruffled by the meetings, and he scoffed at anything that resembled a threat. The only threats that I heard myself were along the lines of: 'Do you realize how many jobs this nonsense of yours will cost this community' and 'These crazy and unnecessary ideas will mean lost votes in the next election'. Not very scary. I don't remember who said what. And Frank didn't appear to care. He strongly believed that what he was doing was right and was overdue. He kept saying that these people know these regulations are going to come in eventually, whoever is in power. The writing's on the wall, so to speak."

"Timing could be an issue, I've thought."

"Delay, yes, it could help them, but I don't think it would be worth murdering someone for, if that's what you're suggesting."

"You're probably right."

"Another thing I remember is that Frank was keen to tour the gravel pits. He got an invitation, but it didn't seem to get him anywhere. I think his primary interest was in the disused pits. Something made him think they might be using them for illegal dumping."

"You mentioned Frank was doing research into illegal dumping, and I think that was one of his reasons for going to England several times?"

"Yes, he seemed to find it helpful to meet with politicians and civil servants in various communities in England."

"You sound as if you're doubtful about this?"

"Well, to be honest, I thought it a bit curious that he needed to visit several times. All I can say is that I didn't see evidence that these trips were helpful, but that doesn't necessarily mean anything, and it's not my place to say anything really, and I wouldn't say a word if Frank was still with us."

"Of course."

"What he did, which I thought was brilliant, was that he set up the Task Force on Fill Disposal and Pit Rehabilitation. Did you know about that?"

"No."

"Well, he invited Moncton-Brown, Bingham, Westmount as well as other stakeholders from across the Province, including representatives from conservation authorities, municipalities and others. He had his policy advisors there too, of course. His aim was to use the Task Force to develop a reasonable compromise which everyone could support. It was proving to be challenging, but he started to make progress."

"That sounds like it would help to defuse things, at least."

"In any case, going back to the threats, Frank acted as if the threats were nothing to worry about. That's the strong impression he gave me."

"You're probably right."

"I don't think I've been much help."

"You have, and I appreciate your time and the delicious tea," I say as I get up out of the cozy chair to leave.

"Whatever I can do to assist, just let me know. Good luck!" George says as he shakes my hand while we stand, dwarfed, in the large, carved doorway.

* * *

It isn't much later when Tom and I are on our way to the, in my opinion, rather too small Vannersville Airport to meet Tom's Doctor. I give Tom an overview of my chat with George on the way, and then ask, "Did you find out anything about Chuck?"

"Yes, a good friend of mine, Raj, is a journalist, and he found a link to a press release issued by Vannersville Children's Centre with a photograph which shows Chuck presenting the cheque for the $50,000, the amount he was left in the will. So, it looks like he's telling the truth."

"It's good to eliminate someone off the list. I can't think of any other reason he would want Frank gone." I sigh as a warm sense of relief washes over me.

"I agree. By the way, Raj says that Chuck is a pretty talented writer. He's asked him to write articles now and then, and they're always well-researched and well-written."

"Perhaps we're getting somewhere," I try to convince myself. But it doesn't work. We've made little progress. There are more questions than answers. Will I be able to find out what happened?

The sight of the flimsy-looking aircraft lining the runway ahead exacerbates my unsettled feelings. My stomach flutters at the thought of swooping and tipping in a small plane. I hope the nauseating flight will be worth it.

12

Up in the Air

I have to ask Tom how he came to have a female doctor. It seems to me people more often than not have a preference for a general practitioner of their own sex. He tells me he didn't have a family doctor after he left university until he ended up in the emergency department with pneumonia, the symptoms of which he'd hope would disappear if he kept on working and ignoring them. He needed follow-up, and the only couple of doctors taking new patients in Vannersville were recent female graduates. One of whom was Kara and, while he was hesitant at first, he found he appreciates her communication skills, her thoroughness and her willingness to explain things. And he likes her spunk and energy. He's stayed with her ever since. What's more, he's connected her with a few new patients, so he says that's why he could ask her to take us up in her plane.

* * *

True to his word, Tom asked Kara for a motion sickness pill, and the doctor duly delivered. I'm wary when I learn that it's a sample of a new drug which a large pharmaceutical company sent her, via a sales rep, just the week before.

"Guaranteed to be fast-acting and non-drowsy, so you'll be awake for the flight. Is that good or bad?" asks Kara, with the widest smile I've ever seen. The brilliance of her perfect teeth and the snowy whites of her eyes highlight her soft, nut-brown face as well as her sparkling dark brown irises. I don't know why I'm surprised that this petite, vivacious woman is a pilot. I suppose I must hold stereotypical images of who flies planes.

She and Tom laugh and joke, and, despite my uneasiness, I admit that a little of the joviality is rubbing off on me as I sip my coffee. We sit at the bar which has enormous windows looking out over the airfield, but the grime which has collected on the glass over the winter, combined with the glare of the sun, make it virtually impossible to see anything out of them.

"What's all this about, Tom? It sounds intriguing. Are we going to get shot at or something?" Kara asks, leaning over the greasy table towards Tom.

"Maybe," Tom replies.

"You're not serious," Kara says. She leans back and laughs.

"We think there might be illegal things going on in those unused gravel pits," Tom says in a low voice.

"What do you mean? Kids on their dirt bikes, and maybe some shooting practice, and I don't know, perhaps..." Kara isn't taking us seriously at all.

"Hey, keep your voice down," Tom says, but with a smile. "We're not sure, but we want to look, and I'm not going into any more here. We can talk when we're up there." Tom collects the empty styrofoam cups. (I wish he'd collect the glasses and other paraphernalia off the family room floor.)

"Oh, hell, what's a few bullet holes," Kara says, as she pushes her chair out and reaches for her jacket.

"She's not taking us seriously," I mumble to Tom as we make our way to the plane.

"It doesn't matter, as long as she gets us up there."

"And down again, preferably in one piece."

It's much noisier in the plane than I'd expected At least Kara seems to know what she's doing. She emits a sense of professionalism, confidence and competence, which are all excellent qualities for a doctor, as well as a pilot, in my opinion. We take off, lifting into the sky with the grace of a large blue heron. As we gain height, everything below diminishes in significance.

I'm glad to be in the back, albeit cramped, and thankful that the medication appears to be working. I don't feel drowsy either. Kara and Tom banter away, but I hear only the occasional word until Tom turns round and shouts, "We're here, Meg. Can you see anything from there?"

"A bit." I sit more upright and lean towards the window. It's a shock to see the vastness of the devastation below. It looks as barren and lifeless as the surface of the moon and shockingly expansive. Certainly, there has been no attempt to do any meaningful restoration of the environment after the sand and gravel have been plundered. We pass this desolation in ignorant bliss as we drive down the roads, since they are lined with berms and trees.

It would be easy to imagine that we're about to land on another planet to look for signs of life, and the odds are that we wouldn't find any. But then I glimpse a telltale sign.

"Tom, I saw a seagull circling below! Can we go down for a closer look?"

"Hang on!" Kara hollers, as the plane swoops down like a giant eagle about to prey on the seagull below. I've lost sight of the gull, but I can see specks of white on what looks like an enormous mound snuggled into the side of a large pit.

"I bet there's garbage buried there!" I shout, pointing down, about 45 degrees from the nose of the plane.

"The gulls are giving them away. They weren't quite careful enough," Tom says, as we get closer and can see more of the white birds.

"So, this is what you're up to," Kara says, "picking up where Frank left off, I suppose? I didn't know you were into this environmental stuff, Tom." I can't hear Tom's reply. Dizziness suddenly makes my head spin, and all I can think about is solid ground.

"I'll take another pass, a little lower this time," Kara shouts. We confirm that garbage has been dumped in the exhausted pits below. We see signs of heavy vehicles which we assume delivered the garbage, and of earth-moving vehicles which worked to conceal the garbage in the pit, although not adequately. About a quarter of a mile away is a wooded area, where the vehicles are likely hidden when not in use. The trees run in a wide band following a deeply rutted track which is possibly the access used to reach the pit.

Kara offers to take us in a wider circle, and Tom and I agree, although I'm sure my face has turned a putrid green.

It turns out that it's fortunate that we did. We found one of the unused pits with its pale yellow sandy sides darkened by mounds of dark dirt which were deposited in what appears to be the deepest section, with two bulldozers poised on top. The bulldozers look like ants, so the mounds must be huge hills. I don't have the energy to shout at Tom, but I don't have to. Tom turns and yells that it's contaminated fill, or at least could be. The likelihood is that nobody knows: we're guessing it has not been tested.

I don't feel at all well by the time we land, albeit smoothly.

"You don't look good," Tom says, as we walk back to the bar.

"I feel dizzy, and rather unsteady on my feet."

"Would you like to take my arm?" Tom asks. I'm glad that I trust him enough, and am comfortable enough, to take him up on his offer.

"Ironically five percent of people get a sort of vertigo as a side-effect of this drug," says Kara, smiling. "Well, Meg, it looks like you have the honour of being in the five percent!" I'm a bit miffed that Kara is treating my reaction as nothing serious and apparently finds it amusing. I feel rotten. I promise myself that there will be no more flights in small planes for a long, long time.

* * *

As I pull on my barn clothes the next morning, I still feel queasy. If I was okay, I would ride, although the weather is miserable. I'm even more disgruntled when the house phone rings because I presume that it's Shane. No-one else calls this early. I should let it ring. But I don't.

"I wanted to check with you about this race I'm thinking of entering Speed into. It's in about three weeks. I want to plan his training to fit his racing schedule and I'd like you to come to the track today to discuss it." Shane says.

"Um, I think that's going to be a problem. I'd like to see the horses, but I have to follow up on something today. Can't we resolve it over the phone?"

"It would be a lot better in person, and then I could show you the horses. I'm still not happy with Rose. She's off a bit, and I'm taking it easy with her." Shane then describes the race he has in mind for Speed. It sounds fine to me.

"So, is everything going okay?" Shane asks.

"Fine, thanks."

"See you here soon. You can visit the horses and we should meet to talk."

I would like to see Speed and Rose, but I have no desire to see Shane.

I venture out into the fog and drizzle. It's worse than I expected. The horses aren't as keen as usual to go outside, even though they know they have access to a run-in shed in the paddock. Perhaps that's why Bullet's stall is in pretty good shape. He was happy to hang out there until better weather appeared.

I don't hurry and take my time to enjoy the sweet smell of the hay as I put a couple of flakes in each of their stalls. My phone rings and I'm surprised to see the lawyer's name pop up, and even more surprised to hear his voice, rather than that of his assistant.

"It's William Porter. Just wondered if you could meet me for coffee. I have some information I'd like to share with you."

I'm glad I've not got a busy morning. Yes, I told a white lie to Shane. I could have made time to go to the track.

William's phone call has given me a bit of a boost, and the barn chores did me some good. By the time I get back to the house and hang up my damp jacket, I'm feeling much better. I tell Tom about the meeting with the lawyer as he makes himself some breakfast.

"What's happened to Brad recently?" asks Tom as he crunches on his toast. Crumbs scatter over the table in all directions.

"That's a good question. He seemed to be on top of me all the time, but we haven't seen him for a couple of days now."

"What's next?"

"I want to go to the nursing home to see Gerald or John, but I want to take the truck, and since it'll be ready later today, and I'm meeting with William Porter this morning, I'd like to go tomorrow. Would that work for you?"

"To be honest, that would be better than today, because I need to follow up on a couple of things at the office. I have to oversee the start of a couple of new consulting projects which I hadn't expected to get the contracts for. Pleasant surprise, but a lot more work."

"Oh, Tom, you shouldn't come to the nursing home then. I don't want your business to suffer."

"I still think it's a long way to go to find out that he didn't see anything, but I'd like to come anyway, and it'll give the staff an opportunity to take on more responsibility, which will be win-win for everyone. But I'll go into the office this morning, back for lunch."

"Of course. I'll talk to Chuck again, to see if he has anything else to add, and then I'll go to my meeting with the lawyer. By the way, Shane wanted me to go to the track to meet with him and visit the horses."

"It's a pretty dreary day to go to the track. Doesn't he phone at least once a day? He's an odd one."

"He texts as well, usually about four or five times a day. It can be a pain."

"I can imagine."

"You're right about Shane being odd. I have to admit that I don't feel comfortable with him." But I know my feelings could be a reflection of my experiences, rather than having anything to do with Shane. After all, I don't know him very well. Not that long ago, I wouldn't have allowed myself to be alone with a man, under any circumstances. It was Frank who helped me to trust.

I came to believe that Frank was different the third time we met. We were in a noisy coffee shop which was not only full of chatting customers, with their words bouncing off all the hard surfaces, but also had a rock radio station beating on my eardrums. Much to my surprise, Frank opened up and told me about his first wife, Louisa. She had been a beautiful fashion model and also a singer, and had meant the world and more, by the sound of it, to him. They had been married for only two years. She died of breast cancer. And he admitted to me he was devastated and had no-one to talk to, other than Tom, but Tom was unmarried and Frank felt he couldn't understand the profoundness of his loss. He revealed that his brother, Murray, was an alcoholic. Their parents had died when they were in their early twenties.

I was just about in tears by the time he'd finished the summary of his life-story. Despite Frank's masculine appearance with his dark stubble, narrow dark eyes and broad, muscular shoulders, he sounded vulnerable and alone. I'd never had such an intimate conversation with a man before, and I felt empathy and sincere compassion. I wanted to hug him despite myself, which shocked me. That was when I started to trust him.

But I should have more been more careful. After all, he even said that I reminded him of her. And that had to be based on my looks, because I didn't have Louisa's outgoing and exuberant personality. When I look back on that morning, I should have realized he was desperately searching for another Louisa, and that I couldn't possibly fill her shoes. I'm not her. I'm me. And I have baggage. And Louisa meant so very much to Frank. It was obvious.

A grim and horrifying thought came in a flash. What if Frank had committed suicide? But I dismissed the question nearly as quickly as it had come to me. He left no note. He would have left a note.

It would be a relief if I could let go of the past. Dwelling on it doesn't help and inevitably leaves me squirming and wriggling, as if I'm trying to free myself from something clutching me against my will. It's as if I'm being asphyxiated slowly by memories of hard truths and by silly speculation, which I should bury and forget once and for all.

I deliberately distract myself with a search for some cookies to offer Chuck. He'll be arriving soon, which is good. I need something or somebody to take my mind off my sombre thoughts.

* * *

As soon as Chuck comes into the kitchen, my spirits lift. He's wearing a royal-blue rain-jacket with orange trim covering every possible edge, a brimmed orange-and-blue-striped hat, smart blue-jeans which looked tailored and far too good to be gardening in, and a long scarf wrapped round his neck which has criss-crossing stripes of orange, blue, yellow and green. His dark blue gloves and yellow rubber boots complete the colourful picture. I just can't help but smile. But when he raises his head, having taken off his boots, his face doesn't fit the picture. He's pale and his large green eyes are somewhat sunken and distant.

"Although we can't really appreciate them today, with the dismal weather, the spring flowers look great," I say in a feeble attempt to cheer him up.

"That's good."

"By the way, I think it was wonderfully kind of you to donate the money to the Children's Centre."

"Oh, so you checked out my story."

I'm not sure how to reply. He stops peering into his tea and raises his head, with a cookie poised in his hand, almost as if he's forgotten he's holding it. There's something attractive about his face, but I can see the signs of strain in the furrows between his eyebrows.

"That's okay," he says. "You don't really know me, so I couldn't expect you to believe everything. But I told you the truth. I've told you more than I've told just about anyone. I don't particularly want my life history to be common knowledge. I'm pretty private."

"Of course not. I've only told Tom. We follow up any lead, and if we can check things out, we do." I'm unsettled. He's not making much sense to me and seems to be over-reacting. There's a minute of silence between us when all that can be heard are the relentless ticking of the clock and the incessant dripping of water in the drain-pipe outside the kitchen door.

"I know. I understand." He finally says. He sighs and leans back in the chair, unwinding his scarf. "I'm just wallowing in self-pity today. It's exactly three years ago today that I met Dania. You know, my fiancée. Was my fiancée. I don't know why I'm telling you this." His head lolls down again, and all I can see is his soft, brown, curly hair clearly encircled by a hat-line. "We should have been married and had a child by now," he mumbles.

I've heard that it's not unusual for a man to have a particularly hard time dealing with the loss of a woman who leaves them. It can lead to suicide. I wonder if it can be harder to lose a woman through break-up than through death. I'm not sure, but I'm beginning to better understand Frank's sense of profound loss when Louisa died. What must Chuck be feeling? Given that Dania left him one week before their wedding day. Not to mention the embarrassment of telling everyone and having no explanation to give. Traumatic is probably not too strong a word. Chuck lifts his head and makes an attempt at a smile.

"I'm okay. I'll pull myself together. Gardening in the drizzle will do it." He sits upright and manages a more believable smile. "I've been wondering if I should tell you or not, but someone's been watching this place."

"What can you tell me about him?"

"Not much. Just hangs around the end of the driveway, well covered up. If I wander down there, he's gone."

"No description at all, no vehicle?"

"I think it's a pickup," Chuck says. "The trees obscured my view. Not a professional stake-out person, that's for sure. I could do a better job myself."

"That sounds like it could be Brad Buckthorn, and a black pickup would be hard to see."

"Yes, I wondered that myself. Not sure it's black though. We'd better be careful if it's Brad. I don't think he has a moral bone in his body." Chuck gulps down the last of his tea, eats his cookie in two fast bites, puts on his hat and boots, leaving the scarf to be picked up once he finishes the gardening, and goes out, taking his embarrassment with him. I have an urge to hug him as he hesitates in the doorway, which takes me off-guard. What does that mean? I'm probably simply feeling empathy for him in his sadness.

I change my focus to my pending meeting with the lawyer, William Porter. I'll have to take a taxi, which will be expensive. I'm careful, and I like to think, responsible, with money, but I'm fortunate that I don't really have to worry about finances. Not now. Not since I met Frank. And he was true to his word that, in the event of his death, there would be adequate funds so that I could continue living the wonderful country-based lifestyle I love and had always dreamed of.

Chuck makes a fuss of Kelly as I leave in the yellow taxi. He ruffles her fur and then chases her round in a couple of circles. I'm glad she won't be alone. And it's nice to see Chuck in better spirits. Perhaps he's right, and being out in the drizzle will help.

13

Coffee with a Lawyer

The coffee shop is an unusual one. I've not been here before. It was converted from a pub, but I don't think much conversion went on. The sultry atmosphere, with its dark reds and browns, conjures up images of old men smoking pipes and downing pints. The old dark-oak bar is equipped with elaborate coffee-making machines and other paraphernalia which appear to be necessary these days in order to serve a cup of coffee. I'm a bit early, so I go straight up to the bar, but I hear my name and as I turn around, I'm face-to-face with William. He seems to have got greyer and balder since I last saw him, but perhaps it's the different lighting. It's rather a dim-lit place. He's about my height, which I'd not noticed before, but must weigh at least twice as much. His puffy face and puffy breath are far too close for my liking. I inch sideways along the bar to increase the distance between us. He extends his hand, and I manage to shake it with a smile.

"I thought I was early," I say.

"Good of you to come. I'll get the coffees." He looks shabbier than I remember, with little of the stereotypical look of a lawyer. He conveys an unease as he holds the coffees and ushers me into a booth near the back.

"You'll be wondering what this is all about. I'll start at the beginning. I won't make this long, but I want to give you some background, especially since, under the circumstances, you'll understand where I'm coming from. I hope so, anyway." He looks at me with his intense dark eyes. I can't think of what to say, because I don't know that he's talking about.

"My wife died five years ago. It was sudden, but that's not relevant to this meeting. What's relevant is that my life fell apart, including my career. I lost my drive and let my legal practice deteriorate. I lost a lot of clients."

"I'm sorry to hear that." With dread, I wonder if he's searching for a soul-mate to share his grief with, and I know I won't be able to handle it. I wish I hadn't come, and what's more, I notice the coffee tastes bitter and is too strong. I put the cup down and look at him.

"To get to the point, because I can see I'm making you uncomfortable, I've been trying to build the practice up again, but at my time of life and with the poorly appointed office I have, it's a tough haul. I don't have sufficient funds to make the significant investment it needs."

Oh, now he wants money. I can feel a tension head-ache coming on.

"Would you mind if I got a cup of tea?" I ask. "I shouldn't have said I'd have coffee. I really don't like it."

"I'll get it." He gets up and puts a hot, heavy hand on my shoulder. "I'm not asking you for anything. You've no need to be concerned. I just want to give you some information."

The tea is a welcome improvement, but I can only take small sips. It's boiling hot and they've put it in a double-walled paper cup. I wonder if it will ever be cool enough.

"Back to what I was saying. I'm trying to set the scene, so you'll perhaps understand." I don't respond, so he continues. "I had some difficulty with drugs for a while. But before I go on, I want to assure you I'm not on drugs now and am getting things back on track. Although I think I've substituted food for the drugs." He smiles and pats his paunch with both hands. I don't react. "Anyway, everything in my life was on a downward spiral when I was approached by the Group of Three, as I call them. You know who they are. Brad Buckthorn, Susan Kingsley-Black and Sharon McDonald. At the time I thought their business would help me get out of my slump, both professional and personal. And, I suppose it did help to stop the decline. So I agreed to write the letter to Frank, but I've reflected on it and I regret doing so." He put his hands on the shiny dark table, palms down, as if he's about to get up. "I regret it: first, because it was not dealing with a legal matter and was just meant to be intimidating and second, because of Frank's death and your suspicions that it might not have been an accident. I'm sincerely concerned that there might be a link. Yes, I know I told you in our meeting that, while I thought they could be capable of arranging for Frank to be killed, I believed that they just wanted to stop his introduction of the pollution control regulations, including pit rehabilitation provisions, by getting him out of the political picture somehow."

"Yes, you said something like that."

"There's something I didn't say. And that's why we're here. Brad asked me if I knew someone who could help him with an assignment that he'd been given by the Group of Three. When I refer to this group, I include the bosses, by the way. The group was being run by the bosses. He said this would be lucrative for me, and I couldn't see what harm there would be in referring someone to him."

"Okay." I'm not sure what to say. I just want him to get on with it.

"It turned out Brad wanted someone who wouldn't ask any questions, who could be trusted, who had the skills to do surveillance including some tailing. I wanted the money. In fact, I felt I desperately needed the money. The only person I could think of who would likely agree to such a project was Gerald Warren. I represented him once on a break-and-enter charge. Among the many challenges he has in his life, at that time he had a mother with mental health issues who he helped to care for. I knew he'd be interested in the money. He's not a bad sort, really."

"So, you linked Gerald Warren, who now calls himself John Nelson, with Brad."

"Yes. But my involvement ended once the introduction had been made."

"So, you don't know what instructions were given to Gerald, or John, rather?"

"No, I don't. But I'm concerned. The more I thought about our meeting, and your questions about your husband's death, the more I wondered. It still doesn't make sense to me that they would go so far as to have Frank killed. Nevertheless, I have to admit that I'm not entirely sure that they wouldn't. And this link to Gerald, albeit a petty criminal, increases my concern."

"Thank you for telling me."

"I still haven't told you the part that has been troubling me the most." He runs his hand over his bald head and then leans forward across the table, although not far because his paunch won't allow it. "Marshall, you know, Moncton-Brown, knows that Brad hired Gerald. And what's disturbing is that Marshall thinks Brad was involved in Frank's death."

"What do you mean? How do you know?"

"Marshall asked to meet with me. I thought it odd, because I'd been dealing with the side-kicks as I told you. And I'd closed the file. He asked me to confirm that I had set Brad up with Gerald, and then told me he wished I hadn't. It was as if he was trying to blame me for what he thought could have happened. He said he didn't want to ask Brad directly. He confided in me he was terrified of being implicated because he'd ordered Brad to get Frank out of the way. He wondered if Brad thought he'd meant he was to kill Frank, when what he really meant was for Brad to help get Frank out of the picture somehow. So, he thought that Brad might have told Gerald to get rid of Frank."

"Oh."

"He said he knew Gerald was at the scene of Frank's accident. Marshall was shaking from head to foot when he told me this. He said it would ruin him and his business. I told Marshall that Gerald was no more than a petty criminal. But it didn't seem to reassure him. He said that Brad is very ambitious and rather a brown-noser, and wants to get ahead. He makes a great Assistant because he's very keen and he'll do anything. Marshall looked like he was on the verge of tears at this point. I said I couldn't see Gerald killing anyone. But he was pretty disturbed."

"I can see why Marshall would be very concerned and I suppose I sort of get why he won't ask Brad directly. He's frightened of what he thinks he'll be told and that the conversation could implicate him further. Yes, he must believe that Brad is involved."

"And now that you're asking questions, I can imagine Marshall is apoplectic. I wouldn't be surprised if he thinks you suspect Brad of being the instigator of Frank's death. And I'm relaying this to you even though he told me in confidence, because he is not my client, he didn't hire me, and I think this has become serious enough to warrant me passing on the information to you."

"Thanks. And, yes, Brad must be involved somehow. He's been trying to scare me off the trail. Given what you've said, and assuming he is implicated in Frank's death, I suppose Brad's actions make some sense."

"If I were to advise you regarding this, I would tell you to exercise caution. In other words, be very careful. There's a lot at stake here, at least Marshall thinks so." He reaches into the pocket inside his well-worn jacket. "And the other reason I wanted to meet with you is I want to return the cheque you gave me." He put an envelope down on the table in front of me. "It was unethical for me to accept it. I'm truly doing my best to get back on track. But I'm not pleased with how I conducted myself during our previous meeting."

"No. I won't take it back. I agreed to the terms. And you've given me some helpful information." It doesn't feel right to take the money. "Please cash the cheque and I hope you see success in the rebuilding of your practice." Perhaps I feel sorry for him.

As I sit in the back of the taxi on the way home, I become more resolved than ever to find out what happened to Frank. I'm not sure that I can believe what William told me. But he appeared to be sincere, and by the time I get home I'm leaning towards believing him. After all, he didn't try to convince me to stop what I'm doing. In fact, he appeared to be encouraging me.

Kelly gets up and stretches as the taxi drives up to the house. She'd been keeping a watchful eye on Chuck, who's crouched over one of the flower beds, presumably weeding. Kelly wags her tail and Chuck smiles and waves as I walk round the side of the house towards the kitchen door.

The tranquility is shattered by the squealing of tires, and spraying of stones as a black sports car fishtails its way into the driveway. It crunches to a halt on the gravel just behind me. Susan Kingsley-Black flings open the door. She's wearing a body-snugging black dress, with a tailored red jacket open and flapping as she lunges towards me. It's as if she's a red-winged hawk, swooping down on me, hoping to scoop me up with her talons and drop me in one of her adoptive father's dumpsters.

Her face is flushed, and her hands are shaking. She pokes her long, red fingernails at my chest.

"You mind your own business." She pushes me backwards and I stumble, partly from shock, almost losing by balance. Out of the corner of my eye I catch sight of Chuck with his phone in his hand as he walks towards us and I wonder if he's calling the police. "You keep out of business that doesn't concern you. I'm warning you for the last time. Do you hear me? Leave us the hell alone." She pushes me again with her sharp fingernails. I'm too startled and flabbergasted to give any kind of retort. I follow her with my astonished gaze as she reverses at break-neck speed out of the driveway, spins the car out onto the road and heads towards Vannersville. Chuck is next to me, puffing, having run from the garden while holding onto Kelly. She was probably barking the entire time, but I didn't register.

"Are you okay?" asks Chuck as he lets go of Kelly. His green eyes are wide with concern. It's as if they're searching, delving into my depths to uncover my thoughts and feelings. This genuine interest in my well-being makes me feel vulnerable. So, my defences come into action and I clamp down on my emotions to stop them from rising to the surface.

"I'm fine. Just taken-aback." I turn away from Chuck and stroke Kelly. Did I snap at him? "I wish someone would be clear on what I'm not supposed to be doing. Is Susan afraid I'll be running against her in the by-election? Do they think I know something about Frank's death which implicates them, or that I'm about to find out? Or is it something to do with illegal dumping? Or about pollution control regulations? Or pit rehabilitation? Honestly, I'm fed up with their threats and attempts to intimidate. It's all ridiculous. Now I've had my rant, I'll see if I can find something for lunch. Tom will be back soon."

"Sometimes a rant is a good thing," Chuck says. "By the way, I'll be leaving once I've finished this flower bed." He hesitates and hovers like a hummingbird seeking nectar.

"Okay, and thanks for holding onto Kelly when Susan was here." I go inside the house without looking at him.

* * *

I try to remember what Tom likes to eat, but I'm not thinking clearly, and likely the contents of the fridge will severely limit the options. I open a couple of cupboards, but no inspiration hits.

"Well, Kelly, I don't seem to have anything good for lunch. I do have a chew for you, though." The dog wags her tail and licks her lips. I'm sure she recognizes the word 'chew'. She takes the treat gently and lies down on the kitchen mat to enjoy it. The phone rings, startling us both, although we hear it several times a day.

"Hello, Meg. This is Munro, Dr Milton." His voice sounds sombre. I can tell something is wrong. My guess is that the quadriplegic has died.

"I know that you're a friend of Tom Penning's. We're having trouble contacting his family," Munro said. I let out a gasp. "Before I say any more, I must tell you that the prognosis is good."

"What do you mean? He was perfectly all right this morning. He's been staying here with me. He left to go to the office first thing. He should have been back by now." My heart's pounding so hard that it's making my body rock, and my mouth is powdery dry.

"That explains it."

"Explains what? For God's sake, tell me. I'm coming right now. Is he alive?"

"Yes, I told you the prognosis is good. It's just that he had an accident on the same bend as Frank did." Neither of us says anything for about three seconds.

"I'm coming now." I have to see him. Munro isn't about to give me details on the phone. I slam down the receiver and run out of the house. I'm relieved to find Chuck still here, despite my cool behaviour towards him. I do sense a twinge of shame. But this is important and urgent. I ask him if he can drive me and Kelly to the hospital, adding the explanation: "Someone's tried to kill Tom!" To me, this cannot be a coincidence. It has to be attempted murder.

14

Tom

"He's sleeping at the moment, Meg. Let's go into my office to talk, then we'll go and check on him. We've sedated him. He's in shock," Munro says. We make our way through a labyrinth of colourless, sterile-looking corridors. I'm shaken and perhaps could do with some sedation myself. My legs are like rubber and my palms sweaty, but I'm also shivering. I feel responsible. I shouldn't have let Tom get involved.

My wobbly legs make it hard to keep up with the slim and fit Munro.

"Were the Police called?" I ask.

"I believe so, but I haven't heard anything. Remember, that bend has the reputation of being an accident spot. As you well know, there have been several accidents and at least four people killed during the past five years. So, the police won't be suspecting foul-play unless there's plain evidence to the contrary." He's correctly guessed that I think Tom's crash was no accident.

Munro opens the door to his cramped office, and ushers me in. I'm relieved to sit down, but I'd forgotten how gloomy and cluttered his office is, and I find the air oppressive – it seems harder to breathe.

"Meg, Meg, are you okay?" asks a muffled voice. I must have fainted. I can hear voices as I'm lifted and put on a stretcher in the busy corridor. Someone has put something cold on my forehead and I feel a little better, so struggle to get up. I have no time or patience for this.

"Nurse, please fetch a wheelchair," Munro says. "Meg, we'll visit Tom. That'll probably make you feel better." I'm given some iced water, and a fresh, cold cloth is put on my forehead. My blood-pressure is taken. "Have you had any lunch today?" No, I haven't. I'm almost instantly supplied with a couple of oatmeal cookies and some orange juice. Munro urges me to eat and drink, so I do.

I'm still light-headed as Munro wheels me along the corridor to the elevators, but I'm much improved. I'm embarrassed that I've become a patient needing attention, taking up precious time and resources. I'm determined to get out of the wheelchair at the earliest possible opportunity. I want my mobility and independence back, and I don't appreciate staring at everyone's stomachs, rather than at their faces. It's virtually impossible to make eye-contact. It makes me contemplate how Kelly feels, being knee-high to us humans, so I make a mental note to pay more attention to Kelly and make eye-contact with her more often.

Munro's calm proficiency helps me to pull myself together, although it's impossible to talk to him as he pushes the wheelchair behind me.

By the time we reach Tom's room, I've had enough.

"I'd like out of this thing," I say. Munro bends over me to hear what I'm saying. "Thanks for helping me, but I really want to get out of this thing. I feel a lot better." I undo the belt and get up.

“Are you sure you’re all right?” Without waiting for a reply, Munro pushes the wheelchair towards the nursing station. I’m determined to be all right, and shove my body against the heavy door to Tom’s room. They’ve had the sense to switch off the glaring strip lighting. I make my way to a chair by Tom’s bedside. He looks pale, but peaceful. He has an intravenous drip, probably to give him medication, but no other tubes or intrusive attachments.

“As I said, the prognosis is good,” Munro says. “Seat belts and air bags do a great job in saving lives.” The doctor sits on the very edge of the bed, being careful not to disturb the patient. “He gave your name as a contact, so I can give you the details. He has three broken ribs on the right side, where we think he hit the arm-rest, and some bruises. The side air bags weren’t as effective as they might have been, but I believe they did deploy. He’s badly shaken up, but things could have been much worse. We’ve strapped him up, but there’s not much you can do for ribs. They take time to heal. There’s no internal organ damage, according to the initial examination, but we’d like him in here for 48 hours to do more tests, including scans, and to observe him. He’ll be all right, Meg.”

“Frank didn’t have air bags or seatbelts.”

“Frank was driving a much older vehicle. Yes, air bags and seatbelts make an enormous difference. Tom might well have been killed in that sports car if he hadn’t got a new model with modern and reliable safety features.”

“You know what I think, don’t you?” I’m glad that I’m able to hold Tom’s hand, although he probably isn’t registering my presence. He feels cool and dry.

“And you might be right. But what kind of nutcase is going to use the same method twice?” asks the doctor.

“That doesn’t puzzle me as much as why just Tom? Why not both of us? Now, Tom doesn’t know, but Brad Buckthorn has been watching my place. Brad would have known if we'd left together or not. So, it's puzzling."

"It's difficult to do a good job of watching. Just lose your attention for a second, and you could miss something important. He's not a professional criminal, so he's probably not much good at surveillance. Being evil doesn't necessarily mean competence as a criminal." Munro gives me a half-smile.

"You're right. My gardener is the one who saw him at the end of the driveway, and Chuck said he could have done a better job of surveillance himself."

"Ah, I thought so. But what will you do now, Meg? The more I think about what's happened, the more concerned I am about your welfare. What about going to the Police?"

"Unless they found something new at the scene of the accident, or Tom can tell us something to follow up on, I bet they'll say that it goes to prove what a terrible bend it is, as you said yourself. It'll serve to confirm in their minds that Frank's death was an accident. And I've no evidence, so far, that would convince anyone that Frank was murdered. I've got nothing substantial to give them or tell them, yet."

"What are you going to do next?"

"I want to visit Gerald, or John as he calls himself now, the other accident victim."

"Mm. I hope it goes well." Munro gets off the bed, straightening his long body. It seems like he's towering over me. "I'll leave you with Tom. You like tea, don't you?"

"Oh, that would be wonderful." I've devoured the cookies and orange juice, and tea sounds great.

I look back at Tom, whose breaths are shallow and quiet. I imagine the strapping impairs the use of his lungs. I hope the pain killers are working. What a mess! A wave of guilt sweeps through me and nearly breaks into a ripple of tears. It should be me lying in that bed, not Tom. If I hadn't been so determined to find out what happened to Frank, he wouldn't be hurt.

My eyes sting, but I won't let myself cry. I remember I couldn't cry when Frank died, and I thought something was wrong with me. But the shock and the horror of such a sudden and tragic death were too great, and tears weren't enough. At the time, sensing my hurt, Murray somehow convinced me to take a courageous step and go to the grief and loss support group. If nothing else, it made me feel less alone and somewhat understood. I found out that there was nothing wrong with me. It was grief.

It's a relief to be shaken out of these thoughts by a nurse bustling in with a mug of tea. It has "Nursing Week" emblazoned on the side, and the tea is just as I like it, with only a little milk. I'm impressed that Munro remembered.

"I'm all right," Tom murmurs. I nearly drop the mug.

"Oh, thank goodness. It's nice to hear your voice. I'm so sorry this happened to you. I'm the one who got you into this mess."

"I'm all right," he says again, partly turning his head towards me, but his eyes look heavy and only half-open. He doses off again. I kick myself for not saying something positive and reassuring.

* * *

It's getting darker in the room and the fluorescent lighting beaming in from the corridor is growing brighter in contrast. I must have been sitting by his bedside for several hours. A plastic tray, smelling of well-processed food, sits on the bedside table. I didn't want to wake him when it arrived, and I didn't let the nurse take it away, in case he wants it later. Thinking about Tom's tray draws my attention to the hunger pangs growing in my stomach, as evidenced by muffled growls and rumblings. I don't want a repeat of my fainting episode, so I hurry down to the cafeteria which is buried in the bowels of the building, and grab a sandwich wrapped in layers of plastic wrap.

"I wondered where you'd got to," Tom says, as I trot in from the corridor.

"You might know you'd choose to wake up during the only time I left the room!" I try to sound light and breezy.

Tom attempts to sit more upright in the bed, but winces with the effort.

"Would you like me to raise the head of the bed?" I'm queasy at the thought of how much pain Tom's probably in.

"Yeah, that would be good." I find the controls and move Tom into a semi-sitting position.

"I can't remember much," Tom says.

"Never mind about that now. We'll talk about it tomorrow."

"That's good, you're awake," Munro says, as he enters the room and stands at the end of the bed. I listen to the exchange between the doctor and his patient. Munro confirms Tom should stay a couple of nights, to be sure that there's no concussion and to get some more tests and scans done. Meanwhile, he'll continue to receive painkillers and a sedative. Tom agrees.

"He'll be sleeping pretty soundly, Meg, so you might want to take the opportunity to get some rest at home," Munro suggests.

"I'll have to go home soon to attend to the animals. But I'm concerned that Tom will be safe here."

"Well, you're in luck. At eleven o'clock, Nurse Sally Marsden comes on duty. I'll leave a message that no-one is to see Tom, and I assure you, no-one will get to see Tom. She's like a Rottweiler as far as guarding patients against unwanted visitors. Visitors on the night shift would immediately raise suspicion, anyway. The visitors' door is locked at eleven, and they have to come through the emergency department. Security is much tighter than it used to be."

"Well, I'll stay till eleven then," I say. Munro tells us he has to leave.

"What about the animals?" Tom asks.

"I'll phone Chuck and ask if he'll feed them, and let Kelly out. He'll have to come here for the key and instructions on the burglar alarm, though."

"I take it you trust him then."

"Yes, I do. I think he's a decent kind of guy. I'll tell you more tomorrow."

"Meg, you won't find out who killed Frank. It's got out of control and it's getting too dangerous." He lifts his head off the pillow with obvious effort and turns to face me.

"We'll talk later, Tom. You need to rest." He puts his head down and shuts his eyes. I have to admit I'm worried about the animals, especially Kelly, who will have been on her own since Chuck left. Tom looks like he's sleeping again, and it's close to eleven, so I consider calling a taxi and reach for my phone.

"There you are!" Chuck walks in with a reassuring smile. "How's the patient?"

"He says he's all right. But he isn't. But I suppose it could have been a lot worse." I tell him what I know.

"I thought you might be ready to get home for some rest. And don't worry about the animals. Kelly's been fed, and the horses are tucked up in their stalls. And I brought Kelly along. She's in the Jeep."

"Wow. Thanks a million, Chuck."

"Hi, Chuck," Tom says, as he turns his head slowly to face us.

"How are you feeling? Must have been quite the shock," Chuck says as he moves closer to Tom's side.

"Meg won't be able to find out who killed Frank. It's out of control and it's too dangerous." Tom has a deep furrow in his forehead, and has lost the little colour he regained earlier.

"Tom, I said we'd talk later. You need to get rest. We're going now," I say as I usher Chuck out. We both wave as we enter the corridor, but Tom's eyes are already closed again.

It's such a relief that Chuck had the gumption to do all the chores at home, and didn't leave Kelly alone. I thank him again as he drives us back. Kelly licks my hand as I dangle it behind me, with my arm held rather awkwardly between the two front seats.

"And just in case you're wondering, I didn't do this stuff as an employee, but because I want to help out. So, you don't owe me anything."

"I don't know what to say. I do owe you. I owe you a lot of thanks if nothing else." I make a concerted effort to allow his warmth and kindness to seep into my being, but I mustn't allow myself to get close to him. My natural instincts are to shut down and back away, because otherwise I'll get hurt.

"You've definitely said 'thanks' enough times." He turns and smiles at me.

"Okay." I smile back. "What did you think of Tom saying I'd never find out who killed Frank?"

"I expect they have him on sedatives and painkillers, so he probably isn't making much sense. He'll likely be more coherent tomorrow."

"Yes, I'll talk to him tomorrow about it and see what he says."

It's comforting to have Chuck with us as Kelly and I enter the dark house. It's close to eleven thirty. It seems eerie and quiet. I seldom go out at night, so this is an unusual occurrence.

On the way home, Chuck told me that, a couple of years ago, Frank had shown him where the spare key for the kitchen door is hidden in the barn, so he could lock up before leaving to pick me up. But he didn't know how to activate the alarm. Once we're inside the house, he returns the key to me and goes over everything he's done, just in case he missed something. He's done a few extra things like filling up the trough and mucking out the run-in shed. I have no need to check on the horses, so as soon as Chuck leaves, Kelly and I get ready for bed.

* * *

I am totally fed up with myself the next morning. I was awake most of the night, tossing and turning. Tom's pale face floated in my mind like some kind of ghost and it wouldn't go away. I finally gave up and got up early. In any case, I want to get to the hospital before Nurse Sally Marsden, aka Rottweiler, leaves.

Chuck said he would come before eight, and look after everything for as long as I want, including cleaning the stalls. I said I would feed the horses before I leave. I reflect that I'm lucky that Tom and Chuck are both in my life. But that thought brings me back to my feelings of guilt about Tom and his pale face. I hope to find him much improved when I get back to the hospital.

I'm a bit more relaxed as I enter the horses' sanctuary. I pour large scoops of feed into their bins and listen to them munch. It's as if they haven't got a care in the world. Nothing else matters but being fed, watered, well-bedded and turned out to enjoy the grass. I can't help but be affected by their nonchalance. It's comforting.

As I walk back towards the house, it's light enough to see that the fencing could do with painting again. When Frank bought the property, which he later insisted be transferred to my name (he said it worked better financially), I remember telling him I'd like to paint the fences. He thought I was joking. He literally said that one hires people to do that. He didn't want me to do it. He was adamant. But I can be stubborn. So, I painted only when he was out, which was often. He knew, and he didn't like it, but he let me be. I enjoyed hearing the birds singing, feeling the soft breezes, seeing the skies shifting, and finding the interesting insects that hide in the cracks in the wood. The fencing shouldn't need painting again so soon, but the horses love to chew the posts, and even attempt to chew on the oak rails in some places, opening pale wounds which make the fencing look ill-kept and neglected. As soon as I've found out what I need to know about Frank, I'll tackle the fencing again.

The kitchen seems empty, even though Kelly's at my side. There's no tea waiting and no smiling Tom. A twinge of loneliness surprises me. I think of myself as independent, and like it that way. That reminds me that Frank hadn't enjoyed being on his own. At least, that's what I assumed.

I'd sat across from him at his large, somewhat intimidating, shiny dining-room table. I couldn't let my skin touch its flawlessness. He had laid it out clearly enough. In exchange for the lifestyle I would like, the riding horses, the country property and an income, I was to assume the role of a Government Minister's wife. In his mind this meant attending Government events and social functions, as well as entertaining in the home and maintaining an appropriate lifestyle. He explained that this included using landscaping and snow-removal services, as well as a cleaner and barn workers. He had included a cook, but then admitted that he'd be unlikely to eat at home that much, so we'd use catering services whenever we entertained. I told him I could agree to all of it, except the barn workers. I wanted to work with the horses myself. He couldn't understand me, even though he had a couple of racehorses at the track. He'd never looked after them himself, although he assured me he took an avid interest in their well-being, and I believed him. Correctly, as it turned out. He eventually relented and agreed that I could do the barn work as and when I wished. I think he thought this had been a magnanimous gesture on his part, and consequently the rest of the agreement would be smooth sailing.

But then I raised the matter of my job. I wanted to continue as the Executive Director of the Humane Society. He leant across the table, his dark brown eyes questioning as he hunched his broad, muscular shoulders and put his hands flat on the shine I couldn't bring myself to smear.

I almost burst out laughing. I thought it must all be a dream. How could I be negotiating with a man about anything, let alone marriage? It was bizarre.

My scars were deep but could rise to the surface. I'd believed I would never find anyone that could care about me enough to want to live with me, and that I'd never find anyone whom I could trust. Frank challenged these beliefs, but didn't quite demolish them. I knew he wasn't in love with me as he sat there at the table, but I knew he liked me. I knew for certain he liked my looks. I knew that I almost trusted him. My intuition told me he was a good man, and that he had integrity and that most of the values he held were ones I agreed with. But I wouldn't give up my job. Not even for Frank or his promises. I owed too much to the animals in my life, and I needed to do something worthwhile, meaningful, giving. I was prepared to walk away from our discussion at this juncture. But Frank must have sensed this. He backed down, and I knew it wasn't easy for him.

Murray had said, during one of the heated exchanges he had now and then with his brother, that Frank was a 'control freak'. Perhaps he was right. He'd also told Frank on another occasion that he wasn't his brother's possession to do what he liked with. Had I been one of Frank's possessions? My heart misses a beat and then lurches to make up for it. I'm relieved to hear the phone ringing. I need something to jolt me out of my thoughts.

"Hi, it's Shane. Linda's called in sick again, and I need some help. I thought you'd like to come. You've helped out before when I've been stuck."

I cleaned a couple of stalls once, when he'd said he had no-one and was desperate. Fortunately, Frank had been away. He would have been appalled if he'd known that I'd worked in the backstretch when he was paying Shane to look after and train the horses. And particularly since it was under Shane's supervision. Supervision wasn't the right word. It was more like having a permanent shadow following my every move and invading my space. It had been obvious he hadn't needed me. He'd found a groom and a hot-walker by the time I got there, as well as his usual exercise rider. I'd been summoned under false pretences and vowed I'd never do it again, however desperate his pleas for help were.

"No, I'm sorry, but I'm extremely busy today."

"Are you sure you can't help out. I'd really like you to come."

"No, I can't. I'm in a rush. How's Speed? Did he come out of the race okay?"

"Yep, but Rose is still sore. I'd like you to see her. I'm thinking of taking her back to my farm."

"What for?"

"You're just wasting your money keeping her at the track. And I'd like to keep an eye on her at home. Maybe you could come see her more often." That doesn't make sense to me. The small farm he rents is on the other side of Vannersville.

"I'd like Rose to stay there for now. But I am in a rush. I have to leave now. I'll talk to you later. Sorry about Linda. Bye." I hang up. I haven't got the patience to deal with Shane's quirky requests. I have to see Tom.

15

Kidnapped

I smile as Kelly and I finally make it to the truck. Another thing I have to thank Chuck for. He has somehow got my vehicle home. I scan the end of the driveway before I set off, and glance down the road as I turn to make my way into town. No-one appears to be on stake-out duty. I keep up a good pace until I reach the infamous bend, which holds an aura of mystique. I slow down to a crawl, almost expecting the answer to reveal itself. I can see the tire-marks from Tom's car, etched out in the soft shoulder, showing where he left the road and started his dive down the slope. I pull into the small parking area that marks the beginning of one of the walking trails and which is dangerously positioned just after the bend. Despite the large, circular roadside mirror, there have been several collisions as trail-weary drivers edged out onto the road. But those accidents can be explained.

I stand on the soft shoulder at the top of the steep slope. I can see smashed shrubs and a couple of broken low branches, and it looks like there's red paint on a tree further down. Along the road to the right I notice the tattered ends of the plastic police ribbon which had been tied to a couple of trees to cordon off the spot where Frank left the road. It is preposterous that there wasn't a barrier, and even more absurd that there isn't one now. As I look the long way down to the fast-moving river at the bottom of the slope, my stomach knots and my neck tenses. I grab hold of a branch. The water looks as if it's boiling. It is always dangerous in the spring as volumes of melted snow rush between its banks and froth over the boulders.

It's incredible that Frank's car made it to the river, since there are quite a few trees on the slope. It was monstrous bad luck that his car hit the rocks at the bottom and that he was thrown into the water. His beloved old Cadillac didn't have seatbelts. Apparently, they were an optional extra when the big, beautiful, luxurious car was made. And of course, there were no airbags. I was only a passenger on a couple of occasions, but I remember the car gave one a false sense of security, created by the combination of its size, its weight, its power and especially its cushioned comfort which cocooned its occupants.

As I stand here, I find it hard to imagine the car plummeting down the slope, hitting the rocks and Frank being tossed into the rapid-moving churning depths of the river. Tom's accident is easier to visualize but, even so, there must have been something to cause him to leave the road. And what on earth, or who on earth, made Frank leave the road at what must have been a great speed? I still can't come up with a theory that makes any sense. Other accidents, when cars have left the road on this bend, have involved ice or slush, as far as I can remember. The road was dry for both Frank and Tom. I shake my head and make my way back to the truck.

Kelly has her head out of the window and barks as I approach, which strikes me as unusual. She rarely barks when I return to the truck. She might yip once or twice and perhaps whine a little in her excitement, but barking is not in the normal repertoire. It's as if she's been anxious about me wandering along the soft shoulder. She licks my hand with enthusiasm as I get the truck back on the road, exercising a great deal of caution. I'm keen to see Tom and visiting hours will soon start.

"I remember the airbag blowing up in my face. It all happened so quickly. I didn't have time to think," Tom says. He takes another mouthful of soggy toast. I'm relieved to find him looking a lot better. It's amazing what a good night's sleep can do, albeit aided by medication. I can't help wondering if I look more harrowed than he does.

"It all happened so quickly. I'm still not sure why I left the road," Tom says. "I never race round that bend."

"You don't remember anything? What about noise? If you didn't see anything, maybe you can recall a sound, a smell or something?"

"I remember the smell of diesel fumes." He stops chewing and looks at me, frowning.

"Another vehicle, a truck. Has to be Brad."

"I remember an engine noise. I don't remember seeing a black pickup though."

"More might come back later. But everything seems to point to Brad. This makes me think that it's even more likely that Brad was involved in Frank's death. But the only person who might actually have seen anything when Frank went off the road, is that other guy who was hurt on the same bend at the same time. I must make the trip to see Gerald, John I mean."

"I don't think he's going to be of any help, but I want to go with you. Give me a couple of days to get back on my feet."

"Well, I want to make sure. I want to hear what he has to say in person. I'm going to call the nursing home. I might be able to talk to him on the phone first, to pave the way. Then we can go to see him later, to get the details. You can't remember anything else?"

"No. I can remember the car tipping forwards as it started going down the slope and I couldn't stop. It was skidding as I was trying to brake and turn. And then it spun round suddenly and my door hit a tree. I can't even recall exactly when the airbags inflated. Thank goodness they did. I was lucky the car didn't flip. By the way, I'm getting out of here tomorrow morning, first thing. So, I'll try to be of some help."

"I'd understand if you'd like to pull out of this."

"No, I don't want to. I want to know who did this to me and why. It's given me quite the jolt."

"Do you think you're safe here?"

"I'm not concerned. The nurses all seem to know not to let anyone in here, other than you and my family."

"Okay. See you at the farm tomorrow then, as long as you're well enough. And don't take risks. Brad knows you're helping me, and if he'd hoped to get rid of you, or both of us more likely, he'll try again."

"I'll be fine, but it'll have to be another rental car. I don't suppose I'll be lucky enough to get another red sports car, especially since I've now wrecked two." He makes a feeble attempt at a chuckle.

"I'd have thought you'd have figured out that red sports cars are jinxed, by now."

"Yes, maybe a change would be a good idea. Maybe something in camouflage colours might help."

"Do you want me to switch off these fluorescent lights? They seem to give off so much glare."

"Oh. Oh, shit! I remember something."

"What?" I ask as I sit back down in the chair.

"There was a brilliant, blinding light. I'd been following a truck, I remember that, and then suddenly I couldn't see anything. I suppose the light must have hit me just as I was going into the bend."

"What could it have been?"

"I've no idea, but I'm certain that's what happened."

* * *

As I drive home, I wonder if the same ploy was used with Frank, but with deadly consequences. Surely Gerald would have noticed such a blinding light and surely its brilliance would be etched in his memory. Another question to ask Gerald, or rather, John. But why didn't he mention it to the police? Perhaps he did, and they didn't believe him.

Being so deep in thought, I forgot to check my rear-view mirror regularly. I become conscious of a noisy engine which sounds as if it has climbed up into the bed of my pickup. I've just reached a straight piece of road, and the truck passes by as the driver beckons me to pull over onto the shoulder. I can see Shane clearly through the untinted glass and my heart sinks. I don't want to deal with him right now, and why the hell has he signalled me to pull over? I don't think there's anything wrong with my truck, after all I've just got it back from being repaired.

"I really need to see you," Shane says as he marches towards me. His red cheeks and dominant nose catch the bright sunshine, making him look like a worn-out, sad clown. And I really detest that grubby baseball cap.

"What's so urgent that you had to pull me off the road?" I know I sound irritated, and I'm fine with that.

"I want you to know that I didn't have anything to do with Frank's accident." He takes off his hat and runs his large, hairy hands through his confused, red hair. I don't say anything. He puts his hat back on and stands about two feet in front of me. I can see the hairs growing out of his nostrils, and the pitted skin of his face including his grease-clogged pores. He is far too close, but I feel the heat of my truck's engine behind me. I'm trapped.

"You and Frank had an arrangement. You didn't love each other like you're supposed to."

"That's none of your business." I lean backwards in an attempt to escape from his steamy breath and the whiffs of his body odour. He's not at his best. I'm not sure if I can smell alcohol. Perhaps.

"Why are you hanging round with that creep, Tom?"

"That's also none of your goddam business. Leave me the hell alone!"

"You don't mean that. You know I love you and I'm sure you love me." Before I can reply, he grabs me by the shoulders and kisses me. It's hot, greasy, bristly and yes, I can taste alcohol. The inevitable flash-backs dart into my consciousness, making my stomach wretch, my knees wobble and my back sweat. He's coming back into my room again. Twice in one night. That didn't often happen, but I remember this instance. He was drunk and reeling, but still forceful and overpowering. My body trembled in anticipation of the pain I knew this brute would inflict, and shame consumed me. I blamed myself for not being able to stop this from happening to me. I had to make it stop. I had to do something. And finally, I found the courage to leave. Besides, Bertie didn't need my protection anymore, and I didn't have his love anymore. He was gone. That was the night I left everything I knew behind, never to turn back.

The fear and loathing which Shane's sickening kiss has aroused inside me swells and erupts into a surprising surge of strength. I kick Shane's shin so hard I think I've broken my toes, and punch his stomach so forcefully my hand won't unclench for a couple of seconds. And I think I might have screamed. Perhaps that's why Kelly jumps out of my truck, through the window. I've never seen her hackles up before. She bares her teeth and growls. I didn't know that she could be so scary. Shane backs up about six feet, and Kelly positions herself in front of me.

"Get away from me! If you come anywhere near me again, I'll have you charged with assault." I yell as loud as I can. I hope my voice didn't quiver.

"You'll come round. You'll see." He grins, shrugs his shoulders, and ambles back to his grimy truck with long, lolloping strides. I feel sick to my stomach. His smell, his touch, his look, his everything make me feel like vomiting and washing myself inside and out. And how dare he call Tom a creep? He's the creep, not Tom. And possibly a dangerous creep. I resolve to find another trainer as soon as possible. And, even more important, he's back on the suspect list.

After a welcome, warm, cleansing shower and a thorough mouth rinse, I join Kelly on the bed. The over-used metaphor, 'I feel as if I've been run over by a Mack truck' comes to mind as I stretch out beside the warm dog. I feel flattened and deflated, but also puffed up with thick disgust and loathing. And, to make matters worse, I have to work hard to stop the dreaded flash-backs from monopolizing my mind. I glance around the bedroom in a half-hearted attempt to distract myself. My body is unwilling to move, and Kelly is snuggled and motionless beside me. The light is flashing on my phone. A message. Despite my physical lack of energy, it's almost a relief to have something to attend to.

I forgot I'd called my local councillor's office asking for a meeting to get information on what the city was doing about illegal dumping and also by-laws for fill. The message asks if I can meet the councillor at his club this afternoon. It's the only time he has available unless I'm willing to wait until he comes back from his ensuing trip to China.

* * *

As I enter the imposing building, which I presume was previously a wealthy person's large, lavish home, I wonder why he asked me to meet him in his club rather than in his constituency office. There had been no explanation. But I soon figure it out.

Councillor Sherman Grapple eases his rotund body down into an armchair with his round, colourless face opposite me. There's a circular coffee table between us. I have a tea. He grabs a double scotch, neat, delivered to him on a silver tray. Before I can ask him anything, the councillor starts talking, saying how much he loves his club, how much he loves the contacts he makes, and then he bounces names around. His good friend, Timothy Westmount, often pops in when he isn't entertaining in that large house of his. And Sandy Bingham often shows his face. He likes to connect with people. Good for relationships and good for getting things done in the community. And of course, Marshall Moncton-Brown frequents this place, and he loves his Scotch.

I get the message. It's as if he's been tipped off. He's in their camp and that's that. I gain even more respect for Frank and his efforts to do something about environmental issues. There are so many vested interests and so much resistance to change. We need people like Frank who aren't intimidated by the likes of Councillor Grapple, and who have some influence, so that we can make some meaningful progress. I don't believe that I have enough fire in my belly, or enough skills, and certainly not the influence, to take it on. My passion is animals.

As I get back into the truck, I realize Kelly hasn't licked my face. It takes two more seconds for panic to set it. She's gone. Shaking from head to toe, I fumble for my phone, telling myself to get a grip. Alarm, guilt and anger have befuddled my brain. I need to think straight. My phone beeps just as I get hold of it. It's a text.

"If you want your dog back, you'd better back off."

I know it's from Susan.

It's almost as if my phone automatically calls Chuck. In blurted, stilted speech I tell him my worst nightmare, at the same time wondering why I called him. I should be able to handle this on my own.

"Are you up to driving back to the farm? I think I can help," Chuck says.

"Yes." I can't think of how Chuck can help, and part of me thinks I should stay and look for clues. But I don't have any idea where to start, and even my foggy brain figures out that there's no point. There won't be anything to find. I pull myself together, despite my distracted mind and rising anxiety, and start the engine. I don't trust my judgement or my reactions, so I drive cautiously back to the farm, even though I would like to have flown like the wind. Kelly's face is in my mind's eye the whole way, blurring the vision of the road, slowing my recognition of street signs, and eating at my heart.

Despite my resolve, I start to sob as I approach the house. There is an unbearable gap, an emptiness. Chuck is waiting. I can tell he's on edge. He opens the truck door and helps me out. I'm glad of his arm. I'm still crying, but I've been able to quash the loud sobbing.

"Meg, Meg, we have an ace up our sleeve." Chuck waves his phone with one hand as he supports me under my forearm with the other. As we walk into the house, he won't let go. His hand feels warm, even through my jacket, and comforting. I wish I had the strength to push him away, to refuse his help. But I'm wobbly on my feet and quivering, and his kindness is helping to steady me.

"What do you mean?" I have a hard time catching my breath. It's almost as if someone has knocked the wind out of me.

"Just take a couple of deep breaths and sit down, and watch this. I'll get a mug of hot tea with sugar." He hands me his phone and my eyes widen as I watch Susan poking and prodding me and hear her threats.

Chuck shouts from the kitchen, "You might not have realized I took that video."

"I saw you with the phone in your hand but I thought you might have called the police." I brighten. There's hope that I'll see Kelly again. I put his phone down. "Oh, Chuck, you're right. We do have something, thanks to you." I take deep breaths and gather my composure, feeling less shattered and fragmented, and more able to think. "How do we use it?"

"You know Susan is running for the Vannersville seat in that by-election, don't you? The one Frank held. That video could wreck her chances."

"There's more though." I've almost come to my senses, thank goodness. "I did some research, including calling George, you know, Frank's Assistant."

"Yes, I know about George."

"Well, Susan is Sandy Bingham's niece, but probably more significant, she's his adopted daughter. Tragically, both her parents drowned in a terrible cruise ship disaster in the Caribbean over thirty years ago. She was only a toddler and had been staying with Sandy's family while her parents were on vacation. By all accounts they're very close. She used to work for him at SWR, started her career there, but then she got a chance at a bigger job at Westmount Steel."

"These businesses are closely related in more ways than one." Chuck hands me a welcome, steaming mug of sweet tea. I try not to look into his kind, perceptive green eyes. There's something drawing me towards him, but I must be sure to resist if I don't want to get hurt. And I must give my full attention to getting Kelly back.

"The three, MMB Aggregates, Westmount Steel and Sandy's Waste Retirement are definitely collaborating on issues and I believe on specific projects as well."

"Like illegal dumping and fill operations." Chuck sits on the sofa next to the recliner I'm sprawled on. Thank goodness I'd piled up all of Tom's things in a corner. At least the family room is usable again.

"Yes, and fighting environmental regulations. So, I think it's not just the by-election itself Susan is concerned about, but the businesses, their projects and their influence. As an MPP she'd have to quit her official job, but I'm convinced the reason she wants to be in parliament is to promote these businesses and their interests."

"In other words, she'd continue to work for them behind the scenes. And she thinks you're contemplating running against her in the by-election, or at least seeking nomination, by one of the other parties, because you've been asking questions and poking around, and because you're Frank's wife."

"So, what about Kelly? How do we use all this knowledge to get her back?"

"We'll think of some way to play our cards. We need to make Susan aware we have the video and we're willing to delete it, erase its existence, when Kelly is returned unharmed."

"I have an idea." I pull the lever on the recliner and sit upright, putting the empty mug on the coffee table. "William Porter, the lawyer, owes me one. At least he thinks he does. He could help make the deal happen."

* * *

William, as I thought, is eager to help. It turns out that he loves dogs. He told me he has a mutt who is the greatest company and loves him whatever state he's in. He tells me to leave it to him. I believe he'll do his best. I hope it works. I can't get used to the emptiness.

When I put my phone down on the coffee table, I notice there's an email from Tom. I wonder if he's recalled more about the accident. But right now I'd rather go with Chuck to check the horses.

I lean on one of the oak rails surrounding the paddock, watching as Bullet and Eagle wander over to see us. The whiskers on their velvet muzzles stand out as if they've been electrostatically charged. When they realize we haven't got any carrots they snort, as if in disgust, and then kick up their heels and canter to the fence opposite, throwing the odd buck in just for fun. Kelly would have given a couple of yips at their antics as some of the excitement rubbed off on her. I miss her so much it hurts.

"It's nice to see that they're in good spirits," Chuck says.

"It's so relaxing to watch the horses, whatever they're doing."

"Yep. I don't quite understand how horses get under your skin, but they do. I just love everything about them. I got hooked when I was at the track." He puts his arms on the rail, clasping his hands and sighs. "Lovely spring evening. Are you going to the hospital?"

"I don't feel like going. In any case, I know that Tom's sister and parents are visiting from Toronto. But he's sent an email I must read."

"Do you want to put the horses in now?" Chuck asks.

"Yes, I think it's about time." I turn to walk towards the barn.

"Let's do it together," he says. I don't look at him. I know he'll be smiling that warm smile of his, and his green eyes will be sparkling with friendship and reassurance. What's the matter with me? What am I afraid of?

My mind shifts to Frank, and the first and only time I suggested he bring in one of the horses, since they prefer being led in as a pair and, of more importance to me, I thought it would be something nice that we could do together. But he made it clear he didn't want to. Part of his rationale was that he would so rarely be around at the right time that there was no point in his getting involved.

I can't help looking at Chuck as he clips the lead-rein onto Bullet's halter. His voice is soothing, and he's gentle with the edgy thoroughbred, and has him walking sensibly at his side, ahead of me and Eagle.

But there's something awfully wrong with this picture. Kelly isn't part of it. My heart sinks.

16

Letter

I still haven't read Tom's email. The priority is to get Kelly back safe and sound. Until I do, nothing much else is likely to get done, other than looking after the horses, of course. I just can't focus and feel nauseated. I can't eat.

I predicted a sleepless night, which is proving to be a self-fulfilling prophecy. I'm not even trying to drift off. During the rare occasions when I unfetter my brain from fretting, I try to put some pieces of Frank's puzzle together. But my admittedly addled and semi-functioning brain can't link the events to compose a picture. Through all hours of the night, I doodle on pieces of paper, click through websites, re-read news clippings, shuffle through Frank's documents, and come up with a broken trail of seemingly unconnected events. The people have some links, but not enough to form a solid chain, and the more I ponder, the more puzzling it becomes. It frustrates me that after all the analysis through the night hours, albeit spasmodic, I still can't make any coherent sense of it all.

The reasons behind Brad's, Susan's and Shane's behaviours in particular are a foggy mess. Sometimes I think I see a glimmer of light, but it doesn't radiate brightly enough to make everything come clear. In my tired, befuddled state, I decide to give up and just accept that their dubious behaviours aren't connected. Frank's death, the three businesses and their apparent opposition to environmental regulations, the illegal dumping, Susan's plan to run for parliament, Shane's opposition to the drug regulations and his assault on me, just don't fit together.

* * *

Chuck wakes me up. I must have fallen asleep in the recliner at last, a couple of hours ago, surrounded by a sea of paper. It's about 8am. He hands me a mug of tea. He's getting pretty proficient at making a good cup of my favourite drink. I might as well have a mug as a fixed appendage.

"I've fed the horses, but I thought I'd better come in and check that you're okay. I thought I'd come early this morning," Chuck says as he unwinds his bright green scarf. I stretch and yawn.

I reach down to pat Kelly's head, which isn't there, of course. The sudden recollection of her abduction and my heart-breaking anxiety about her comes over me like a suffocating, dark blanket.

"We'll get her back," Chuck says.

I don't try to speak. I need all of my energy to keep myself composed. I can't allow one tear to run down one cheek. But I'm finding it harder to control the welling up of emotions which are bubbling dangerously near the surface. Usually, I'm good at concealing and burying my feelings. I had a lot of practice in my earlier life. But it seems I can't control everything all the time.

But, despite efforts to block my feelings and emotions about Chuck, a strange and disturbing impulse raises its ugly head. I have a sudden desire to be hugged by this man sitting cross-legged on the floor in front of me, with his red socks, light blue jeans, argyle sweater in blue and yellow, and his green scarf lying discarded on the floor beside him. The shock of the recognition of these alien feelings sends adrenalin into my system, and thankfully brings me to my senses. These unfamiliar sensations I've been experiencing recently must simply be because I'm utterly distraught about Kelly's abduction. And I must do something about it. Now.

"Well, I'm not going to hang around waiting for something to happen," I say, with a tremble in my voice, which I hope Chuck didn't notice.

"You said you have some confidence in this William Porter guy."

"Yes, I do. I'll check with him first and then think what to do next."

William answers his phone almost immediately, although it's not long after 8am.

"The woman is being difficult," he says. "She wants you to sign an affidavit saying you'll delete the video clip and not forward it to anyone, or post in anywhere, and that you'll pledge not to run for any political office, that you'll not work on any cause relating to environmental issues or any matter which could affect current or future operations of the three businesses, you know which they are, and lastly and perhaps the most problematic, you'll stop investigating Frank's accident."

"Oh." That dark blanket descends on me again. I know I'm willing to do anything for my beloved Kelly, but I have to admit it's a big price for me to have to pay. "I'd really like to know why she's demanding all these things. It raises suspicions, doesn't it?"

"Absolutely," William says. "To my mind, she's implicating the three businesses in Frank's death. There must be a link, and Susan must know what it is, and she could be involved herself."

"But all I'm concerned about at the moment is getting Kelly back, alive and well." I don't like the sound of the last three words as they spew out of my mouth in a sputter.

"I have a recommendation for you."

"Let me put you on speakerphone. I'd like Chuck to hear." He's still sitting on the floor, twirling his scarf round in circles in front of me.

"Okay. Can you both hear me?" William asks. We say we can. I'm doing my best to be optimistic that there's a way out of this situation, but I'm not finding it easy. Losing Kelly is making it harder to think straight, it seems.

"Wait until I've finished, because your initial reactions will probably be negative," William asks.

"Okay," I say.

"Just to put this in context, I've assumed one crucial thing, which is that you'd not want to stop your investigation into Frank's death."

"But," I blurt out.

"Let me finish. I assumed you wouldn't agree to her terms for Kelly's release. At least, in my opinion, you shouldn't. I would advise against it. I had my assistant do an extensive background check on Susan Kingsley-Black, on my behalf. We can all pull strings if we need to. In brief, these are the items of interest. One: Susan has been admitted to Lighthouse Rehabilitation Centre on four separate occasions for psychiatric treatment for manic-depressive disorder. Two: she was charged with assault three years ago, but the charges were later dropped. Three: she owes Revenue Canada $223,723 in unpaid taxes, determined by an audit, and legal action is pending; and four: she owes the City $3,240 in unpaid parking fines. While these issues have not become public knowledge, most of this is accessible from various websites. Now, we might feel compassion for her mental illness. But, even if we put that aside, we might conclude from the other matters that she's unsuitable to run for public office, for a seat in parliament, especially given the proven tax evasion, and perhaps even the outstanding parking tickets. Making and upholding the laws of this province, and this land, is part of the job description for a member of parliament."

"So your recommendation?" asks Chuck.

"I recommend we draft a letter addressed to the leader of the party, documenting all the above, plus a couple of other pieces my assistant unearthed, which include extremist right-wing statements she's posted on social media sites, such as a categorical denial that climate change exists, racist comments about young black men and crime, and derogatory remarks about the Pride Parade. The letter would state that the party would be well-advised to reconsider the nomination of a person of this character. Rather than go directly to the press, we give the party a chance to get its own house in order. I would be glad to send it myself."

"I don't see where this gets us," I say, feeling weary and impatient at the same time. I flop back in the recliner. I was hoping for better.

"It's an added bargaining chip," William says. "I would show Susan a copy. The new terms would be, Kelly returned alive and in good health in return for the destruction of both the video clip and the letter."

"It's worth a try, I suppose," I say, without optimism. "But I don't like it."

"Why not?" asks Chuck.

"Most of what William has mentioned will probably become public knowledge anyway and surely Susan must realize this and be ready to deal with it. So, I'm concerned that threatening to reveal these things won't work."

"Let me answer," William says. "My thoughts are that Susan is banking on these matters not becoming public. The party most likely hasn't exercised due diligence and must surely be unaware, and I am of the opinion the party would not want her standing if it was aware. So even if she thinks it's worth the risk, she would not want someone alerting the party at this stage."

"And," I say. "You've convinced me she shouldn't be running for parliament in any case."

"Ah," William says. "We can deal with that in some other way at another time. There are ways, as I'm sure you realize."

"Well, the top priority is that I must have Kelly back alive and well. And this seems like our best chance," I say. "Thanks for all this William." I just hope it works, but I can't help feeling uncertain, especially since Susan might very well not act rationally.

"My pleasure. I might even cash the cheque, assuming this works."

"Please do. I told you to do that earlier."

"What's the time-frame?" Chuck asks.

"My plan is to complete it this morning. My assistant and I came in early. She loves dogs too, by the way. I'll get back to you before noon and give you an update."

"I'll let the horses out and clean the stalls. You get some rest or shower or whatever," Chuck says as we amble out to the kitchen. "I brought some muffins, hope that's okay."

"That's definitely okay." I put the mugs in the dishwasher. "I hope I haven't got my hopes up only for them to be dashed into tiny fragments."

"I don't think so." Chuck picks up a plastic bag which is sitting next to a pair of shiny yellow rubber boots on the kitchen floor. He pulls out a new pair of blue-and-white-striped coveralls and unfolds them.

"I see you've come prepared," I say.

"Well, I want to help."

"Thanks. I'll take you up on your offer and have a shower. See you in a bit." I should add something to express my gratitude for his help and support, but when I turn to leave the kitchen, the silver-framed picture of Kelly, which hangs on the hall wall, catches my eye. A surge of emptiness and doubt stops me in my tracks. I hear the kitchen door close as Chuck leaves the house, and allow one tear to run down each cheek as I garner the energy needed to go upstairs without my beloved dog.

* * *

I pick at my muffin. Crumbs are everywhere. I have my eyes glued on my phone. It's 11.27am. I know Chuck is saying something, but I'm not listening. I've received two texts from Shane apologizing for the incident at the side of the road and asking to meet. The nerve of that man is beyond belief. I'm glad that I've had two showers since he touched me. I feel as if I need another one, just at the thought of him.

"Meg, I don't think you heard me," Chuck says. I raise my eyes and look at him. "I just wondered what Tom said in the email he sent you yesterday. Hope you don't mind me asking."

"I'll check it."

"I just wondered if he had more to share about his accident. I'm wondering about Susan's connection or role."

"Right. He says that he's much better, hopes to get home tomorrow. I suppose that's today now." I read the rest of the email. "He admits he wants to know who was responsible for him going off the road, and why, but he then says that I shouldn't continue with my investigation. He believes it's got out of control and is too dangerous."

"I suppose his accident must have really shaken him up enough to make him back off. Just what they want, presumably."

"But he seemed so keen to help until a little while ago. You know, it makes me wonder if there's something he's not telling me."

"What are you going to do?"

"As long as I get Kelly back safe and well, I'll carry on."

"As you know, I'm happy to do anything I can to help."

"Thanks. You're already being a great help."

There's a loud knock at the door. Neither of us heard a car come up the driveway.

"We should both go," Chuck says.

When we open the door, an exuberant Kelly jumps up to my face and licks me, and nearly knocks me off balance. William laughs, his paunch bouncing up and down. Chuck shakes his hand, pats Kelly and has such a broad grin on his face I thought his cheeks would burst. My elation makes me feel as light as a feather. The weight of the anxiety and guilt has nearly all gone. We seem to be glued to the verandah as Kelly dances around us.

"Come in, come in," I say.

Kelly goes straight to her water bowl and laps with gusto, spraying water onto the floor. Chuck fetches some glasses and a bottle of wine appears from somewhere. I'm not really paying attention. Kelly looks up, water droplets sparkling all round her mouth and on her whiskers, and barks.

"She's probably hungry," William says. "I don't think the woman has a clue about animals. But I don't think she harmed her. Kelly would act differently if she'd been hurt."

"Like a muffin?" Chuck asks.

"I sure would, thanks." William sits down at the kitchen table, and I find Kelly's favourite kibble. I notice, out of the corner of my eyes, that both men are breaking the rules and feeding Kelly bits of muffin. Frank was adamant that Kelly should not be fed human food and should definitely not be given anything while we were sitting at the table. Not that we sat together at the table very often. Frank hadn't much patience with Kelly, or with my love for her, or with my passion for working at the humane society. Despite having officially settled the matter in our marriage contract, Frank raised the issue of my work on more than one occasion. I suppose there's some irony in the fact that I've taken a leave of absence since his death. He said he would prefer I did volunteer work, if I had to do something. He thought that, since I wouldn't hire help for the barn, I shouldn't be working. I realize that most of the wives in his social circle volunteer, including sitting on boards of directors, and only a few have their own careers. Frank asked me one day that, if I was determined to continue working, why didn't I take on a management role in health care or business, rather than working for the lowly regarded humane society? I didn't ask what his problem was. I should have. But perhaps, at this point, it's better that I don't know.

"William, what are your thoughts about what happened to Frank and connections to these three businesses which seem to be closely entwined?" Chuck asks. He has his green scarf wrapped around his neck a couple of times. Is it cold in here? I have the advantage of Kelly's warm body spread across my feet under the table as she sleeps soundly. I hate to think how she must have pined while away from her home.

"I can only conjecture based on Susan's demands, and Marshall's conversation with me that I mentioned to Meg earlier, that there has to be a link between at least Susan and Frank's death. My guess is that the link is between the three businesses, you know, SWR, MMB Aggregates and Westmount Steel, and Frank. It could be that Marshall's fears are well founded, and that Brad was involved in Frank's death somehow. And now that Meg is snooping around, I think that's got them all very edgy. What if someone talks? What if someone slips up and gives something away? What if some incriminating information comes to the fore?"

"Just got an email from George, Frank's assistant," I say. "He's been looking into Susan's background too, because he says, there have been some rumours in the government buildings, even questions being raised by her party, apparently." I read a bit more as we all sip on the mellow red wine. "He says that the word is that she is ultra-right-wing, is a non-believer as far as climate change is concerned, and wants to see smaller government, less taxes, especially for businesses. He says she's almost verging on libertarian, according to some of the gossip. She believes people should have the freedom to do virtually anything they want. That's scary. I sure hope she doesn't make it to parliament. It's surprising how catching some of these views can be."

"She won't," William says. "I don't think we'll have to worry about it at all. She's beginning to self-destruct. The good people of Vannersville won't stand for that nonsense."

"Yeah, you're right. Sanity will prevail. Talking of sanity, I feel so much better and ready to continue now that Kelly's back." I hear the muffled thumps of her tail hitting the floor as Kelly wags it. She knows her name, even if it's mentioned in conversation and even if she appears to be sleeping. She's lying underneath me and hasn't moved since she had her fill of water, muffin and kibble.

"Well, I'm glad," says Chuck. "I'm getting more curious by the day. I can understand why you want to investigate, Meg."

"So can I," William says. "Just keep your guard up."

17

Drugs

I sit nursing the umpteenth mug of tea, reflecting that I probably drink too much of it. I was raised on tea. It was as if a cuppa was believed to be the answer to anything that ailed you. I was one of the few disbelievers while I lived in England (it didn't heal the wounds I suffered), but I've found some solace in it since Frank's death.

I'm awake with the dawn chorus. Despite the birds' songs being tuneful and cheery, I am slumped at the kitchen table, feeling morose. I didn't sleep well. I tossed and turned. It was as if my off-button wasn't working. My body nor my brain would settle. Kelly's ordeal played out in my mind, but most of my agitation was caused by thoughts of Tom and Chuck. Concern for Tom and my distress over his accident disturbed me, but his pleas for me to stop unsettled me more. And, as I grew more troubled, my trust in Tom wavered, causing me to churn in my bed. I even questioned if Tom had something to do with Frank's death.

And then Chuck. In my half-awake, half-asleep stupor I pushed him away one moment, only to pull him closer to me the next. Whenever Chuck got nearer to me, though, I grew more and more terrified. And then the flashbacks started and then I was fully awake, in a cold sweat and shivering.

Those damnable flashbacks suck me into the dark depths of my past. I must conquer the little demons which run around in my brain linking all my neurons to my wretched memories of intolerable torments, threatening to monopolize all my thoughts. I shake my head as if to rid my brain of the pesky devils. I need to put my wits to work.

But I can't shake all of the fear I felt when Chuck came close to me, albeit in a dream or half-dream. As a result, I feel apprehensive about working with him in the barn this morning. I'm muddled and confused, which also must have something to do with my lack of sleep. When Chuck arrives, I make some excuse and say I won't be able to help with the barn chores. Kelly is happy to go out with him, wagging her tail and looking up at him with bright, shining eyes. I should trust Kelly's instincts.

* * *

I don't know where the time has gone, but Chuck and Kelly have burst through the kitchen door, bringing a distinct horsey odour with them.

"I've finished what I'd planned on doing," Chuck says, as he hovers in the doorway.

"Have some tea. There's plenty in the pot." There's something about his warm smile, topped by his soft brown curls and bright yellow hat, that bucks me up. I can't push him away, not at the moment.

"Thanks."

As Chuck sits down at the table, he says "I haven't seen Brad at the end of the driveway since Tom's accident."

"Well, perhaps he thinks we're well and truly scared off. Or, perhaps he's rethinking because of the incident with Susan, assuming this is all connected as William thinks."

"What about that nursing home guy, the one who was hurt when Frank went off the road? I'd be very curious to know what he saw. I can't believe he wouldn't have seen something."

As Chuck was talking, I notice I received a text message from Tom. His sister has just driven him home from the hospital, and he's decided not to attempt to go into work. He admits he doesn't feel up to it partly because he's developed a chest infection. He will do as much of his work from home that he can manage. He tells me, again, that I should stop trying to find out what happened to Frank. I text back that I plan to keep going. He phones.

"This has got complex and dangerous, Meg."

"It hasn't been without its danger all along. And I thought you wanted to find out who was responsible for you crashing your car and why, let alone finding out what really happened to Frank."

"I did. I do. But this accident has made me see sense. The stakes have got higher. At least wait until I'm better and can help you."

"I'm not going to stop. All I can say is that I'll be careful." Chuck mumbles something in the background about helping me.

"But you won't be able to find out what happened to Frank."

"What do you mean by that?" I'm losing patience with Tom, and growing more suspicious.

"I just mean it's gone up too many notches. They're not going to let you find out anything."

"You don't know that, Tom. Please, just get better. Get rid of that infection. I'll talk to you later."

Tom moans. I guess his broken ribs are pretty painful even though they're wrapped up. Our conversation ends less pleasantly than I would have liked and with me remaining adamant.

"Sounded like an awkward conversation," Chuck says.

"You likely figured out that Tom said yet again that he wants me to stop my investigation. I'm not going to, as you know. I think the fact that things are heating up must mean we're on to something. And, to be honest, I still think Tom knows something that he's keeping from me. He even has me wondering if he was involved somehow in Frank's death."

"He was Frank's best friend, and he's been helping you until now. I reckon it's the shock of his accident. You can sometimes see your life flash before your eyes, and it can give you a different perspective on things."

"Maybe. Anyhow, I'm going to get on with it."

"It's your call. And I'll help anyway I can."

"Thanks. You've already been a great help. I'll call the nursing home and hope to talk to that Gerald or John guy."

"Can I help with that?"

"Well, it would be good to have you listening in. I would tell them of course." I make a determined effort to stop my fears from driving a wedge between me and Chuck. I do value his opinion and I trust him more than I do Tom, at least for the moment.

"I'd be glad to do that." The land-line phone rings.

"It's probably Shane bugging me again."

"Hello, Meg?" asks a soft voice.

"Yes."

"It's Bill Price, from the racetrack."

"Oh, hello, how are you?"

"Fine, thank you. I have some news which I don't think you'll like."

"Oh."

"First, I regret to advise you that Shane Parrington had his training licence suspended two days ago. If the investigation supports our allegations, he could be banned from training for quite some time. It concerns your horse which he entered into a race yesterday."

"I didn't know one of my horses was entered into a race yesterday. It couldn't be Speed, he raced just recently." I have a sinking feeling in my stomach. I remember I deleted two texts from Shane while I was so worried about Kelly. I didn't read them. And I might not have phoned back when I should have. I assumed it was all just more of his pestering. Perhaps he had told me about the race in the texts, but he still could have told me earlier. The race entries are usually made three days ahead.

"It was the mare, Alusio, stable name Rose, I believe."

"Oh, the last I heard was that she was sore, and he wanted to take her back to his farm."

"Off the record, I think there's a lot he hasn't been telling you, Meg. Alusio won the race, and as you know, a drug test is mandatory for all winners. Your horse was found to have traces of a restricted drug in her urine, which presumably had been administered illegally by Shane with the intent of giving the horse an advantage. There were traces of a painkiller as well. Perhaps that's because of the soreness he mentioned to you."

"Oh, no, poor Rose. I hope she's okay! I hope you realize that I certainly didn't authorise any of this." I'm shaken and ashamed that I'd somehow allowed one of my horses to be drugged, and what's more, raced, while presumably unfit to run. But while I'm far from a fan of Shane, it's hard for me to believe that he'd be stupid enough to drug a horse, and somehow, I think it especially dumb of him to drug one of mine. And what of the horse? Rose is an honest, gentle mare. Frank would have been horrified on all fronts. He'd fought against performance-enhancing drugs, he cared about the horses, and he upheld the law with the utmost integrity. Shivers run up and down my spine as fury bubbles up inside me. I can sense my hot face turning scarlet.

"I know you wouldn't have. You have a good, solid reputation, Meg. I did mention to you when we met that Shane has been acting rather strangely about the new drug rules. He's in some very hot water with the officials now. And you need to know that when officials asked what the owner planned for the horses, he said he's taking both of your horses to his farm, which I thought was rather odd, since you have your own farm, and I remember Frank told me that the horses went home to your farm when they weren't at the track. I'm overstepping my bounds here, but I'm concerned for the horses and for you. I'm assuming you haven't approved this move. As you likely know, they must be transferred to a licensed trainer or they must leave. The point of my phone call is to make sure you know the situation."

"I really appreciate you doing this. I'll get on to this right away. I'd like the horses to come home here for now, to give me a chance to sort things out. It won't hurt for both of them to have a break, especially Rose."

"I thought you'd want to do that."

I thank him again. I'm dazed as well as livid. My head aches and I have a stiff neck. Shane had talked to me about Rose having a sore leg, but I still don't believe it. I'd not felt any heat or puffiness, and Linda would have told me if there was a problem, because she knows how much I care. And she cares too. And why on earth would Shane risk everything by using a banned substance? And, more to the point, why didn't I change trainers months ago?

"You look terrible," Chuck says. I give him a summary of what Bill told me.

"I could arrange for the horses to come back here today, if that'd help," he says.

"That would be great, thanks. And it would be wonderful if you could ask the vet to come and check them both, perhaps tomorrow. The number's posted on the wall by the phone."

"Be pleased to. By the way, I don't know what reminded me, but I've seen a rusty white pickup a few times, driving along the road slowly. Do you know of a neighbour with a vehicle like that? It seemed odd."

"No, I can't think of anyone. I'm wondering how Linda is doing. I hope she'll find another trainer to work for."

"Who's Linda?"

"You remember, the groom. Anyhow, I'll let you arrange for the horses to come home while I do some other jobs. Then we'll call the nursing home, if you're able to hang around for a bit."

"Sure thing. I'm also willing to help with the horses until they go back to the track. Otherwise, you won't have much time to do your sleuthing." Chuck smiles and pushes his chair away from the table. "I'll get on with the phone calls and prepare the barn then."

I thank him again. I'm relieved that I was able to quash my fears and half-dreams, and haven't pushed Chuck away. I won't let him get close, I know that, but I'm comforted by the realization that I do trust him. This is a big thing for me.

* * *

Chuck and I sit at the kitchen table with the phone between us.

"I'll try to make that phone call to the nursing home."

"Good morning, Berry Nursing Home."

"Good morning, I wondered if I could talk with John Nelson."

"I'll put you through to his nurse."

"Geraldine Foxton here," a crisp voice says.

"Hello, this is Meg Sheppard. I'd really like to talk with John Nelson, please. It's important."

"John is having a tough day today. He might not be up to talking with you. I'll check with him. You realize he has difficulty breathing?"

"I'm so sorry. All I know is that he's a quadriplegic, which must be unbelievably challenging. But I would like to talk with him if at all possible. I'd be very grateful."

"What did you say your name was?"

"Meg Sheppard. Frank Sheppard's widow. The name may mean something to him." The word 'widow' caught in my throat.

"Was your husband in the accident which caused John to go off the road?"

"Yes. Did he tell you about it?" I ask, with some sound of surprise in my voice, which I immediately regret.

"Yes. He's confided a lot in me. Excuse me while I close the door." She soon returns. "I'll put the phone onto speaker. It's easier for John, and I can assist. He's told me everything. I came with him from the Shelton Hospital. Can you hear me?"

"Yes."

"Good, and we can hear you. John, Meg Sheppard is on the line, Frank Sheppard's widow. This might be difficult for you, but I thought you might have something to say to her."

"Yes," a breathless voice says.

"By the way, I have a friend of mine on the line too, Charles Murphy."

"Hello," says Chuck.

There's a pause.

"Do you trust him?" asks John. I can hear that it's difficult for him to get his breath. He seems to have to gulp at the air, and he speaks in hesitating, staccato speech, but I can understand him.

"Yes, absolutely." To say this out-loud, and I know I mean it, acts like a salve for my sensibilities.

"You've called to find out more about the accident," John says. "I've been waiting for this call for about a year." I don't know how to reply. I realize it has taken me that time to rouse myself into action, and can't even explain it myself.

"It's kind of you to talk with me," I say.

"Sorry about your husband, but I want to say right off that I didn't kill him. A man called Brad Buckthorn hired me and told me that all I had to do was to help in a plan to intimidate Frank Sheppard a bit, scare him off, like." There's some choking and spluttering.

"Be with you in a moment," Geraldine says.

"He hired me, as I said, to scare Frank off something. I don't know what. This guy Buckthorn looked like he'd be better at it than me. But I didn't question. I was desperate for work. I'd just come out of jail. No-one wants to hire a jailbird. And it sounded pretty harmless."

"Take it easy, John," Geraldine says. "Excuse us, I'll have to suction him." We hear gurgling and sucking sounds, and finally John speaks again.

"Would it be easier if I came to visit?" I ask.

"Come any time. We'll be here." says Geraldine.

"Don't go. I want to tell you the rest. But please come to visit as well, as long as you're not followed. I have to get this off my chest. I'm sure Brad thinks I killed your husband. It's not true." There's more coughing and gasping.

"We've been thinking all along that Brad killed Frank. Everything seems to add up to that."

"Well, he wasn't there at the accident. It doesn't make sense." John splutters again. "You have to believe me when I say I didn't kill your husband."

"I do believe you. We'll come to see you soon. I really want to hear what you have to say."

"John would really like that. He gets virtually no visitors, and it'll be easier for him than on this speaker phone," Geraldine says.

"I have you, Gerry." John says. "I could afford to move into this home with my private nurse when my aunt died. She was a wealthy woman." He gasps and gulps. "I'm putting her money to good use, aren't I?"

"I'm glad you think so, John," Geraldine says. "John wants me to tell you he doesn't want Brad Buckthorn to know that he's here.

John changed his name and location so that he could lie low. He's concerned that Brad thinks he killed Frank Sheppard, and that Brad believes John could implicate him."

"I see," I say. "We certainly won't tell Brad. And we'll do everything we can to avoid being followed."

"Thanks," says John.

"We'll see you soon. Thank you very much for talking with us," I say.

As I hang up, I decide I'd like Chuck to come with me to meet with John. "I hope you don't mind me including you in the trip to the home. Hopefully, we'll be able to fit in the visit with the barn chores and other jobs," I say to Chuck.

"I'm glad to help," Chuck says, as he gets a big lick on his hand from Kelly.

"What do you make of what John said? He seems convinced that Brad had nothing to do with Frank's death. Then who is responsible?"

"I don't know what to think."

"I want to meet with him as soon as we can make it. He obviously knows more, and perhaps he has some answers."

I'm just about to get up from the table when the phone rings. I wonder if it's John or Geraldine, but it's Linda.

"I'm glad to hear from you. What's going on?" I ask.

"Oh, Mrs Sheppard. I'm sorry I didn't call you. Shane told me he'd talked to you. But Chuck called today, so I know you hadn't been called. I'm sorry."

"It's not your fault. I think you and Chuck are organizing for the horses to come home today, so that's great. What about you?"

"I've lucked out. I've already got a job with another trainer in the same barn, and I start on Monday."

"Oh, good. I'm glad. Hope it goes really well for you. You'll have to let me know if you think he'd be right for Speed and Rose."

"Yeah, I will. I want to tell you some things that I didn't have the courage to tell you before. I've been biting my tongue for a long time."

"I've noticed that you've been on the quiet side. I just thought that was your personality."

"Well, I'm not all that talkative. But I want to tell you some things."

"Okay."

"I want you to know what Shane is like, 'cause I think Speed and Rose should never go back to him. I shouldn't have stayed working for him, but I care about the horses, like, and I did my best."

"I'm sure you did."

"Well, Shane didn't like Frank. Said he was stuck up and threw his weight around, was born with a silver spoon in his mouth, whatever that means. He said Frank was trying to tell him how to do his goddam job, and who did he think he was, making up those effing drug rules?"

"How awful. I can't understand why Frank didn't pick up on Shane's attitude."

"Me neither. And why did Shane keep on working for Frank? Likely, he needed the money. He's been losing clients over the past several years. I've been getting worried that he'd cut my hours."

"It doesn't make much sense to me. I suppose Frank hadn't been spending as much time at the track during the year before his death. Who's been looking after Speed and Rose for the past couple of days?"

"I have. They're fine. Even though I haven't seen Shane around, I've made sure they're okay. I expected you to show up, though. I should've realized Shane hadn't called you."

"I'm so grateful. I'll make sure you get paid for the work. Thanks a lot."

"That's okay. I think this will be for the best, like. But I should have told you before. I feel bad."

"There's no need for you to feel bad. I'll let you know when the horses get here safely."

Chuck is about to leave when a taxi comes up the driveway. A large foot emerges from the open door, followed by a tall and lanky body.

"Murray! I wasn't expecting you. I'm glad you're here," I say.

"I'm now getting out a bit in the day, but I'm not driving yet." I'm thankful that he looks less gaunt and has a healthier colour in his face.

I convince Chuck to stay and have a snack with us, and he says he'll help put the horses in. He tells me that Speed and Rose can't be shipped until the next morning, but he's arranged for Linda to take care of them until they leave. Chuck says he'll rummage in the cupboards and fridge for some snack food, and put the kettle on, while Murray and I sit at the kitchen table. Murray asks me about my plans for the future once I've found out what happened to Frank.

"I'm ready to go back to my job at the humane society, I think," I say.

"That's good. I bet they'll be glad to have you back," Murray says.

"Well, I know that the woman filling in for me has found it tough. I think the Board has been pretty hard on her." I thank Chuck for the mug of tea he's just put in front of me. "So, is there a particular reason for your visit, Murray? There doesn't have to be, of course, just wondering."

"I wanted to visit in any case, but I do have another reason. I hope you know that I very much want you to find out what happened to Frank, how it happened and who was responsible. Well, you must have a list of suspects."

"I do, but," I begin.

"I want to help you shorten it. I have a rock-solid alibi for when Frank had his accident. I'm ashamed to admit that I was under house arrest at the time and my driver's licence had been suspended. It still is. It was impaired driving again. I was ordered to get professional counselling this time. I was very sceptical, I can tell you, but I found it of some help. So, I decided to give the Lighthouse another try. You can check the dates."

"That's okay, I believe you. And thanks for telling me. I hope you can conquer your demons once and for all."

"I'm more optimistic than I've ever been. I have more supports in place. I think I might have a chance this time."

"Good. That's great."

Chuck puts some cheese, crackers and fruit on the table, as well as some cookies and boxes of raisins. It looks pretty good considering shopping hasn't been on the top of my priority list. But I have to admit that it never has been.

"And something's been bothering me," Murray says, as he picks up a neatly cut cube of cheese. "We both know all about the will and who got what. I know you were left some for running the farm, and you know how much I was left. The point I want to make is that I know Frank was a very wealthy man. He made a ton of money as a stockbroker before he started his political career. My question is where did all that money go?"

"Are you sure?"

"I am sure. He was foolish enough to brag about his wealth to me during one of our arguments when I'd got under his skin. My addiction to booze took me down to ugly depths of desperation at times, and I wasn't a nice person. In this particularly nasty argument, he mentioned a figure of around ten million. And you know he never lied."

"Wow. My goodness. I had no idea. I wonder where it is now?"

"He's not the sort of guy to get involved in anything like gambling, and I always believed he was honest. But I don't think all the money was included in the will, which I know doesn't make sense. I'm at a loss, but I thought I should mention it, in case it had something to do with his death."

"Wasn't Tom the Executor of his will?" Chuck asks. "I wonder if he knows anything?"

"He was Frank's best friend. It's worth asking him I suppose, although I know the will itself didn't make any reference to additional funds other than the ones we're all aware of," Murray notes.

"I'm going to ask Tom," I say. "My intuition has been niggling at me since Tom was in hospital, telling me he knows more than he's letting on."

"Good idea to check with him then," Chuck says as he sits down to join us. Kelly lies on his feet, under the table, as if pinning him down to make him stay.

18

Nursing Home

The horses' hot breaths hang in foggy clouds as Rose and Speed look around. Loud whinnies shake their firm, glistening bodies as they stand at the end of the driveway. Chuck has Speed on a lead-rein and I have Rose, and we intend to give them a minute to get orientated since they've just been off-loaded from the truck. But they don't need all that time to recognize that they're home and that there's green grass to graze on. They whinny again, with their heads held high and their ears pricked like antennae. Eagle and Bullet answer. I can feel the excitement at the end of the lead-rein as we move up the driveway. Neither of them will walk. Each trots in small springy steps, as if dancing.

The thrill of being home in open space can spell trouble for these highly strung athletes, so we lead them to the smallest paddock where they won't be able to get up to a full gallop. We turn them loose, and they snort in unison with nostrils flared, kick up their heels, and put on a bucking bronco display with all eight hooves off the ground at least three times. We laugh as we watch this awesome synchronized display of athletic prowess. But it doesn't last long. They soon settle down to greet Eagle and Bullet over the fence, in between snatching mouthfuls of lush green grass. It's almost as if they haven't been away. Now that the excitement of the return is safely over, we walk back to the house with smiles on our faces, thanks to the temporary, welcome distraction.

When I check my phone, I notice I've received another email from Tom. While Chuck goes to the barn to double-check that it's set up in readiness for the four horses to go into their stalls later, I read the email. I'm glad to hear that Tom is continuing to improve. It's clear from his message that he either doesn't have any more information about Frank's financial affairs over and above the estate, or if he does, he isn't about to reveal it. And the tone of the rest of the email exasperates me. He urges me, yet again, to stop my investigation into Frank's accident. He says it has become too dangerous and too much time has elapsed presumably making it harder to find answers. Tom appeared to be pretty enthusiastic and keen to help me until he got hurt. I'm now wondering if he has a head injury which hasn't been detected. Either that or he was involved in Frank's death. But I can't think of a motive. Unless he had access to the additional funds Murray believes Frank had. Something isn't right, but I reply that there's no need for him to be concerned. Why get into an argument, and why tell him what I'm doing?

Chuck emerges from the barn. "Did you just get an email from Tom?" he asks.

"Yes, you too?"

"He wants me to convince you to stop. He thinks it's particularly dangerous for you to go to see John Nelson."

"As you know, I'm not stopping. And I'm growing more exasperated and suspicious each time I hear from him."

"Perhaps his crash really shook him up. He can be an intense sort of guy."

"Either that or he was involved in Frank's death, best friend or not. I'm going to keep Tom out of the loop from now on."

"You're obviously not going to quit." He smiles, and I'm sure his large, green eyes twinkle. "I'll just ignore the email. And, by the way, everything appears to be in order in the barn and the horses have settled down nicely in the paddock. I think it's safe for us to leave for the nursing home."

Chuck takes off his snazzy-looking light-green hat and climbs into the pickup. Kelly wags her tail and seems to march on the spot with her two front paws in her excitement and anticipation. I feel badly. She probably thinks we're going somewhere for a walk.

The GPS is set for Berry Nursing Home and we start the roughly 120 mile trip under a blue sky. I'm hoping we'll learn a lot from Gerald Warren, or John Nelson as he's now known.

I hear Chuck's cell phone beep.

"I've just got a text. Hope you don't mind if I check it out?"

"Of course not. Go ahead."

Out of the corner of my eye, I see Chuck shudder as the phone falls out of his hands, landing on the gritty mat between his feet.

"Is everything okay?" I ask.

"I'm not sure." He releases the seat-belt and stretches down to grab the phone. I glance at him. His tanned face has turned a greenish colour, and his teeth are clenched. He looks down at his phone.

"The text's from Dania, you know, my ex-fiancée. She wants me to call her." His voice is raspy and hard to hear.

"Oh." I try to control the unwelcome tremble in my voice. "Will you call her?"

"I suppose so, yes." He turns away and looks out of the side window.

The unexpected tension compresses the air in the truck, making it harder to breathe and harder to speak. We don't utter a word for the rest of the drive. I'm sure my stomach has a jellyfish swimming around inside. Much to my consternation, it won't settle down. Why do I care about him calling her?

Despite the distraction and my uneasiness, I remember to check every so often that we aren't being followed. Only the occasional vehicle shares the road with us until we reach the outskirts of Thornton. Berry Nursing Home is clearly marked but smaller than I expected. I guess from the tall gables, weathered brickwork, and sweeping verandah it was built well over a century ago as a grand private home.

Chuck and I make our way in silence to the front door. Unlike most nursing homes, we aren't able to walk in. We ring the doorbell. Having rubbed our hands with cool antibacterial foam which oozes from a hand-pump, we're guided to John Nelson's spacious and sunny room. Geraldine Foxton walks towards us with a warm smile and gives us each a firm handshake. John uses a mouth-stick to guide his power wheelchair towards us. Chuck and I both say "hello" at the same time and bob our heads.

"Do sit down," John says. His chest heaves with the effort of speaking each word as he gulps air. I note the various tubes, padding, supports and straps, and marvel at his courage. Geraldine has already arranged tea and snacks, and acts as if John has never had visitors. Perhaps he hasn't.

"Thanks so much for seeing us. I'm sure this isn't easy for you," I say.

"I'm glad you've come. I need to tell someone everything I know." John's voice starts to gurgle, and Geraldine jumps into action, using a suction machine to clear his airways. It's obvious that this is a regular routine for them.

He sips a little apple juice through a straw with Geraldine's help.

"You mentioned on the phone that Brad Buckthorn hired you to help intimidate Frank Sheppard," I say.

"Yes, but I don't know why. Geraldine, you tell them." John's breathing is laboured. Geraldine puts a reassuring hand on his dry, somewhat atrophied one, and is about to speak when the door is flung open, crashing against the trolley, tipping over the mugs and making the cookies jump.

Brad scans the room as he stands just inside the doorway. His dirty-blond hair looks like he's had a couple of rough nights, and his face is pinched. His eyes settle on John. We wait.

"Hi, Brad. I wondered when you'd find me." John's voice has become a raspy whisper.

"Glad to meet you," Geraldine says, with seemingly calm composure. "Have a seat. You've timed this well. You can all hear what John has to say."

"He's not John. He's Gerald Warren," Brad says as he slowly sits, as if reluctant, on the chair that Geraldine retrieved from the room next-door. He doesn't take his eyes off John.

"Yes. He's both. He changed his name after what happened."

"You assumed I'd run Frank off the road." John's chest heaves. My concern for him grows.

"I'll tell them everything, John. Just take it easy," Geraldine says.

Brad fidgets and then stares down at his shoes.

"John, as you probably all know, was a petty criminal: his words, not mine. He'd grown up in poverty with a mother who had mental illness. He was charged a couple of times with theft and got to know a lawyer, William Porter."

"I thought he'd help me get some decent work when I got out of jail." John grimaces. I'm not sure why.

"He linked him up with Brad."

Brad nods his head without looking up from his shoes.

"Brad told John that he wanted him to assist in a plan to intimidate someone, and John replied that Brad could count on him. Brad then told John that the person was Minister Sheppard, and that he wanted ideas from John. William Porter would be the conduit, Brad's bosses would have the message, but Brad was counting on John to be the heavy, so to speak."

Brad nods again.

"But the truth is I've no idea how to intimidate someone, or be a heavy. I've never done anything like that." John sputters. I wonder if he needs suctioning again, but Geraldine keeps on talking. I can't help feeling anxious for him.

"John admits he didn't do anything for a while, and even thought of dropping it. But he needed the money badly."

"Yes, so I got myself to the library and read about him, articles and stuff."

"He realized he needed to know more about the Minister and his routines. At least it would be a start."

"Honestly, I was close to panicking sometimes. I didn't find anything of much use. I couldn't find any bad press or juicy stuff on the internet." I squirm as John gurgles and gasps.

"And the House wasn't sitting. And I think you said that there wasn't even an up-to-date schedule for Parliament," Geraldine says, as she suctions him again. "So, he thought he'd follow the Minister and this way he'd find out more about the man, and hopefully this would lead to a plan. Essentially Minister Sheppard was under surveillance by John."

"I didn't even know how to follow someone without being seen," John says.

"John's thoughts were that it's best to tell Brad he was planning on following the Minister, and once he had the information he was looking for, he would meet with Brad and they would agree on a plan. This would give John some time to find out more and to think. Brad had mentioned there was a timing issue, but it sounded as if there was no urgency."

Brad nods again, and mumbles, "My boss planned to have William Porter communicate with Frank but, as far as I know,

Marshall hadn't even started the ball rolling on this when Frank had his accident."

"After a couple of days of surveillance, he followed the Minister, Frank, as he was on his way back to the farm. John said he was keeping a safe distance behind. Just as he came to the bend he saw Frank's car off the road, pointing down the slope."

"And then it suddenly took off," John interjects. "And this is the odder bit."

"That's not all John saw. He distinctly saw someone leaping away from the vehicle, and from the driver's side, just before it sped down the slope."

"I'll swear to it," John says. "And I believe it was the Minister." He's almost inaudible, his voice muffled by gurgling fluids. Geraldine leaps into action and suctions his airways again.

My mind's eye sees Frank jumping away from the car and my body freezes, as if it has been turned into a statue made of cold, rigid stone. Then a myriad of muddled questions collect and collide in my brain. The biggest one being: could Frank be alive?

"John didn't kill Frank. Brad didn't hire John, or Gerald as he was then, to kill Frank. John was doing nothing but tailing him, and I don't mean right on his tail." Geraldine uses what I guess would be her professional tone of voice. She is clearly adamant about what she says on John's behalf.

Brad unfolds and stretches his back upright, bracing his hands against the top of his knees.

"What happened to John?" Chuck asks.

"He was so shocked, puzzled and agitated by what he saw, that he lost focus on his driving and went off the road about half-way round the bend, swerved abruptly and hit a tree on the opposite side of the road at quite a speed. He got so badly injured because the airbags deployed after the car stopped, and John had taken out the headrests because they bothered him." Geraldine glances at John with a mock look of disapproval. But even in my state of bewilderment, I notice sadness in her eyes.

"What happened to Frank is also a good question," Chuck says.

"I'm sure that my boss is convinced that I'm in some way responsible for Frank's death, that I'd got carried away. And I thought I was too, because I hired you. I assumed you'd blown it and forced him off the road." Brad looks at John. "This is huge."

"John, did you see what happened to the person who left the car?" Chuck asks.

"He didn't. But he's convinced, adamant, I would say, that the person was alive. And we all know that no body was found at the top of the slope. It was presumed that the person was in the car until it hit the rocks and was somehow thrown into the high, fast-running river that flows into the lake, and that eventually the body would be washed up on the shore somewhere."

"But he didn't come and check to see if I was okay," John says.

"You can't be sure of that, John." Geraldine turns to face him. "You could have been going in and out of consciousness." Geraldine turns to face us again. "But we know Frank wasn't the one who called 911."

"We checked it out," John says. "It was some other motorist."

"And John doesn't know if Frank, assuming it was him, realized that John's crash was caused by his actions, or at least by John's reaction to his actions."

"No, I can't be sure of that, but I know he would've had no idea that I was following him or watching him. I'm sure of that."

"Yes, John told me he's sure that nothing he did would have caused Frank to be alerted and that he would have known nothing about the existence of John. And certainly, he firmly believes he had no impact on Frank's accident. He wasn't near enough to have had any influence on what happened to Frank." Geraldine straightens the mugs on the tray but doesn't pour the tea. But she takes a cookie and passes the plate around. "I can tell you that John has gone over things many, many times, and we've had many conversations about it."

I couldn't eat the most delicious cookie on the face of the planet.

"I need to talk to you." I look directly at Brad, who nods.

"Thank you for listening. It feels like a ton of weight off to get this out into the open," John says.

"Why didn't you tell the police?" Chuck asks.

"The police didn't question John when he came out of the coma. I suppose they thought they knew what happened," Geraldine says. "And John wasn't sure he'd handle police questioning well since he thought he might reveal too much. He didn't want to say that he'd been hired to help intimidate Frank, and that he was following him. It could implicate people who had nothing to do with what happened to the man. And it wouldn't have sounded very credible because he didn't know why or what it was all about."

"And why didn't you tell Brad?" asks Chuck.

"I didn't think he'd believe me." John's chest heaves. "I was afraid to."

"Criminals have a hard time being believed. But I think the fact that you're all here makes it easier to share this," Geraldine says. "And perhaps it helps a little that I have no question in my mind that John is telling the truth. I've got to know him very well during this past year."

The air in the room has grown heavy and stuffy. It's as if someone is tightening a noose around my neck. I have an urgent need to get out of here. I've heard enough. With a few quick words of appreciation, Chuck, Brad and I leave.

I have no interest in talking to Brad right now, and he must sense it. Without a word, he hands me a business card with his cell phone number circled, and leaves me and Chuck standing in the small, gravel parking lot without a word. His short chunky legs clamber up into his monstrous pickup, and he goes back to Vannersville.

I look at Chuck. Words won't come out. His large, green eyes show deep concern and compassion and are searching my face for signs of my reaction and feelings. I don't know what I'm feeling other than numbness and confusion. I should feel elated that Frank could be alive. But I don't. In fact, what we've found out makes me even more puzzled and muddled than I was before. My head is spinning and I feel dizzy. As if he senses my disorientation, Chuck wraps me in his long arms. I can smell the sweet scent of his shampoo as a couple of his curls brush my face, and he gives me a tender, sympathetic caress. Despite all that has just transpired, it's as if a warm light is travelling down my spine. And my muscles feel like they've been treated to a soft massage. I'm lighter, almost floating. I don't know what to make of these strange sensations.

Frank was the only adult I'd allowed to hold me since I left England. (I don't count Shane's assault). He was the only one I felt safe with, perhaps because he expected little. He wanted a wife who looked the part at the innumerable photo opportunities and at the plethora of functions requiring the Minister's presence, and not much more. I've always believed I'll never find anyone who truly loves me, who really cares about me, because it feels as if the scars of my abuse are indelibly and visibly marked on my skin, as well as in my heart. I'm damaged goods and don't deserve to be loved. When Frank approached me, I thought I'd never get another opportunity to marry. Frank's patience, kindness, and forgiveness helped me and made me feel safe. And it had felt good that the flash-backs and nightmares had virtually gone by the time of his accident.

I do my best to keep my myriad of muddled feelings hidden as I climb back into the pickup and prepare to drive home. And I know Chuck was merely consoling me, nothing more. I was embraced by his kindness and empathy and there is no more to it than that. I let out an involuntary sigh, and vanquish thoughts of Chuck out of my consciousness. After all, I have to focus on the revelations I just heard in John's room, especially the one question which is gnawing at my heart. If Frank is alive, he must have deceived me, mustn't he? He must have known his apparent death, and my loss of him, would bring inordinate pain. I can't believe he didn't know how much I cared about him. But, to be fair, I am an expert at hiding my emotions.

My phone interrupts my thoughts with a loud beep signalling a waiting email. I find it hard to ignore. I ask Chuck to check who it's from. He says it's from George, and I ask him to read it aloud as I drive. It's a relief to have something to divert my mind from my tormented thoughts.

George has done some digging. He confirms that millions of dollars are involved in the rehabilitation of the gravel pits, since construction companies will pay big bucks to have the soil dumped which they've had excavated for their major building projects. Frank had notes that mentioned 80 truck-loads a day to one site near Vannersville, and another note that the budget for the planned new subway had an estimate of $100 million for the cost to have the excavated soil moved. Also, George found a draft speech of Frank's in his computer files, which referenced the lack of sufficient regulatory tools to ensure the safe management of commercial fill operations. And he found some draft regulations which Frank, as Minister, would have had the authority to issue, attached to an email from a policy advisor who'd assisted Frank in the research.

But George adds that he's only just realized that all the activity on this ceased after Frank returned from his most recent trip to England, about two months before the accident. Frank stopped holding the monthly meetings of the Task Force on Fill Disposal and Pit Rehabilitation without giving a reason and without stating if it was a postponement of the meetings, or the termination of the Task Force. But then George adds that Frank had so much going on that he was passionate about, it's hard to figure out what could have been the trigger for someone to want to go after him. But also, it's hard to figure out why Frank backed off. He wonders if something happened in England or if Frank had fallen ill.

"Well, I didn't hear Frank talk of anything. And I'm sure he wasn't sick." But it makes me think hard about the time leading up to his accident. Perhaps he had been a bit preoccupied. I can't be sure.

"Sounds like something could have happened in England," Chuck says as he put the phone back in the cup-holder.

The email helps me to focus. No more tingling up the spine. No more feelings of lightness. No more thoughts of Frank's probable deception. I've banished all those strange feelings so I can concentrate, and garnered inner strength so I can compose myself.

"It could just be a coincidence. Frank's visits to England might have nothing to do with it. He could have backed off because someone increased the pressure," I say. "And his apparent retreat might have nothing to do with his crash."

"But what do you think it would take for a man like Frank to retreat from his work, his passions?"

"Good question. I believe it would have had to have been a serious threat, and one that he believed was real. You're right. It would have taken a lot to stop him. And we haven't found anyone who seriously threatened him, as far as we know. Not yet, anyway," I say. I admit I feel as if I'm still wandering in the dark, and the promising glimmers of light I thought I'd seen earlier have dimmed. Now I'm fumbling about.

"What do you think of Gerald's story that someone leapt away from the car?"

"As you know, it's really shaken me up." I try to breathe calmly. "He seemed so definite about what he'd seen and that the person was on the driver's side. I suppose it must have been Frank. No-one has ever mentioned anyone else being in the car. I just can't think what to make of it." I grasp the steering wheel with a hard grip, making my knuckles go white, and my clenched jaw makes my teeth ache. Despite all my resolve, I'm tense. That's the part of John's (or Gerald's) story I want to bury. It's not what I want to hear. But why wouldn't I want Frank to be alive? After all, when I thought he'd died, I was devastated.

"There isn't anyone else who can verify it, that's the problem," Chuck says.

"The only thing I can think of is to ask Dr. Milton, Munro, what he thinks. I don't know who else to ask about this."

My phone beeps again. This time it's a text and Chuck asks me if I'd like him to read it aloud. He says it's from Shane.

"Oh, I suppose so. I really don't want to deal with that man ever again."

"Well, he sure has let you and the horses down."

"And that's not the half of it. I'll tell you sometime."

"He wants you to go to his farm to pick up some things he says belong to you. He doesn't say what."

"I'm not going anywhere near his place."

"Would you like me to go?"

"Thanks for offering, but I'm guessing he's got nothing of mine."

"That's odd then."

"Yes."

"What are you going to do next?"

"Meet with Brad." And try to stop my head from spinning, my stomach from churning and my heart from aching.

"That should be interesting."

19

Brad

I sit at a wobbly table and look out of grimy windows. The outlook is black and barren, just asphalt and painted brick walls. But the occasional coloured car entering the 'drive-through' lane upsets this monochromatic scene. Just a few minutes of waiting have me longing to be home, soaking in the green trees, the purple crocuses and the yellow forsythia.

I'm thankful when Brad arrives on time. We each buy our own drinks.

"Bet you have lots of questions," Brad says. He has a half-hearted smile, as if he plans to make light of the situation.

"I do. We'll start with why you were harassing me."

His smile gone, he stares into his coffee. "I'll give you the rundown and you can shoot your questions at me."

"Okay."

"When we heard about Frank's accident and that Gerald was at the scene, we assumed Gerald had run Frank off the road. I've been terrified that someone would find out that I'd hired Gerald as part of a plan to intimidate Frank. I knew I'd told Gerald too much, and I figured I'd be implicated in Frank's death. I saw my career going up in a puff of smoke and my life in tatters."

"I don't care about your career. Who is 'we'?"

"My boss was in cahoots with Tim Westmount and Sandy Bingham. The three of them wanted Frank unnerved. Marshall ordered me to plan and execute ways to intimidate Frank, including trying to find dirt on him, from his past."

"And no-one found any dirt, I'm sure."

"That's right. Including Gerald, or John, who did a lot of research in the library, as he mentioned."

"So, what was the plan?"

"I didn't have a plan worked out before the accident. But I know the bosses planned to follow up, after I'd done my part, to ensure that Frank knew their demands. Not sure how. But they'd hired William Porter, and I assume they were going to use him as a conduit."

"It sounds ridiculous. What would make them go to these lengths?"

His eyes dart down to the empty paper cup he's twirling with his chunky fingers. "Frank had draft provincial regulations in the works, which would control the removal and dumping of soil from construction sites, including the use of fill for the rehabilitation of sand and gravel pits. I don't need to tell you that Frank had the necessary power as Minister to enact these regulations. But the three big guys had plans to bring in millions of tons of excavated soil. They were talking to the major construction companies involved in the new subway project." He rubs his hand through his short, stubbly blond hair. "There's big money in this. At the moment the municipalities are the only jurisdictions that can put in controls, and their by-laws don't have the teeth that the new provincial regulations would have had."

"Why would the regulations make a difference?"

"I was told that Frank's regulations would control volume, type and location of fill operations. This would include thorough testing of the soil before it could be excavated and removed, provincial approval of the fill site, which would involve testing as well as local government approval. This would mean engineers, reports and time."

"That doesn't sound all that bad. Sounds like a good idea to me."

"It probably is, for the environment. But for businessmen who want to make a buck, it's a problem. It could mean constraint on volumes, and they had designs to move millions of tons. It could mean costly rehabilitation of the soil if contaminated. And it could mean that they'd have to do more preparation at the fill sites which would take time and money." He has torn his cup into little pieces. "Multi-millions of dollars of revenue were in jeopardy. I say 'were' because the big guys believe the regulations are dead now Frank's no longer around. He was the champion provincially for the controls."

"And they now know that the deadline for nomination of the by-election candidates has passed and that I'm not one of them. So, I'm not picking up where Frank let off, at least in the political arena. So, they must be breathing easier. But, getting back to Frank, did they really think that he would back away? He was tough and determined. Frank had, or has, I don't know which any more, integrity. Or perhaps the better word is tenacity."

"I had the same question when I was given this job. But about a month afterwards, Marshall, my boss, told me that Frank had suddenly pulled back, almost like he'd lost interest. I wondered if it had to do with Gerald. I didn't know what tactics he was using, other than doing some research on him. But, in truth, I was worried, so I chatted with Gerald, and he told me he was going to the library and had some ideas, but he obviously hadn't done anything yet."

"How did Marshall know that Frank had lost interest, and when?"

"Marshall told me about two months before Frank's accident."

"Then why did Gerald start to follow Frank?"

"Because the big guys thought it was strange that Frank had backed off before the lawyer had connected with him on behalf of the group, before we'd done anything significant. I don't think the big guys had even connected with Porter for the follow-up. So, they were puzzled. You've mentioned Frank's tenacity. It seemed like he'd suddenly dropped everything and they couldn't figure it out. They wondered if he could have guessed what was in the works, but then agreed that Frank couldn't have been aware of their plans because it wouldn't have been possible to shake him off that easily. Personally, I don't think there's any way he could have found out. But, regardless of whatever caused him to pull back, I think you'd be the first to agree that, Frank being Frank, he would be certain to pick up the pieces again at some point. So, they ordered me to move forward as planned, but not to do any more than prudent surveillance until they were ready for next steps."

"You didn't say how Marshall knew."

"All I know is that Marshall said something about Task Force meetings being called off, as well as a couple of local consultation meetings which had been planned some time before. You probably know that Frank had set up a Task Force on Fill Disposal and Pit Rehabilitation, and it suddenly ceased to meet. I assume Marshall drew his conclusion from that, but I suppose he wasn't absolutely certain, so that's why I was ordered to continue." He put the torn pieces of his cup into my empty one. For some reason, I resent the invasion of his bits into my cup.

"I still don't get why you harassed me." I get up and dump my cup in the garbage and buy a fresh cup of tea. When I return, I notice Brad has his square shoulders hunched forward over the table. His slouched posture contrasts with the solid, upright and strong-looking stance he took when he first confronted me in the parking lot.

"I also want to ask about the illegal dumping of garbage in the pits," I say as I sit down and just manage to stop my tea spilling as the table wobbles again.

"Sandy and Marshall are the ones involved in that. I don't have anything to do with it. I think it's a stupid thing to do." He wants to know how I knew it was going on, but I ask again about why he harassed me.

"When you started to meet with people and ask questions, the big guys thought you might be picking up where Frank left off. It's not unknown for the wife of a politician to carry on with his work after he's gone." He gets up and buys a second cup of coffee. I wedge a couple of folded napkins under one of the legs and stop the table wobbling. "Marshall speculated that you would have access to Frank's papers, including a copy of the draft regulations, and that you would very likely want to continue his work, perhaps as a tribute to him. So, I was ordered to shake you off the trail. I decided not to hire someone this time, and to do it myself."

"Why would you take it on? Why didn't you just leave your job?" I reckon Brad is ambitious and wants to climb the ladder fast, but I no longer think of him as hateful. He doesn't seem as bad as all that.

"Because I know Marshall thought I'd played a role in Frank's death. He knew I'd be eager to have you off the trail, so that you couldn't find and reveal anything that could incriminate me, and also the big guys whose orders I'd been following, although I swear I was never told to get rid of Frank. That was never the intent, at least as far as I know."

I believe him.

"Did you set that vicious dog on me and Kelly?"

"He was a guard dog from one of the pits. I knew he was aggressive, but I didn't think he was potentially lethal. He got into the back of the pickup okay. But I suppose I don't know much about dogs. The horrible growling and snarling I heard from the forest made me wonder if I was going to have another death on my hands. I couldn't think what to do. I drove to the end of the trail and I shook with relief when you and Kelly emerged and I was even more relieved when Tom shot him."

"Was that an apology?"

"Perhaps. You're owed one from Susan, Susan Kingsley-Black that is, as well. It was her idea to set the dog on you. She was driving past when she saw you getting out of the truck with Kelly at the head of the trail. She texted me to bring the dog, stat."

"She had the nerve to come to my house and attempt to intimidate me, right after that incident. She won't be giving me an apology, that's for sure."

"I'd texted her to get the hell over there and do something to help. She didn't get there in time. I have to admit, she seemed pretty unconcerned about it when she finally did show up, but she must have been worried. She's a very independent, forceful woman, in control, so she's hard to read. But I'm sure she went to your house to make sure you were okay."

"I don't think so."

"Well, I have to admit that she was pushing me to get you off the scent. But her reasons were mostly related to her plans to get elected. She's absolutely passionate about her adoptive father, Sandy. You know about that, don't you?"

I nod.

"Well, she's also passionate about the success of his business, Sandy's Waste Retirement, and of course Westmount Steel, since she works there. And Marshall, of course, is a key player, being MMB Aggregates, in the rewarding relocation of excavated soil, as I mentioned before. And she herself is pretty right wing. She'd be happiest if there were no rules, I think, and certainly not Frank's pollution control regulations. Anyway, I also know she'd be concerned about any allegations that any of the three businesses had been involved in Frank's death, because that sure would be bad for business, as well as personally devastating for her adoptive father. And, as you've likely figured out, she's aggressive and determined, and pretty much obsessive about everything she does."

He looks up. He's torn this cup into even smaller pieces. "By the way, it scared the shit out of me when Tom shot at me."

"He shot at the truck. If he'd wanted to hit you, he would have." I will not let him put me on the defensive.

"This whole business has been a huge-ass mistake. I'll admit it. But they, the three big-shots, have got time on their side for now. They can see dollar signs and will be raking it in, that's for sure." Brad sighs and looks up. His face is too close for my comfort. I lean back.

"You realize I could go to the police and likely be successful in having several pretty serious charges laid against you. You've damaged my property, you've..."

"You're right, to a point. As I said, the whole thing was wrong, and I regret all of it. But the necessary proof is lacking, except perhaps for the dog incident."

"Maybe."

"And I had nothing to do with any of the so-called accidents on that bend. By the way, it was an enormous relief to me, of course, to hear that Frank likely survived his accident, but it must have been an incredible shock for you to hear that from Gerald or John, whatever he calls himself."

"It was." I stand up to leave. I don't want to talk about it. With few words we leave the table and walk to our respective pickup trucks.

I'm surprised that I don't feel as angry with Brad as I had been determined to be. But it's a relief to drive home without having to check mirrors and gauges, wondering what will happen next. I left Kelly at home for the first time since she was attacked. I told Chuck I could manage everything and he could take time off. He was reluctant, but I insisted. However, as I near the farm, there is a niggling sense of emptiness staring to grow, making my stomach flutter. I don't want to admit that I miss him. It's just because he's been around so much. But he'll miss Kelly and the horses, I'm sure of that.

As I get out of the truck, the farm seems quiet, as if it's in suspended animation. I can't see or hear any movement. I'm glad to open the door and to get a warm welcome from Kelly. Her exuberant greeting makes me think that she's missing Chuck, even if I refuse to. Speak of the devil, I've just received a text from him. "Promise to contact me if you need any help. Am at home." I decide it's best not to reply. Besides, I still need to uncover what happened to Frank. I must know the complete story.

I remember Frank has two cousins who live in England who he visited when he was there, and that Murray emailed them to let them know about Frank's death, including the arrangements for the memorial. Neither of them came. I've never met them, and not once communicated with them directly, but perhaps they'll be able to help in some way. Perhaps something happened to Frank in England, as George wonders. I hope that Murray still has the email addresses somewhere. I email Murray and by the time I've folded the laundry he's got back to me with what I need. So, I send off an email to each of them and keep my fingers crossed.

The land-line phone rings and startles me. I've been lost in speculation about what could have happened to Frank in England that would have changed his behaviour. It's Munro.

"You're sure that a person was seen jumping away from the driver's side of the car?" he asks.

"It was Gerald, now John, who says so. And I'm sure he believes it."

"Well, I checked with a retired police detective friend of mine, Larson, off the record. He knows the bend and terrain. What's more, he was part of the team which first looked at the accident site, to rule out foul play or anyone else being directly involved. They didn't suspect foul play because there was no reason to question how the car reached the top of the slope. There were tire tracks in the soft shoulder which appeared consistent with the car going out of control and veering off the road, and there were no other vehicles reported in the vicinity, other than Gerald's, and it was too far away."

"Oh."

"Larson took a great interest in the suggestion that someone could have leapt away from the driver's side just before the car raced down the slope. It's in his nature to look for motives, reasons, so that's what he considered first. He says there are two possible scenarios. One is that there was something wrong with the car and the person jumped away to avoid being hurt, or two, the person could have planned the accident to fake his own death."

"I can't think of any other reason." I have goosebumps on my arms.

"But then, in the first scenario, why did Frank disappear? So, and you won't like to hear this, Larson is putting his money on Frank's motive being to fake his own death. But I told him I knew you weren't involved with the plans, which is confusing."

"No, I certainly wasn't. And there were no insurance policies or anything like that." My heart skips a beat, although I'm not shocked. I've been mulling over the possibilities in my mind ever since the meeting with John, and haven't come up with any other explanation.

"Larson reviewed what he could remember of his notes and his observations of the site, from the viewpoint of this scenario. He even revisited the bend earlier today. He says if Frank had planned on the car crashing on the rocks by the river below, it would have needed to be set up very carefully. It would have taken some ingenuity. He said that the older, heavy car would have helped. He thought Frank could have used a device to depress the accelerator. The question would then be, how was the device removed? Because the accident investigators didn't find anything. And Frank would have had to jump out of the way as soon as the device was deployed, because the car would obviously speed down the slope. But this is consistent with what John says he saw, I think."

"Yes."

"And Larson commented that the driver would have had to be in good shape to get out of the way without getting hurt. I suppose he's saying that it isn't impossible. We chatted a bit about it, and we couldn't come up with any other scenario, if John is right about what he saw, that is. It must be very hard for you to consider this might be what happened."

"Yes. It certainly is."

"From what Larson says, it's not out of the realm of possibility that Gerald is right and that Frank escaped the accident, and that it could have been deliberately planned."

"I'd be interested to know if, in your opinion, and off the record of course, you think Frank would have been capable of doing this?" My throat feels like it's closing up and my hands are sweaty. Even though I've been churning over what John said about the accident, and I have some idea of what must have happened, I'm finding it hard and, yes, hurtful, to contemplate Frank doing such a thing. And as to why, I have no clue. Munro hesitates. I wait.

"Yes, I suppose so. Although he wasn't my patient, I know that Frank certainly was fit, and he was clever. Perhaps I should be saying "is". But I have to add that it doesn't make sense to me. I'm not talking as a doctor, but as a person who knows you both."

"It doesn't make sense to me either. If this happened, then he wanted to disappear. And I can't think why." As I say these words, I realize how hurt and betrayed I feel. What if Frank had indeed wanted to disappear? He told me nothing. Surely, I meant something to him. Why didn't he tell me what was going on? I would have liked to have helped him, if I could.

"Larson says Gerald, or John, should talk to the police about what he saw," Munro says.

20

The Bend

I slouch back in my chair, and try to gather enough stamina to face the fact that Frank must have planned his disappearance. That act of deceit means that he didn't care about me, let alone love me. The only redeeming factor in all this is that he left me the house, the animals and the lifestyle I cherish. I am grateful, but hurt and disappointed. I'd deluded myself, thinking there was something more in our relationship, something meaningful.

If I'm honest with myself, it had always been wishful thinking. There was never anything more than the "marriage of convenience" which Frank had proposed, and which was reflected in our marriage contract. I know, all too well, that I'm not lovable and that my past has permanently devalued and debased me, so I was a fool to expect more.

I can't even mobilize my sad and bedraggled body to make a cup of tea. The house is too quiet. And I didn't think I'd ever feel this way. Sinking to the bottom, under the weight of self-pity, I admit I miss Chuck. I don't want to miss Chuck. There's no point in thinking about Chuck.

Kelly shakes me into action with frenzied barking, and I wonder how long I've been in a trance of self-absorbed inactivity. I heave myself out of my chair and join Kelly at the front door. Somehow, she knows there is a vehicle coming up the driveway. I don't recognize the car, but Chuck struggles out of it and limps towards me.

"What on Earth happened to you?" My legs wobble.

"Someone tried to make me crash on that bend." Chuck hobbles into the family room.

"What? Oh, no! Have you been to the hospital?"

"Yes, just bruises and some minor shock symptoms. Don't be alarmed." I notice Chuck is shivering as he slowly lowers himself down into one of the armchairs in the family room.

"I'd say they shouldn't have let you leave. You look like you're still in shock."

"I'll be fine." Kelly sits on his feet as if she knows he needs comfort. I hand him a couple of throws. "Just before that infamous bend, I noticed I was behind a rusty, white pickup truck. I'm sure it's the one that often hangs around this place. I noticed an odd contraption protruding from the truck bed onto the open tail-gate." He pulls the throws up to his chin.

"First things first. Hot tea with lots of sugar. I'll be right back. You stay, Kelly."

My hands tremble, and my face flushes as I prepare to make a pot of tea. The kettle seems to take an eternity to boil. As I stand, hovering over it, I contemplate that I'm relieved beyond all measure that Chuck was not more seriously hurt. My heart races, relishing the fact that Chuck chose to come here to see me as soon as he was able. But I throw a wet blanket on my pleasure by acknowledging that he probably came to warn me. I shouldn't read more into his visit than that. Pouring the tea with a shaky hand, I force myself to get a grip on reality, and finally make it back into the family room.

"As I was saying," Chuck continues, having had a few sips of hot, sweet tea. "I wanted to know what was loaded on the pickup. I just couldn't figure it out. He sped up just going into that infamous bend, and I couldn't help myself. I tried to keep up. Just as we got to the centre of the bend, a brilliant light blazed from the back of the truck. I've never experienced anything like it. Now I know what it's like to be dazzled. I couldn't see, lost my bearings and lost control. I went veering off into a tree."

"How bloody awful. Who the hell was driving that pickup?" Who could possibly want to hurt Chuck? "We know it can't have anything to do with Brad."

"I've no idea. But, as I said, I think it's the same one that I've seen hanging around. I've seen it several times, so I'm pretty confident."

"I'm surprised you're not more badly hurt." And so thankful.

"My old Jeep is no more, I'm sorry to say. But its airbags did a good job, and my seat belt kept me from being thrown, although I think I've got bruises from it. I got off lightly, considering."

"Thank goodness you're still with us." And I mean it, with my whole heart. "I hope you'll stay for a bit. You need to rest up for a while before you get behind the wheel again. You shouldn't have driven here. Is there anything else I can get you or do for you?"

"No, I'm already feeling better. Hope you don't mind me coming, but I wanted to let you know what happened. And I will stay for a bit. Thanks."

I sip some more tea as I think about what Chuck said. "In a way, I wish I could believe that the same thing happened to Frank." Chuck doesn't say anything. And his silence speaks volumes. But I'm trying not to listen. "But I don't recall a bright light being mentioned at all in the analysis of the crash," I add.

I know as I'm speaking that, despite everything, I'm still fighting against the more than probable fact that Frank deliberately faked his own death.

"No. There was no reference to a bright light that I can remember," Chuck says in agreement.

There's a further moment of silence which I break. A body-shuddering sigh erupts from my subconscious and brings the disquieting deductions about Frank's accident to the surface again.

"I wish I could find an explanation for why Gerald says he saw someone jump away from the car, other than the one I find so hard to accept, that Frank staged it all so that he could disappear." I'm not only trying to bury the obvious, hard-hitting truth about Frank's accident, but also to smother my unsettling sense of delight at Chuck's presence. My insides are twisting into knots, and uncontrolled emotions are threatening to percolate up and burst out. I want to dig a hole and bury myself in it, to hide. But, I must not. I can't run away from everything in my life. I can't pack up and escape.

"It's got to be the oddest thing," is all Chuck says, as he rests his head on the back of the soft armchair, and closes his eyes. I assume he's referring to Frank's accident. I'm sure that he believes Frank planned it, but he's shielding me from his thoughts. I look at Chuck's pale face. His brown curls seem darker as they fall over his wan forehead. He's a kind, warm man and I find his presence comforting and reassuring. More than that. I don't think I've ever felt so at ease with any other person, even Frank.

I often felt tense when Frank was around. He came home late one evening and asked why I'd been in his office. The light was on. I'd been looking for a new book to read and had scanned the bookshelves in there. I hadn't thought that his office was out-of-bounds. Besides, he permitted the cleaner to work in there. I felt humiliated and untrusted. He treated me like a child. Perhaps I hadn't loved

Frank after all. Perhaps it was something else. A mixture of gratitude, respect and compassion for the man.

Chuck opens his large, green eyes and we look directly at one another for a couple of long seconds.

"Sorry, I wasn't sleeping. Just thinking," Chuck says. "So where does this pickup truck fit in?"

Yes, there's obviously something still going on, and Chuck has been hurt. Two of my friends have been hurt, not to mention my beloved Kelly being hurt and abducted. This has all got to stop. I can only assume that Chuck's accident is related to Frank's accident. I must get answers. There's no time for navel-gazing and dwelling on my feelings for Chuck, which have no chance of being reciprocated.

"I don't know. It makes no sense, but I'll find out."

"Meg, we need to be careful. One reason I wanted to come here as soon as I could was to warn you about this guy, whoever he is. And I don't know about you, but I've no clue what he's up to. At least we had an idea that Brad was trying to intimidate you."

"It can't be anything to do with that business, I'm sure. I don't think it could be Brad or Susan. And they're the only ones who've been on the attack, so to speak." My phone beeps. "It's probably another one of those infuriating text messages from Shane. Oh, it's one of the cousins from England who Frank often visited, responding to my email. Good."

As I read the email, my heart pounds, making my body rock slightly. My neck grows stiff and my head aches. It's as if I can almost see stars. I think I have a sense of what someone means when they say they can't see straight.

"What's the matter?" asks Chuck, leaning forward with a deep furrow in his forehead.

"Well, even though I should have suspected things weren't right, nothing has prepared me for this message. It's side-swiped me, I admit. It's the usual story of another woman. I know it shouldn't bother me, given all that we've assumed about what Frank did, but it does."

"Will you share the email with me?"

"You can read it."

Chuck takes my phone. He reads the following email:

"Meg: Nice to hear from you. We should try to connect now and then. How are the horses doing? I can share some information with you, now that Frank's passed (God rest his soul). It might be helpful in your quest to find out what happened to him. Frank became besotted with an opera singer he was introduced to after one of the performances he loved to go to. He became her lover as well as her sponsor. (I didn't approve because, even though your marriage was one of convenience (he'd made sure I knew this), he was still MARRIED. In fact, we had a couple of heated arguments about it!). His plan was to travel round Europe with her. She has several big roles lined up in opera houses in Italy, France and Germany over the next 5 years. He said he planned to retire (very!) early and not only support her financially but also help with the business side of her career, along with her agent. As you know, Frank was a very wealthy man. Plans were underway. I know he hadn't told you by the time he visited here last time, but I thought he would have told you soon afterwards. In fact, we had an argument about it (yes, another one!). But, for some inexplicable reason, he didn't want to tell you. He was just going to say he was travelling for a bit. By the way, I met her. She's beautiful, and the most exquisite soprano. I'm sure you'd like her. Her name is Annabella Cantrina, you've likely heard of her. She'll be hard to reach, but it might be worth connecting if you can. God Bless You! And Good Luck! Shirley. PS if you ever come to England, do visit."

"I suppose I shouldn't be shocked," I say. "Frank still grieved for his first wife. Louisa was his love and his passion. And she was a striking beauty. It was really tragic that they only had two years of marriage before she died. I reckon he'd been hoping, perhaps even without realizing it, that he would find someone like her again, and they would fall in love. I suppose this Annabella Cantrina was the one."

"Where does this leave you?"

"I'll be fine. I have to face reality," I lie. I'm not sure I'll be okay. Until a matter of hours ago, I'd been able to maintain the delusion that I loved Frank. And I'd certainly and desperately wanted him to love me. It's true that I'd dreamt of living at least some of my life with someone I loved and who also loved me. But he turned out not to be my knight in shining armour. But perhaps he is for someone else.

"I'm sure you will, with a little help from your friends." Chuck smiles. "Are you going to connect with the opera singer?"

"I'm not sure. Yes, I think so." I'm uneasy about contacting Frank's lover, but since there's significant doubt that Frank is dead, it would be a logical next step. After all, she was probably the reason he planned the disappearance, if that's what happened. But I rather think she won't want to connect with me.

* * *

It's about time to fill Tom in. I don't think I should leave him totally in the dark. I think he should know about Chuck's accident. I take the time to send a detailed and carefully worded email, while Chuck snores softly. He's wrapped up in a cocoon of throws with nothing showing but his face framed by his curly brown hair which falls softly to below his ears. It looks like the colour is coming back to his face. I wonder if he's connected with his ex-fiancé yet. He hasn't mentioned it. I hope he doesn't call her.

Tom responds about ten minutes later. He doesn't answer my questions about how he's doing, but states that he thinks things have got even more dangerous. It's annoying that he's still on that tack. He still holds onto the belief that Brad is involved, which is ridiculous. And he says that Chuck's accident must be linked to Brad. What's this all about? It's absurd. He says the light that Chuck saw is the weirdest thing, and he thinks it's likely the same one he remembers before he went off the road. But most of the long, tedious email is a reiteration of his concern for my safety, urging, even imploring me to stop. This is over-the-top and out of character. He adds that he's super-busy with work, with two new contracts which he's managing mostly from home. A couple of times one of his staff has taken him to off-site meetings. But he ends his email by re-stating that he wishes I would stop, that it would give him some peace of mind if I just dropped the whole thing, and that he'll phone me later.

I put my phone down, wishing I hadn't emailed him. It isn't like him to be contrary. He was so supportive earlier. I wasn't surprised that he wanted to find out what happened to Frank because he was his best friend, after all. But I can't figure him out at the moment. I'm relieved he's so busy and still recuperating because I guess we won't be seeing him around for a bit.

Chuck stirs. He's still wearing his stylish leather jacket even though he has a mound of throws on him. He must be over-heating by now, especially with Kelly's warmth on his feet. I decide to show him Tom's email.

"I can't make sense of it or him," I say as I hand him my phone. It takes him a couple of minutes to read it.

"You know how close Tom was to Frank." Chuck looks into my eyes and hesitates.

"You think he knows something. I think so too. He could have played a part in Frank's accident and that thought disturbs me. But I have the feeling he won't tell us anything, by the tone of his email.

So, I'm going to ignore him again and focus on moving forward. I'll start a search for Annabella."

Chuck gives me a half-smile and closes his eyes. I hope he gets some more sleep. I'm sure it'll make him feel better. I'll be sorry to see him leave. But I need to keep my distance, I remind myself, otherwise I'll get hurt. I turn my attention to tracking down Annabella.

* * *

It took me a few hours, spanning a couple of days, and several emails to different contacts. I finally connected with Annabella's agent. He said he would pass on the message that I'd like to speak with Annabella. I said I would call her if I had her number, a date and a time. I don't feel optimistic.

21

Chuck

The land-line phone rings at 6am, startling me.

"Is this Meg Sheppard?" The female voice sounds warm and thick, with a trace of an Italian accent.

"Yes. Who is it?"

"Annabella. I am very glad you contacted me. I have lots to tell you."

"Thanks so much for calling me. I was going to call you, to save you the expense."

"No problem. I have the opportunity. I am about to join rehearsal. In London."

"Well, thanks again."

"I do not remember the time difference between England and Canada. I hope it is a good time?"

"It's great. Thanks."

"I believe strongly that you should know what I am going to tell you. That is why I called. In your email you said you do not know what happened to Frank. You thought he might have died in a car accident, but his body was not found. I hope not to shock you, but Frank came to be with me about a year ago. It must have been after the accident."

"I'd sort of figured out that he's alive. But I don't know much else." Despite my attempt to sound calm, my hand is shaking, making the telephone receiver jiggle on my ear.

"I thought he had told you about our plans. But he could not have. I knew about you, by the way. He spoke of you with fondness."

"Oh."

"He said your marriage was a business arrangement. When we first met, it was also about business. I needed large financial sponsorship so that I could have more coaching in Florence, and so I could promote my career. This is an important time for me. Many years of training. Time to get the big roles. I thought it was so fortunate that Frank became a generous supporter. And then we became lovers."

"Oh."

"He came to be with me in Paris about a year ago. He had changed his name. I thought this was strange. He did not want to explain. He said that he wanted no-one to upset his plans to be with me. He wanted a fresh start."

"Oh."

"My agent was concerned, so he checked him out. He could not find anything bad. And he said Frank got good press. I wish that was always the way for opera singers!"

"Yes, Frank has a good reputation here." I struggle to keep my voice steady. I've broken out into a sweat, but I've stopped shaking.

"I had performances in Basel and Paris, and some auditions scheduled in Florence, and my coaching there. Things went well. But then Frank became strange, quiet. About six or seven months ago, he said he was leaving. I asked if he was going back to Canada, and he said he would definitely not be going there, or England, ever again. He planned to start a new life. Another one! He would not tell me where he was going. And then he was gone. Along with his sponsorship. And I have not heard a word since." She adds something in Italian which I don't catch.

"You must have been pretty upset."

"I can tell you I was steaming. My Italian blood was boiling. We had stopped searching for other sponsors because he pledged many years of support. And I was heartbroken. He loved the music, the life, the theatre of it all, but not me."

"I'm sorry."

"No, no, no. I am not telling you to get you upset. I am telling you because I thought you ought to know he is alive. I am telling you because I feel like your sister. We have been jilted by the same man. Now, I do not know if you loved him. None of my business. All I know is that it is easy to fall for a man like Frank. Let us be strong women. We do not need him."

"You've been very kind to call me and to tell me all this."

"I am happy that I have the chance to tell you. And I have an idea about why. He told me about his first wife. I do not think either of us stood a chance. We cannot compete with her ghost. He is infatuated with his memories of her. He needs help from a professional. I believe with all my heart that there is nothing we can do for him."

"I think you're right. You make a lot of sense. But I should have been more observant." Surely, I should have picked up on the signs that he was suffering such deep grief.

"Do not blame yourself, no. I feel that no-one can reach him. Only some kind of doctor, perhaps. He has wrapped himself in an armour made of grief and will not let anyone in." At this moment I admit to myself, definitively, that I had known all along that he hadn't loved me.

We chat for a while longer and then I hang up the land-line phone and stare out of the window towards the barn. But I'm not really seeing anything. My mind and emotions are in turmoil, and I'm trying to make sense of it all.

Frank is not the man I thought I knew so well. Our relationship was nothing but a charade. But, to be fair, he hadn't promised me a relationship, only a business arrangement. What I was to receive was the lifestyle I'd always dreamed of and thought I'd never have. But why did he feel he had to fake his own death? That's drastic. He could have just left and gone to live with Annabella. Did his grief cause something to snap? Or was it simply male menopause? I don't know if there is such a thing. It's more likely to be, as Annabella suggested, a desperate search for his reincarnated wife. And perhaps Annabella had such similar qualities and looks to Louisa, that he thought she could fill the hole in his life and in his heart. Still, it doesn't explain him staging his own disappearance. I'll probably never find out what was going on in his mind and why he did it. And I will not try to track him down.

In fact, unexpected anger is simmering inside me. Frank showed no consideration whatsoever for my or Murray's feelings or emotions, or Tom's. He deceived us all. He obviously didn't concern himself with the stress his "death" would put others through. He must have thought that it was fine to walk out of people's lives as long as you lived up to your financial obligations. And, yes, he seemed to have met those. His will provided what he'd promised. Although I now know that this likely falls far short of the wealth he could have shared, but this isn't what's eating away at me. I'm hurt.

I'd hoped for a fairy-tale, with a fairy-tale ending. I'd wanted us to fall in love and live happily ever after. But the prince left, and I fell into deep grief as if I was under a spell. And now I've been woken up by a Fairy Godmother, who doesn't have a magic wand, but who's opened my eyes. It hurts to open them. The prince left me for someone else in foreign lands and wanted me to believe he was dead.

It's better to know the truth, I tell myself. And Annabella is right, we don't need him. I pull myself out of the chair where I'd been curled up, hugging my knees, and go into the kitchen followed by faithful Kelly. My beautiful dog could teach a few people a thing or two about loyalty and unconditional love. She runs to the kitchen door, wagging her tail. Chuck's fumbling to get in. He's soaked with rain from a sudden downpour. Water runs off the floppy brim of his soaked khaki hat and it's hard to make out his face behind the wall of shimmering water. He steps inside, and it seems like he brought most of the rain with him.

"Hi," Chuck says as water drips off the bottom of his jacket and from his hat. The mats aren't adequate and a couple of small puddles form on the kitchen floor.

"I thought we'd agreed you'd take some time off to recuperate." And I've been hoping to get his warm smile, his sparkling eyes and his brown eyes out of my mind. It hasn't been working, despite his absence. I've been dreaming about him every night and thoughts of him have distracted me every day. And now it will be tougher.

"I took a couple of days," he says, looking at his boots.

"You don't look good and you're shivering."

"Nothing to do with the crash, or the rain."

"Well, let me put those wet things in the dryer. Your jacket's soaked through."

"Thanks."

"Then I'm going to pour a brandy for each of us."

"Oh, I take it you've had a bad day too."

"Yes, I've been enlightened but I feel heavier." We have to shout, since I'm in the utility room. When I finish belting out the words and they stop resonating off the hard surfaces around me, I sense a wonderful release, a letting go. The emotions which I've bottled up inside me effervesce and bubble to the surface, bursting into laughter. I turn the dryer on, hoping that Chuck won't hear me. After a couple of minutes and with some effort, I swallow back my guffaws and return to the kitchen, but with telltale tears in my eyes.

"It seems I've opted to laugh, rather than cry, about what I found out today," I say. But all desire to laugh evaporates when I see Chuck's grim face.

"I wish I could do the same thing," he says.

"What's wrong?" I'm concerned for him.

"I brought it on myself, at least in part."

"I'll get the brandy. A drop of alcohol will either make us feel better, or make us feel worse. I'm banking on the former." I think this is even funnier, but I've no idea why. I'm almost doubled over in hysterics. I can't remember laughing this hard ever before. It's as if something has possessed me and is shaking every part of me, inside and out. I've lost control and wonder if I'll be able to stop. But I wonder what Chuck's upset about, as well as what he's thinking of me. It matters a lot, so I put the brakes on my hysterics and look at him. Thank goodness he's smiling.

"I need to follow your example," he says. "And there's an irony to what happened. My ex-fiancée, Dania, finally called me after I'd left three voice mails in reply to the phone message she left ages ago."

I really stop laughing now and hand him a glass of brandy. Mention of his fiancée throws a wet, cold blanket over me. I take a gulp of the silky smooth spirit which slithers down my throat with welcome warmth.

"You know what she said? She just wanted to let me know that she's getting married. She didn't want me to find out in the papers. How very kind of her! She's marrying some hot-shot. Not a word of apology for having walked out on me, no reason given. It was as if she found pleasure in rubbing salt into the wound."

"Perhaps she'll walk out on him a week before the wedding? Have you thought of that?"

"No." He swirls the brown brandy around and takes a swig.

"I'm not being funny. But you'll probably find this hysterical. I just found out that Frank definitely lived through his so-called accident, and that he went to be with a beautiful and talented opera singer, called Annabella Cantrina. She phoned me from England. It was kind of her, because she not only told me that as far as she knows, Frank is alive, but also that he up and left her. She doesn't know where he's gone."

"So, he faked the death, as we suspected. Wow."

"Yes, changed his name, and planned to tour with Annabella. She's angry, but handling it so well. She's lost her sponsor and her lover."

"Shit. How are you feeling?"

"I don't need the bastard."

Chuck throws his head back and his shiny brown curls bounce as he laughs. It's a deep, rumbling, chuckling laugh that envelops me like a soft, warm caress. It's catching. I join in. We laugh as salty tears run down our cheeks. Kelly jumps up and down on her two front paws and barks a high-pitched, excited bark. She wags her tail, and if I had a tail, I'm sure I'd be wagging mine. It's exhilarating to feel the strangeness of happiness folding round my body and wrapping round my heart. I don't want the moment to end.

But the phone's agitating ring puts a halt to it. With the help of a larger sip of brandy, I stop laughing, wipe my eyes, blow my nose and pick up the phone.

"Hi, it's Linda." Her voice brings me back to earth with a thud.

"How's it going with the new trainer?"

"Fine. I wondered how Rose and Speed are doing. I miss them."

"They're doing fine. They're enjoying their freedom and the spring grazing, but they can be handfuls at times. They should go back to the track soon. What's the new trainer you're working with like?"

"I think you'd like him. He's Irish and really knows his horses and cares about them."

"I'll look into him then. By the way, just wondering what vehicle Shane drives?"

"I've seen him in a white pickup. It's rusted bad though, so he might have something else now. Why?"

"Probably nothing important. We've seen someone in a pickup at the side of the road, near the end of the driveway. We've not been able to figure out who it is."

"I'd have guessed it could be him hanging about hoping you'd take him back on, but he hasn't got his trainer's licence."

"Anyway, thanks for telling me. Glad things are going okay for you. Hope to see you at the track."

"Yeah. Hope to see Rose and Speed back there soon."

Chuck retrieves his warm but damp jacket and hat from the dryer and puts them on, and reaches for the kitchen doorknob. Thank goodness there don't seem to be any serious repercussions from his swerve off the road.

"I'm here to help, so I'll do the barn chores. Thanks for the brandy and the reality-check. And that good laugh. I needed it."

"Before you disappear, I've just found out that it's likely Shane who's been hanging around. On a whim I asked Linda what he drove. But I'm puzzling over what he's been doing."

"Perhaps he wants to steal Rose and Speed?"

"No. I'm sure that wouldn't be it. He has no trainer's licence. He doesn't have a horse trailer. And, racehorses have registration tattoos which aren't easy to remove. Also, didn't you say that it was a rusted-out white pickup that had that funny light contraption on, and also, that you thought it was the one that had been hanging around here?"

"Yes, I forgot." He smacks his forehead. "What the hell would he want me out of the way for?"

"I've no idea."

"He hardly knows me. And it sounds as if he did the same thing to Tom. Talk about bizarre."

"Yes. I've got to find out what's behind this before something worse happens."

"I'm off to the barn. I'll drop in before I leave, and I'll be back to do the evening chores."

"You don't have to do that, Chuck."

"I want to help, as a friend, so you can find out the truth. I'd like to know what the hell the guy thought he was doing when he made Tom, and then me, go off the road. We could have been killed."

"I know. It doesn't bear thinking about. I'm going to do some research on Shane. Thanks for the help."

"You're welcome." He disappears out of the door, but Kelly doesn't go with him. She sees the torrential rain cascading over the eaves.

I kick myself for not being observant enough to register the vehicle Shane was driving when he made me pull over onto the shoulder. I won't be up for the Sleuth of The Year Award, that's for sure.

I retrieve the laptop from the family room. First things first. I must update Tom on this critical development, to let him know Frank is presumed alive. I know I should phone him, but I'm not quite ready to talk to him. I hope he'll forgive me for letting him know by email. The writing of the message has some cathartic benefit and further soothes my feelings of betrayal. In fact, I feel a strange sense of liberation, which I think is partly to do with what Annabella told me and the laugh with Chuck, as well as the writing of the email. From Annabella's tone, more than from her words, I sensed inner strength and resilience, which I found motivating as well as reassuring. Our brief conversation has helped me to get things into perspective. And Chuck is back, as a friend.

Kelly growls at the kitchen door just as I'm about to shift my attention to the research on Shane. Her hackles go up and she even shows her teeth in a snarl. I stare at her for a second in disbelief, and then Shane bursts through the door. He looks like a wild man. He hasn't washed or shaved. His flaming red hair is standing up on end, despite the rain, and it's not a fashion statement. His weather-beaten face is flushed, his light brown eyes are narrowed and blood-shot, and he's flexing his wet hands.

"What the hell are you doing here?" I stand up and take a step towards him.

Without warning, he grabs me with a firm, painful grip on both of my arms. I can feel his strength and expect the dreaded flashbacks to flood my mind and immobilize me with terror. As I wish for some of the resilience that Annabella obviously has, Kelly barks, and I find strength of my own from somewhere deep inside.

"Let go of me!"

"You belong with me." He shakes me as if I'm a rag doll. "Frank didn't love you. I love you. I want you. I deserve you. Frank didn't deserve you."

"You don't love me. You don't even know me. And you're hurting me. Let go!" I try to wrench free with a sudden lurch. It doesn't work. My resilience wavers.

"I know you love me really. You just don't know it."

A rush of panic sweeps through every inch of my body. I have a flash-back of being pinned down and he's going to hurt me again. I can't bear it. I can't. I can't. So much hurt.

I find the strength to scream. He lets go of one arm and I see a glint of something shiny coming towards me. Kelly grabs hold of his jeans and yanks and growls. He turns towards her. I can't let him hurt Kelly. Not for anything. I kick his knee as hard as I can. I kick again. He loses balance and falls to the floor. I see the knife beside him. It has blood on it. Has he hurt Kelly? I don't think so, she's barking frantically. Chuck lunges through the door. I collapse onto the chair and fold my arms on the table and rest my head. I feel weak.

The next I know the house is alive with incessant noise and bustle. I want everyone to stop. Who are all these people, anyway?

"How do you feel?" I can hear Chuck's voice. The warmth and concern shown in those few words give me an instant boost.

"Is Kelly okay?" I turn my head and get a warm, sloppy lick on my face. I move my arm to pet her, but my side hurts. I can't remember how I ended up lying on the sofa in the family room. I have a mound of throws on top of me, but I'm shivering. Then I notice I have a wad of something on my side, where I feel the pain.

"You'll be okay, but Shane stabbed you in your side, and I think you fainted. They'll be taking you to the hospital in a minute." Chuck crouches on the floor next to Kelly. Their four eyes focus on me. "And Kelly is fine, as you can see."

"I'm just thankful that it wasn't Kelly who got stabbed. I remember he was turning towards her."

"How did you fight the brute off? He was on the floor by the time I got to you."

"Kelly inspired me to fight back. She deserves all the credit."

"Wow, some special dog, aren't you, Kelly!" He pats her head, but she won't take her eyes off me.

"She inspired me to do something. She has more courage and more loyalty than I deserve." I mustn't cry. Chuck puts his warm hand on mine, and I don't resist its small caress.

"You deserve each other." He smiles.

"Do me a big favour, Chuck. Follow the ambulance and bring Kelly with you. I can't bear to leave her here on her own. She'll be fretting after all that's happened. She's been through too much." I want Chuck at the hospital with me. His friendship warms my heart. I don't care anymore if I get hurt.

"Yes, no problem. By the way, the police say that Shane was more than likely stalking you. I had a brief conversation with the detective and told him the bits I know, about all the texts and phone calls, and the hanging about. I also said he'd probably tried to get rid of both me and Tom. At least that's how it appears. The cop said Shane might have seen me and Tom as threats. What's more, and this seems counter-intuitive, he said that a few stalkers, if they see they can't have the person of their obsession, are determined that no-one else will have them, so to speak, which would explain Shane's violent attack on you. The cop said you should have reported him."

"His behaviour has been odd but I haven't taken his actions seriously enough. I should have paid more attention. Things escalated after Frank disappeared. But I still didn't put all the pieces together, even after his earlier assault on me, which I didn't tell you about. When I realized it was his rusty white pickup, the picture got clearer and more threatening."

"Oh, Meg." Chuck sighs and the furrows in his forehead deepen. "Yes, I expect Shane saw an opportunity when Frank disappeared. But he won't have any opportunity now. He's been arrested and I reckon he'll be facing some serious charges. Anyway, the paramedics are ready to take you, by the looks of it. I'll see you at the hospital." He places a gentle kiss on my cheek. Warmth rushes through my body, as if I've had sweet, hot chocolate pumped into my veins. I'm not shivering anymore. I'd rather stay home with him than go to the hospital. Despite Shane's attack, I yearn to be with Chuck, and not just as a friend. I know there's more to my longing than that. But this means that I'm well on my way to being hurt.

* * *

I'm grateful that I didn't have to wait long in the hospital for stitches. And I convinced them I was fine to go home, with the clincher being

Chuck's promise to stay overnight. It's an enormous relief to see Kelly in such good spirits. She greets us both with great exuberance as we get into Chuck's rented Jeep. It's as if she knows we've got rid of a bad guy. In fact, I'm quite sure we've got rid of all of them. It's a good feeling. But I don't want rid of Chuck.

It's pretty late by the time we both limp into the house. Chuck's tired and I'm sure the bruises are still bothering him. He's as stoical as Kelly though, and doesn't want to let on.

Since I'm on antibiotics I settle for tea, but convince Chuck to get himself a brandy. He says he hasn't drunk so much of the stuff since he's been working for me. I don't like him saying that. It isn't the brandy, it's the thought of him being an employee. It isn't right. Not anymore. Surely our relationship is more than that. He said himself that he was a friend. I stare into my mug of tea and try to figure out what I'm feeling. The phone's piercing ring makes me jump. I have got edgier over the past few days. Hopefully, I'll be able to settle down soon and won't startle every time the phone rings.

"I'll get it," Chuck says. It's the land-line phone.

"Hi! Tom. How are you?" Chuck brings the cordless phone into the family room. "You're on speaker phone now. Meg is right here."

"Oh, Meg, how are you? I heard you were assaulted with a knife. My God!"

"I'm fine," I say, although his agitated voice and anxious tone don't help my edginess.

"What happened? And who was it?"

"It was Shane."

"The police reckon he's been stalking Meg," Chuck says. "And he was the one that tried to get each of us out of the way, Tom. He saw an opportunity when Frank disappeared, but then saw us as threats."

"He must be completely nuts," Tom says. "How badly hurt are you, Meg?"

"I don't think the wound is all that bad because they've stitched it up, and they wouldn't do that if it was deep. He must have glanced off my side with his knife. I'll be fine. Kelly deserves all the credit. She gave me courage and helped to fight him off. She's a special dog. She deserves a medal." I can't stop tears welling up in my eyes. Fortunately, Chuck doesn't notice. He's patting Kelly and telling her what a good dog she is. She's enjoying his praise.

"Anyway, another reason I'm calling is that I need to talk to you, Meg. It's very important. Would it be okay if I visited tomorrow?" Tom asks.

"Okay. Are you sure you're well enough?"

"I'm getting better every day. I'll get a taxi. I'm not driving yet. But I'm not in anything like as much pain. And I'd guess not as much as you are."

22

Burying Frank

Chuck and I sit on the verandah with Kelly at my feet, her coat glistening in the warm spring sunshine. We wait for Tom to arrive. He sent a text message to say he'll be at the farm after lunch. His pending arrival is a good excuse to take it easy, surrounded by the spring flowers which look brighter and more exuberant as they dance in the breeze.

But perhaps I'm enjoying them so much because they reflect my mood. And my contentment isn't solely a reflection of the serene and beautiful environment surrounding us. I have fallen in love. It's strange, unfamiliar and unexpected, but also wonderful, uplifting and beautiful. It doesn't seem to matter what I think or do, my love for Chuck won't fizzle or fade. Even when I tell myself, that he can't possibly love me. The truly amazing thing is that my intuition tells me he cares about me, and much more than Frank ever did. My eyes are open and my heart is free and I'm able to bury my past with more success than I've ever had. Even though Chuck doesn't know my past, and even though my love is not reciprocated, I'm going to enjoy the times I have with Chuck and enjoy our friendship. I can handle this.

"I think this is a good time to mention something," Chuck says.

"What is it?"

"I'm going to hand in my notice as gardener."

"Oh, I see." My mood changes in a flash. The colours fade, the breeze chills, and I sink into a cold gloom. I shudder. All my hopes and dreams collide with one another, and all I can see and feel is darkness. What is wrong with me? Why does no-one ever want me?

"I have a," but he stops talking because Tom's new flashy red car turns into the driveway, and I make the supreme effort to focus on Tom as he lurches to a stop by the garage. He unfolds his long, slender body with obvious care, and walks towards us wearing a deep frown. I am shaken, somewhat, out of my self-centred thoughts, as I wonder why he looks so morose.

"I thought you were coming by taxi," I say.

"I decided to hell with it, I'd drive. And I managed fine. The worst part is getting in and out of the vehicle, and I'd have to do that if I went by taxi. It doesn't hurt to breathe anymore. Anyway, I want to hear how you are."

"I'm fine. I don't think I'm in as much pain as you, and I'm sure I'll heal quicker. It's just a flesh wound. No organs were damaged." Except my heart is broken. I knew it would happen. But I didn't know how much it would hurt.

"Well, it seems horrific to me. Getting stabbed is frightening, I'm sure." He sits down on a chair next to me, taking care to lean on the arms as he lowers himself into the seat. He looks at me. I see deep concern in his soft brown eyes, and they look watery.

"You don't have to worry about me. I'm fine, really," I lie. I'm a little perturbed by his look.

"I know. But I have something to tell you, and I'm trying to pluck up the courage."

"Should I leave?" Chuck asks. I think I hear a slight tremble in his voice, and he doesn't look like he's making any attempt to get out of his chair.

"No, no, Chuck. I think you should hear this too," Tom says. He rubs his hand through his fine, thinning hair. "I hate to be a pain, but I think I need a drink."

"What would you like?" I ask. He's even more restless than usual, with one leg jiggling up and down, and he doesn't seem to know what to do with his hands. He's making me feel even more agitated. I can't guess what he wants to talk to me about. Or perhaps I can.

"Let me do this," says Chuck. "I have a couple of bottles of red wine in the Jeep that I bought yesterday. How about we share one?"

Tom nods and gives a half-smile.

"That would be great. Thanks," I say. I'll just mix wine with the antibiotics. I really am past caring. My spirits are not merely dampened, they're downright drenched by Chuck's news. I must be in a bad dream. All the surrounding sounds echo as if I'm in an underground cave. But Kelly's sudden, aggressive barks bring me back to the surface. She jumps off the verandah and dashes towards a taxi as it turns into the driveway, and runs alongside it as it tears up to the house, spewing gravel.

Kelly stops barking just as suddenly as she started and wags her tail as Murray emerges. He joins us on the verandah with Kelly licking his hand.

"Sorry about the dramatic entrance," Murray says. "Taxis sometimes like to make out they're getting you to your destination in record time, when they're probably not. Tearing up the driveway was probably part of that." Murray grabs a chair and joins our semi-circle. "I wanted to see how you are, Meg."

"Thanks, Murray. I'm doing fine," I lie, again. "It's so nice to see you."

"I'll get some lemonade," Chuck says.

"That's a great idea," I say. Thank goodness Chuck has his wits about him. I can't think straight.

"And you've come at a good time, Murray," says Tom. "I think you need to hear what I have to say as well." Tom's edginess has increased. His fidgeting and restlessness are making both his legs bounce up and down, and I'm tempted to tell him to stop. I can't cope with it.

Once we each have a glass of something to drink in our hands, Tom pulls his chair closer to the rest of us, with a wince, and faces us. He leans forward with his hands clasped around the glass and his arms leaning on his thighs. He stares down at the wooden floor of the verandah in an eerie stillness and silence. No-one moves or says anything. It's as if he's summoning the strength to talk to us and we're bracing ourselves for what we're about to hear.

"I hope you'll forgive me, Meg, but I've known that Frank is alive all along." I let out a small gasp but truthfully, I've known for some time that he's been hiding some crucial knowledge, and recently suspected that it might be this. And, at this point, I don't care that much. "I must explain. Frank confided in me he'd fallen for Annabella. He said she reminded him of Louisa, and he believed this was true love. He was desperate to be with her, and I do mean desperate. But he couldn't bring himself to tell you, Meg. And he wanted to make sure he upheld his side of your marriage contract. That was his primary concern. He cares about you a lot, but I think his grief for Louisa became close to some kind of mental illness. To be honest, I hoped that the relationship with Annabella would work out. I thought it was a sign he could be healing." Tom looks up. I take a couple of gulps of wine. Realizing that Murray looks befuddled, Tom gives more background about Frank and Annabella to bring him up-to-speed.

"He didn't tell his own brother. That hurts. I can't pretend it doesn't." Murray looks ashen. All the red spidery veins which usually seem to crawl over his face have shrunk away with the shock. I should have kept him more in the loop, and then it wouldn't have been so traumatic for him to hear this from Tom. I shouldn't just be thinking of myself all the time.

"Anyway, what's very hard to admit is that I helped him to plan the accident," Tom says. "In fact, I was there to help make sure everything went as planned. I was devastated that the guy in the car behind him went off the road. I heard about that later. That wasn't supposed to happen, of course. Gerald or John or whatever his name is. I realized right then that it had been completely wrong of me to be involved and I regret it more than I have words to say." Tom looks at each of us, but we don't say anything. Chuck refills our glasses, but Tom hasn't touched his wine and Murray hasn't sipped his lemonade. The stinging truth that Frank's disappearing act caused John's traumatic and tragic injuries has only now become crystal clear to me. I make a mental note for Kelly and me to visit John regularly. Not that I can give him his life back, but Kelly and I must do what we can. Tom broke the uneasy silence.

"Frank asked me to make sure that you stayed safe, Meg, and he told me I was never to let you find out what really happened. He thought it would hurt you badly to discover he'd left you and he was still alive. He said 'I don't want Meg hurt'. He knew you cared a lot about him, and perhaps even loved him."

"Well, he has hurt me. It would have been a lot better for everyone if he'd just talked to me. Why the hell couldn't he do that?" I look at Kelly. I need some of her courage and resilience. "And I find it ironic that I've been telling people he was, is, a man of integrity, and then I find out he deceived me. And I discover that from Gerald and Annabella, not you. And, what's more, you were part of the whole thing, and your goal was to keep me in the dark." My face is flushed, and I remember Annabella talking about her Italian blood boiling. Mine is boiling. I won't let Tom off the hook easily. "You concealed the truth from me and put on an act, pretending that you wanted to help me find out what happened to Frank, when in fact that's exactly what you didn't want me to do." The words spill out of my mouth in a torrent of frustration and exasperation.

"Yes. You're right. It can't be justified however you look at it. I know. I know. My only excuse is that I was very close to Frank. He was my best friend. It was brutal to watch him grieve his loss of Louisa. He was absolutely besotted with her. I think something snapped in Frank when she died. He tried to bury himself in work. He got obsessive about his projects. I thought he improved a bit after he married you, but he admitted to me it still felt like he had a vast hole in his heart."

"I suppose I was so buried in my own problems that I didn't see what was going on with my own brother," Murray says as he stares into his full glass of lemonade. I can sense he's dejected and forlorn, and my heart goes out to him. And my anger subsides. Have I become self-obsessed? Other people are hurting too.

"You sure shouldn't feel any guilt, Murray," I say. "If that's what you're implying. If anyone should have realized, it should have been me. I lived with him, sort of. Perhaps if I'd tried harder to reach out to him, I could have helped him. But I see I didn't really, truly know him and I've spent a lot of my life feeling sorry for myself, and not reaching out enough to other people, including my own husband."

"I don't think anyone's to blame," Chuck says. "It's not going to help anyone to look back and wonder if there's anything we could have done. Frank didn't seek help, and that often happens to people. I talk from experience. Just when we need help the most, we shut down and withdraw. It seems Frank did that. And he dramatically tried to escape the hurt and pain, deceiving all the people who loved him and could have helped him, in the process. Let's not lay blame."

"Thanks for that, Chuck," Murray says. I'm grateful too. Since my chat with Annabella, I have tortured myself with questions about Frank and what I could have done to prevent his disappearance. But the pain of his deceit lingers.

"Where does Brad come into all this?" asks Chuck.

"I don't think Brad is such a bad guy," I say, relieved to talk about someone other than Frank. "He made the mistake of allowing himself to get tangled up with Marshall's nasty business. And I don't mean plans to shake Frank off, I mean the movement of fill and whatever. He'll probably land on his feet and likely won't make that kind of mistake again. At least that's the sense I get from him."

"I think you're right, Meg," Tom says. "I've heard that Brad and Sharon are moving to Vancouver, by the way. But it was absurd that he harassed you. I was seriously worried that you were going to get hurt. And that's just what Frank had entrusted me to prevent." He pauses. "I was growing more and more concerned, and puzzled, about what was going on. My first reaction was to get you to stop, and I know I said it a million times. I'm sorry. But I finally realized, I know, too late, that I should tell you the truth."

"So, you didn't help Meg for any reason other than because Frank asked you to make sure she was safe?" Chuck is agitated. He stands up and finishes his glass of wine in one gulp.

"No, it wasn't just because Frank asked me to make sure Meg was safe and to keep it secret," Tom says, "it was because I didn't want to see Meg get hurt." He turns to face me. "I realized how much you'd been grieving his supposed death, and then to find out he'd left you, I wasn't sure how you'd react."

"I'm tougher than you think, obviously." But perhaps I'm not.

"I didn't think there was any hope of you finding out what really happened, at first. I couldn't think what Brad was up to, and wanted to find out. I couldn't figure out why he was harassing you, because he obviously had nothing to do with Frank's death. I knew they didn't want anyone championing those pollution control regulations, and they thought you were planning on doing that. But then it occurred to me that Brad must know something about Frank's death, and I wondered if you could find out. And then I realized Gerald could have seen something. But as time went on, I got more and more disgusted with myself. And I wanted to tell you, Meg. I really did. I realized Frank had been a jerk. Quite the ass-hole. But I am too, perhaps more so, because I allowed myself to get involved. And I wasn't the one sickened by grief, as Frank was, so I had no excuse. I lacked the courage to deal with the whole thing as I should have."

"Let's not go down the blame road again. I agree with Chuck that it's not helpful," I say. I help myself to more wine. We are now on the second bottle.

"Tom, I'd like to know how Frank staged the crash," Chuck says.

"We found a direct route down the slope which was clear of significant brush. And Frank devised a contraption involving a folding piece of wood and attached rubber ends to it. He made it so that, when straightened in the right position, it would keep the accelerator down so that the car would plunge down the slope at almost top speed. So, he had to put the car in drive, quickly insert the wooden device, and jump clear."

"What did you do to help?" Murray asks.

"My job was to retrieve the device once the car had crashed on the rocks. I was nervous about it. I didn't know how the car would end up and I had to be quick, before people checked things out. I thought this was the riskiest part of the plan. But I was lucky. The door was open and the car itself was well and truly stuck, wedged between boulders. I stretched out on the rock and retrieved the device. It was broken, so it was easy to remove. I got wet and was incredibly stressed. But I was relieved that I hadn't let Frank down and he wouldn't be found out."

"Oh, God," Tom says, as he stares at the verandah floor again.

"No, I don't want to do anything about Frank. I don't see the point. He doesn't want to be tracked down, and I don't think any of us want to add to his problems. And Tom would likely be considered as some kind of accessory to fraud and whatever other charges could be laid. If the police were able to find him, what would happen? I'm not sure, but it probably wouldn't be good. I think it's best to leave things as they are. As far as I'm concerned, he died in that accident. Frank Sheppard no longer exists, and we should do our best to get on with our lives. As Annabella said to me, we don't need him. You think you know someone, and then find out that you don't at all." I hope I can heed my own advice and get on with my life, making the best of everything, for my and Kelly's sakes.

* * *

Chuck and I are still sitting on the verandah, with Kelly at our feet. The others have left, and it's time to put the horses in. But I'm tense and can't get motivated to move as I contemplate Chuck leaving the farm. The dreaded gloom has deepened around me, weighing me down like a tangle of heavy chains. My up-and-down emotions are getting the better of me and I haven't got a tight control over them.

"So, you want to leave?" I ask, doing my best to sound casual. But I know my voice is soft and trembling.

"I want to leave my position as gardener," Chuck says. "But I have a suggestion which I'm hoping you'll consider." My heart beats faster.

"What kind of suggestion?"

"A bold one."

"Tell me, then," I can't help showing my anxiety.

"I'd like to be your partner, here, at the farm."

Beautiful words.

I look into his kind eyes and at his warm smile, framed by his soft brown curls, and a surge of happiness greater than I've ever experienced floats through my entire body. I can't talk. We stand up and hug one another in a warm and caring embrace, and Kelly disobeys the rules, jumping up on us, trying to lick our faces.

Is this how a family is meant to be?

CPSIA information can be obtained
at www.ICGtesting.com
Printed in the USA
BVHW042343101021
618652BV00005B/34

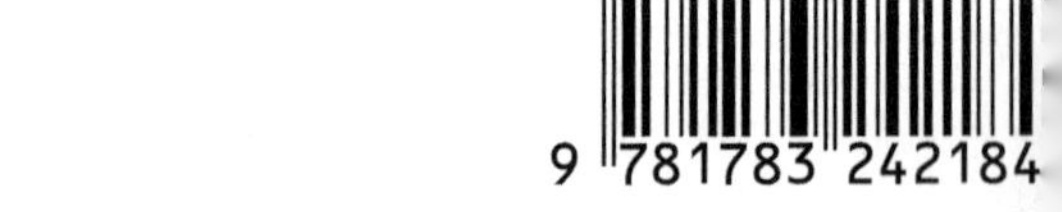